———————————— ★ ————————————

The red light twinkled again, very quickly on and off.

Panic flooding through him, he scrambled to get to his feet and run. But he wasn't fast enough. He heard the thrashing of brush right on top of him and then saw the legs, and the long dark tube.

"No!" he pleaded hoarsely, throwing up one hand to try to defend himself.

That was too late, too. The shadow figure moved and something crashed into Bell's head with paralyzing impact, and he fell deeper and deeper, darker and darker, until the last scintilla of light went out.

———————————— ★ ————————————

"A third, vastly more potent dose of geriatric homicide for Laura Michaels..."

—*Kirkus Reviews*

"This is a realistic portrayal of retirees dropped into a murder mystery at its nastiest."

—*Meritorious Mysteries*

JOHN MILES

A MOST DEADLY RETIREMENT

WORLDWIDE.

TORONTO • NEW YORK • LONDON
AMSTERDAM • PARIS • SYDNEY • HAMBURG
STOCKHOLM • ATHENS • TOKYO • MILAN
MADRID • WARSAW • BUDAPEST • AUCKLAND

A MOST DEADLY RETIREMENT

A Worldwide Mystery/October 1997

This edition published by arrangement with Walker and Company.

ISBN 0-373-26252-3

Printed in U.S.A.

A MOST DEADLY
RETIREMENT

ONE

WHEN THEY BUILT the JiffyGrub convenience store just down the narrow wooded road below Timberdale Retirement Center, nearly everyone at Timberdale thought it was really neat.

Timberdale resident Col. Roger Rodgers (USA, Ret.) might have put it best: "Bully! Provide a nearby depot where we can provision with Twinkies and tobacco and other necessaries not provided by the commissars at this boot camp."

Violet Mayberry, seventy-seven, said, "Great! A place where I can buy cigarettes after my son comes and takes my carton from me every Sunday."

Less than two hundred yards downhill from Timberdale, the two-pump store nestled into a grove of native elms and scrub oak, and was invisible from the beautifully landscaped hillside where the retirement center sprawled. In addition to gasoline and cigarettes, the little glass-and-metal emporium had a wide variety of toothbrushes and similar bathroom necessities, some chilled soft drinks and beer, and the usual variety of junk foods containing near-lethal levels of sugar, sodium, and fat.

Timberdale's 150-plus residents loved it. They found that they did not even have to walk all the way from the retirement center's front entrance, across the parking lots, or down the little-traveled gravel road. Behind the center, a little dirt path descended through brush, weeds, oaks, and willows, passed a small, reedy green pond, and then curved around to a point just across the road from the JiffyGrub.

Going down that way was a good shortcut, was perfectly safe from the scant traffic on the road, and—since someone had once seen a garter snake down there—almost an adventure.

That was the way it was—peachy keen—for the first two weeks of the warm Oklahoma July after the store opened. The JiffyGrub had a lot of visitors from the retirement center. Everybody was happy.

Then, however, everything changed.

It started before dawn on a Monday, when Violet Mayberry went out for a pack of Camels to replace the ones her son had confiscated the day before with his usual insufferable lecture about how bad smoking was for her health.

Wearing a pretty dark floral summer dress and white tennis shoes, Violet left her apartment on Timberdale's third floor a few minutes before 6:00 a.m. She had her purse clutched under her arm and a small flashlight in her hand. Going downstairs in the back elevator, she reached the center's main atrium.

The atrium, Timberdale's architectural focal point and center of much of its social activity, towered three stories high in the center of the building. Far overhead, skylights highlighted a vaulted white ceiling. Encircling the vast open space were three wedding-cake tiers of white banisters enclosing open hallways that led to individual apartments. The main floor, with handsome Oriental rugs scattered around on oak parquet flooring, featured rich, traditional furniture arranged in conversational groupings. A grandfather clock ticked majestically in one corner. Doors to activity rooms and the postal center were closed and dark at this hour.

Humming softly in anticipation of some good nicotine, Violet crossed the vacant atrium and approached the long, curving reception counter near the front doors. A college girl named Stacy Miller looked up from a textbook and the wreckage of a pizza.

"Wow, Miz Mayberry, you're up early today!"

"Just going down to the JiffyGrub for some fags, Stacy."

Stacy did a double take. *"Fags!"*

"Sorry," Violet murmured. "Showing my age. In the olden days, fags were cigarettes." She put her flashlight on the counter long enough to sign the register signifying that she was going out. For "Est. Ret.," she wrote in *6:30.*

Going back through the atrium, she reached the rear corridor, took it to the back exit beside the kitchen, and pressed the electric button that disabled the alarm to let someone open the door from inside. The green light flashed and she pushed the metal door open and stepped out into the damp, gray night. The eastern sky had begun to turn pearl, and Violet thought she would have daylight for her walk back.

Humming again, Violet sprayed her flashlight beam on the service area pavement and made her way quickly to the wall gate that opened to the dirt path. The metal gate complained rustily as she swung it open. She stepped through and started happily down the path, spraying the flashlight beam this way and that, to ward off possible critters, don't you know.

Twenty minutes passed, then thirty, and daylight came. Violet did not come back. Stacy, the girl at the desk, forgot about her.

THE LITTLE DIGITAL clock on the dashboard of Laura Michaels's old Toyota showed 7:20 as she pulled into the Timberdale parking lot. She was right on her usual schedule as the retirement center's assistant manager. At exactly seven o'clock she had left her daughter, Trissie, at the neighbor's house for transportation to her summer school, an enrichment program for exceptionally gifted children. Then she had swung by the neighborhood 7-

Eleven long enough to buy a cup of coffee. Then she had
driven the rural back roads from Norman, her home, to
the Timberdale site a dozen miles northeast in the rolling
blackjack hills.

Parking her battered Toyota on the west side of the
handsome brick complex, she gathered her office papers
and attaché case of unfinished school work and hurried
around to Timberdale's front entry, her mind already full
of the day's activities. A slight breeze riffled her tightly
cropped hair, and her white medium heels clicked on the
concrete walkway. Her reflection in the heavy glass front
doors as she reached them showed a slender woman in
her early thirties, decidedly attractive, although she
would not have thought of herself that way. What the
reflection could not reveal was a divorce, custody of her
eleven-year-old daughter, a start toward a social work
MSW at the university in Norman, and a new relationship
that scared her, it felt so right.

She pushed the doors open and went inside.

Only three or four residents could be seen in the towering atrium. Far toward the other end, lights shone behind the closed doors of the dining room, which wouldn't
open for breakfast until eight. Col. Roger Rodgers stood
down there, near the grandfather clock, stiff in summer
gabardine slacks and shirt, Brillo haircut shining, doing
a few quick side-bends and squats just to keep his face
red. Mr. and Mrs. Chase, new residents, lovely people in
their late sixties, sat in facing plum-colored chairs not far
away, sharing their copy of *USA Today*. Old Judge Emil
Young sat on one of the couches nearer the front, head
down on his chest, asleep.

Laura walked to the curving reception desk where
night clerk Stacy Miller was just in the process of brush-
ing up shattered chunks of overnight pizza and Dunkin'
Donuts in preparation for her getaway.

"Morning, Miz Michaels."

"Good morning, Stacy. Anything to report?"

Stacy blinked sleepily. "Huh? Oh, no. Mrs. Stillwell says she needs to get in the clinic this morning. She's got gas."

Laura started by the end of the desk and glanced down at the sign-out register. She noticed Violet Mayberry's spidery handwriting, checking out at 6:05 a.m., and no signature or time in the space for listing the resident's return.

"Stacy, where was Violet going so early?"

"Oh. JiffyGrub."

"What time did she get back? She forgot to sign in."

"Oh. Gee. I don't know. I was in the bathroom a few minutes."

Mildly irritated, Laura picked up the phone and dialed Violet's room. No answer. The first twinge of concern stirred.

"I'm just going to walk up there and check on her, to be sure," Laura said, taking the sub-master key out of its locked cabinet and heading out across the atrium.

No one replied when she tapped on the Mayberry door. Using her key, Laura opened the door, poked her head in, and called, got no reply, and went in. The apartment was dark, draperies all drawn, no lights turned on, and musty with the odor of stale cigarette smoke. Laura lit a ceiling light and looked around.

"Violet? Are you in here?"

No answer. A check of the bedroom showed sheets tossed back and the pillow on the floor, but no sign of Violet.

Laura went back downstairs faster than she had gone up.

At the front desk, Stacy had finished cleaning up the wreckage of her nightly snacks. "Well," she said with a pretty little yawn, "I'm outta here."

"Call Maintenance," Laura snapped. "Still Bill ought

to be here by now. Get him up here. Then see if anyone is in the clinic yet. If so, I want them up here right now, too. I'm calling the kitchen; they ought to have a spare hand.''

"Wow, Miz Michaels! What's going on?"

"I can't find Violet."

Within three minutes, Laura had lanky old Still Bill Mills, the custodian; clinic nurse Kay Svendsen; and a youthful kitchen helper named Harley Richardson standing in her office. She explained the situation. "Maybe I'm being an alarmist, but I think we'd better start looking for her. Bill, I want you to go down the path to JiffyGrub and make sure she didn't fall somewhere. Ask them at the convenience store if they remember her. Look carefully. Kay, you can check the sauna room, exercise room, the arts room, and so on. Harley: Start up on Three; walk all the halls; anyone out, ask if they've seen her, but for heaven's sake act calm and don't say she's *missing.* After all, she's probably just dozing in a chair somewhere…or something.''

Frowning, members of her search party left the office. Laura went through the back hall, crossed the atrium, and checked the large activity room and mailbox area. After flipping the lights on in the library and checking there, she headed for the closed, darkened music room. *I'm being silly,* she told herself. *Just because she didn't sign back in doesn't mean a thing. She just forgot.*

But Violet, for all her little rebellions around the retirement center, had never been careless with the basic rules, as much as she had complained about some of them. She had always been a sort of formulary crab, and her mind was clear as crystal, not given to forgetfulness or confusion. Forgetting to sign back in was not at all like her.

Laura went back to her office and considered calling Mrs. Epperman. As manager of Timberdale, Judith Epperman might come in as early as eight or as late as ten, depending on how late she had stayed up, maintaining psychic communication with a dead celebrity. Laura knew what a dressing-down she would get from her boss if a call were made and then Violet was found perfectly safe ten minutes from now. She decided to wait.

She did not have to wait long.

Less than five minutes later, she was in the back corridor near the clinic when Still Bill Mills rushed in, his straw hat missing and shirt out of the side of his bib overalls, totally out of breath and pale as a heart attack victim.

"What?" Laura demanded.

Still Bill gasped a breath and leaned against the wall, fanning himself with his hand. "I found her. She's down there beside the path."

Laura's heart lurched. "Dead?"

"No, at least not when I left her to run back up here. But she's out cold, and she don't look any too good."

"WHAT HAPPENED?" Laura demanded.

"It looks like she fell and bashed her head on a rock or something." He paused, and one of his eyes stopped looking at Laura and instead wandered off west, toward the door of the clinic. "Has Dr. Which destinated yet?"

"No, but Kay Svendsen ought to be around the sauna room or someplace like that. Look, Bill, go back down there and stay with Violet. I'll get Kay and some other help right down there."

Still Bill nodded, heaved himself away from the wall, and hurried out of sight.

Laura unlocked the glass door of the clinic, went inside, and dialed the intercom number that put her on the public address system. A beep told her she was "live."

"Kay Svendsen," she said into the telephone, and heard her amplified voice echoing down the hall. "Nurse

Svendsen, please report to the clinic. Harley Richardson, please report to the clinic." Hanging up, she briefly considered her options and dialed 911. The emergency services dispatcher said an ambulance would be on the way within the minute.

Kay Svendsen, a handsome young woman in a soft blue nurse's tunic, hurried into view. "What is it, Laura?"

Laura told her. As she was doing so, kitchen aide Harley Richardson hurried in. Laura sent him hurrying to the atrium to bring Stacy Miller if she hadn't gotten away yet.

"We can't manhandle a gurney down that path," Kay said, cool and practical as always. "Harley and I will get on down there and administer first aid as possible. Somebody needs to stay up here and direct the paramedic team when they arrive."

Stacy Miller hurried in from the hall.

"Stacy," Laura said instantly, "you'll have to stick around awhile and wait for the EMS ambulance."

"LAURA WAS BACK in her tiny office behind the reception desk area about an hour later when Mrs. Judith Epperman, Timberdale's manager, hove into view. Mrs. Epperman, a very large woman with facial features that reminded some people of the immortal Babe Ruth, was wearing a lemon-colored summer suit and large blue heels. Her pince-nez eyeglasses bounced energetically on the considerable shelf of her breasts.

"Laura, dear girl!" Mrs. Epperman grunted. "I see an ambulance out in front. What's happening?"

Laura tried to word it in a way that wouldn't convict Violet of irresponsible behavior. "Violet took an early stroll down the back path and had a nasty fall."

"Is *that* all!" Mrs. Epperman heaved a huge sigh. "She's alive, I trust?"

"Yes. The paramedics want to take her to the emergency room for an X ray. She's groggy, but she's saying she doesn't want to go. They're still with her back in the clinic."

"All right, dear girl. Get back there and convince her to go in for the X rays. Don't take no for an answer. She has to go, period. I mean, that's all we need right now— a resident not getting proper emergency treatment and then suing us for negligence or something. Honestly, everybody is litigious these days. Did I ever tell you how long it took for me to get a hearing on that lawsuit I filed two years ago against my minister, for saying channeling was only a superstition? So many people filing frivolous lawsuits, I thought I would never get my day in court. All right, dear. This is serious. Hurry along! Hurry along!"

Laura hurried.

In the examining room of the Timberdale clinic, both paramedics and Nurse Svendsen were already trying to convince Violet Mayberry. Sitting on the side of the examining table with an ice pack over a large bandage on the side of her head, she looked pale and shaky and absolutely unmovable.

"I will not go to the hospital," she said, shaking her head. "Every time a friend of mine goes to the hospital, they die. I'm fine. I'm not going."

"You don't have to stay, Violet," Laura argued. "All you have to do is get an X ray to make sure—"

"No."

"It's a necessary precaution."

"No."

"Violet," Laura said more firmly, "we have to insist."

Violet stuck out her chin. "No."

The hall door opened and a tall, good-looking man in the crisp uniform of a deputy sheriff strode in. His name tag said he was Aaron Lassiter. Laura didn't need the name tag.

"What's going on?" Lassiter demanded, his forehead a washboard.

"Hi, Aaron," Laura replied, glad as always to see him. "Violet had a fall out back a while ago and we had to call 911 for help in bringing her back up to the main building. Now she's refusing to go into town for a precautionary X ray."

Lassiter frowned down at Violet Mayberry. She glared up at him.

"What happened?" he asked.

"I was walking down the path," Violet told him. "Off to one side, through the bushes, I saw this weird little red light."

"Red light?" Lassiter cut in, surprised.

"Red light," Violet repeated, slightly thick of tongue. "I turned off the path to see what in the samhill it was. Then I must have tripped or something. The next thing I knew, my head was hammering like a washtub and Still Bill Mills was trying to get me to take a sip of ice water."

Lassiter's frown deepened. "Ma'am, you've had a serious trauma. I want you to go to the hospital and get the X ray."

"No," Violet snapped. Her eyes looked dazed.

"Ma'am," Lassiter said, "you are going. You can go nice or I can arrest you and take you as a prisoner."

"You wouldn't do that!" Violet said. But she paled.

Lassiter glared at her.

"Oh, all right," she said, holding her head. "You're all a batch of fools, but I'll humor you."

Kay Svendsen said, "I'll follow the ambulance in. After you've had your checkup, Mrs. Mayberry, I'll drive you back home."

"Oh thrill, oh rapture."

AFTER THE PARAMEDICS had wheeled Violet out through the atrium, to the stares of possibly a hundred gawking fellow residents, Lassiter walked Laura back to the rear entrance, turned her quickly by the shoulders, and gave her a swift, decisive kiss.

Gasping, she fell back against the wall. "I thought you said we were going down to look at the place where Violet fell."

Lassiter's big, crooked grin gleamed. "We are, we are. But you don't think I'm going to miss a chance for a kiss, do you?"

"I think you're a bad person," Laura told him severely.

"Do you really think that?"

"No," she said. "Let's go."

Lassiter opened the steel door and they went out into the back delivery and service area. The sun was high enough now to shine around the corner of the building and hit the asphalt. The reflected heat felt like something that would radiate from a gigantic waffle griddle. The two of them hurried across the area to the fence and the gate leading to the path.

In the greenery along the path it was considerably cooler, although still uncomfortable. Laura began to sweat and get slightly out of breath as she hurried to keep up with Lassiter's larruping strides. It took only a minute or two to reach the lower part of the path where Violet had been found, and it was a good thing, Laura thought.

The site of Violet's fall was clearly marked by crushed green weeds and a spot of bare dirt with unmistakable bloodstains on it. The wheels of the EMS gurney had torn up more dirt along the path, making a pretty good mess of everything.

Laura stood on the path while Lassiter prowled around the scene, moving beyond some of the nearer bushes and trees, then circling back.

"Well," he said finally, hands on hips. "I guess I'll need to make a report after all."

"On an old woman's fall?" Laura said, surprised.

Lassiter turned, and his eyes felt like they bored right into her skull. "Are you sure that's all it was?"

"What makes you think it might be anything else?" Laura countered.

He pointed. "For one thing, it's all soft dirt along here. She took a good blow to the head, but there isn't a rock anyplace in view."

Laura stared at the ground. He was right. She remembered what Violet Mayberry had said about a "weird red light," and she felt goose bumps rise on her arms.

Then, before she could speak, Lassiter moved past her, bending sharply to grab at something in the weeds. He turned with it in his hands—a small, old-fashioned cloth change purse.

"That's Violet's," Laura said at once.

"It's empty," Lassiter said, holding it up for her to see.

"She got *robbed?*"

"Mugged and her money stolen," Lassiter corrected her. "Yes. She's probably lucky she isn't going into town right now with a sheet over her face."

"Who would do something like that to an old woman?"

Lassiter put the deflated little change purse in his tunic pocket. "A lot of people might, these days. As to who did it, I wouldn't mind knowing that myself."

Worried by his grim expression, Laura tried to minimize things. "I guess maybe it's no big deal. She's okay."

Lassiter glared. "What about next time?"

The chill intensified. She hugged her bare arms. "Next time?"

"What if his aim is just a little better, or he hits just a little harder? I think we narrowly missed having a murder here."

JOHN PARIS   19

S...? If he's still in her white belfry or in his just... Then "Spicer Tunnel has narrowly missed laying a nut in face...

TWO

LAURA'S IMMEDIATE reaction was incredulity: "That can't be!"

Lassiter—big, solemn, loyal, loving man she already cared more about than she had ever imagined she would care about any man again—stared somberly at the ground. His forehead wrinkled in that troubled expression she now knew so well.

"Maybe," was all he said.

Laura turned and looked around the little woods traversed by the path. To her right, and up the slight hill, willows grew in close, making the path resemble a leafy tunnel. To her left, a bit more downhill, the trees were fewer and the path went along the edge of a weedy thicket, punctuated by a few little scrub oaks and smaller native firs. Farther on she could just see the opening in the brush where the path turned sharply left, went up the side of a shallow embankment, and reached the gravel road. A bit to the right of that, sunlight glinted green off the surface of the frog pond. It was hot in here now, and flies buzzed. A wasp hummed angrily by, intent on carrying out some evil mission.

She felt another small chill. "Can we go back now?"

Lassiter nodded. "I need to get back to the car anyway. I'm going to call our photographer to come down and take a couple of shots."

"You're not going to make it public—what you suspect!"

"Oh, no. I could be entirely wrong. I just don't want to take any chances, that's all."

They started back up the path toward the retirement center, invisible from their present location.

Laura realized she was far more upset than the circumstances—even in their worst interpretation—probably justified. After her nasty divorce not all that long ago, she had taken what seemed an eternity to feel she was starting to function again. The decision to return to the university and work on a weekend master's program in social work had signaled a major step forward in her emotional rehabilitation. Then, meeting this man beside her had shown her that she could feel again—was even willing to risk such feeling.

The job at Timberdale had also come to mean more and more to her. Her caring about the people here went deep. Although her main job was administrative, Mrs. Epperman had okayed it when she and the school suggested a practicum assignment—individual and group therapy sessions for any of the elderly residents who might want to participate. The sessions were free. Only a handful participated. But more were coming in, and she had come to know many of the oldsters well enough to care intensely about them.

Violet Mayberry had come into Laura's primary group—dubbed the Breakfast Club by some of its original members—only a few weeks ago. She had brought a breath of fresh air with her good humor and quick wit that never turned bitter or cutting. Her forbearance with her bossy, interfering adult son could have been a model for everyone here with grown children who thought they knew everything because they hadn't gotten old yet. Laura had even come to be amused by Violet's stubborn insistence on smoking her beloved Camels despite her son's lectures and pack confiscations.

Now maybe Violet had had a very close call. Laura felt curiously violated, as if the attack had been on her own person. She felt a protective urge for all her people here. She felt scared, too.

She and Lassiter approached the gate that led back into Timberdale's service area. He lightly touched her elbow, making sure she got over a twig in the path the size of a pencil. If anyone else had made such a thoughtless helping gesture, as if she were a delicate flower, she might have resented it. When he did it, she felt warm inside, and thankful.

"Do we tell Violet what you think?" she asked as he opened the gate for her.

"No, at least not yet. But I'd like you to visit with her some more after she gets back from town—you know, quietly, alone if possible. See if she might come up with any other memories of what happened down here, once she's calmed down."

She stepped through the gate. He followed.

A small, dark-haired, electrically excited old woman came charging across the pavement toward them. She had a camera around her neck, a cassette tape recorder over her shoulder, and a reporter's notebook in hand. Her thin floral dress, midcalf length, flapped with her hurry. She was wearing stout black shoes that laced up.

"There you are!" she cried, veering to intercept them. "Aha! You've been down at the scene of the crime!" She whipped her notebook open and poised a pencil over a blank page. "What clues did you find? Who are your primary and secondary suspects?"

"Maude," Laura groaned, "we just went down to make sure Violet didn't lose anything down there when she fell."

Maude Thuringer was well into her seventies, and she had read murder mysteries since she was about six. If Maude hadn't read it, it hadn't been published yet. This gave her a great deal of pleasure. It also made her suspect a crime anytime anything whatsoever happened that was out of the ordinary.

"Oh, I knew that was what you were going to say, Laura!" she piped. "Keep it quiet, don't get any of the old fuddy-duddies upset. Right. I understand. But you can tell *me*. You know I'm silent as a clam. Hercule Poirot couldn't keep a secret better than I can. My goodness, I talk a lot sometimes, but you know I'm really just like Rumpole of the Bailey: I never say what's *really* on my mind."

Maude paused, eyes snapping with excitement. "So come on, guys. Let's have the straight scoop. Was it simple robbery or attempted murder?"

"It was a slip in the mud," Laura said quickly.

"Aha!" Maude cried triumphantly. "There's no mud down there! I already checked!"

"Dust, then." Lassiter was stiff-lipped. "There's no crime to gossip about."

"Oh, right!" Maude shot back sarcastically. "Then how do you explain the funny red light she said she saw down there before she got conked?"

Lassiter straightened up sharply. "How did you hear about that?"

"I've got ways, Mister Law Officer. I've got ways."

Lassiter's hand under Laura's elbow grew firm as he propelled her toward the building's back doors. "Later, Maude."

"Just remember that cooperation is a two-way street!" the old woman called after them. "If you don't share your clues, I might not share mine!"

"Jesus," Lassiter muttered as he got himself and Laura safely inside and behind the closed door.

"She's really on a tear," Laura observed ruefully.

"I want to talk to your nurse and anybody else who had anything to do with this incident. Somebody has already been gabbing, telling that old lady about the red light. I want everybody to shut up about this."

"Well, I'm sure Mrs. Epperman couldn't agree more. Whenever anything happens, the first thing she worries about is keeping it quiet, maintaining a nice, even strain among the residents."

By this time they had crossed the back service area beside the kitchen. Passing an open doorway into the dining room, they caught a glimpse of breakfast in full swing: linen-covered tables all occupied, a few residents still in the breakfast buffet line, white-jacketed college boys hustling around with refills on coffee. Most of the residents were well dressed, the old men in sports jackets, the ladies in dresses and hose. It looked like the dining room of a plush Miami Beach hotel, which in some ways Timberdale resembled.

Unlike some retirement centers, this one did not require a virtual lifetime lease, a major up-front investment, or a provision in the will that practically robbed the heirs by leaving everything to a church sponsor or "philanthropic" sponsoring organization. Timberdale operated on six-month, renewable leases. You had to be over fifty—although most residents were considerably older than that—and ambulatory; walkers were okay, but wheelchairs were out.

If you could meet those qualifications, then all you needed was a couple thousand dollars a month for a private apartment that included housekeeping services. You also got two meals a day in the dining room, the third one (if any) on you in your own efficiency kitchen. In addition, Timberdale offered routine clinical services, an exercise room and whirlpool, art and music classes, the social contact of the atrium, Laura's informal therapy sessions, and Mrs. Epperman's astounding array of general parties, including such gems as Cruise Weekend, Let's Go to the Dude Ranch, Everybody Dress Up, Fred and

Ginger Night, Easter Bunny Time, Yuletide, Let Us Give
Thanks, Happy New Year, Everybody's Talent Show,
Swing Time, Beach Party, and Medieval Fair.

All well and good, and Laura considered it a lovely
place for elders who didn't want to worry about much of
anything. But as an informal therapist, she now knew
how much most of them did worry: about money and
inflation, about investments, about children and grand-
children, about health, about loneliness, about death. As
wonderful as Timberdale was, she saw the sadness behind the artificial gaiety and galloping eccentricities. She
wished she could do more to make many of them more
optimistic and secure, but time had stolen those feelings
and they would not be back. All she could do was what
most of them did on a day-to-day basis: smile and try not
to think too much about it.

One thing she was sure about: They didn't need something like a damned mugging taking place nearby. There
were few enough genuine small pleasures like the glen
behind the complex or the new JiffyGrub. Everyone
would act as if nothing had happened this morning, but
there would be whispers...and worries.

All she could hope, Laura told herself, was that it had
been a random bit of urban-style violence, and wouldn't
happen again. She wondered how well that idea would
sell in group when she herself felt this unsteadied by a
lone attack.

Leaving the kitchen area with Lassiter at her side, she
was about to suggest a cup of coffee in her office before
he departed. Just as she turned to him as they walked, he
stopped abruptly, his face going slack and dumbstruck.
She wheeled back to see what had caught his attention.

Coming through the front doors into the atrium, a tall,
leggy, honey-bronzed blond in lavender sundress and
white spike heels sailed toward them like a vision out of
Playboy.

"Oh, shit," Laura murmured, not entirely under her breath.

FRANCIE BLAKE, the Timberdale social and recreation director, was the bane of Laura's existence. She was also gorgeous, and she collected men the way philatelists collected stamps. Seeing Laura and Lassiter coming toward her, Francie pivoted slightly on magnificent bare legs and hips that almost purred with every movement, and assumed a sultry intercept course. With the kind of pinpoint accuracy that the Pentagon wished they could claim for the Patriot missile, she crossed Lassiter's path fifteen feet, ten and one-half inches from the reception counter, and exploded multiple warheads of flirtation, excitement, sheer sexual energy and invitation.

"Hi there!" she purred, her body making all sorts of interesting little wiggles inside the sundress. A red-taloned hand went out to grasp Lassiter's bare forearm. "Gosh! I just heard what happened! Is Violet all right? Is there anything I can do to help you, Aaron? Gee, maybe I shouldn't say this, and all, but it's been *so* long since I've seen you out here, and I've *missed* you...a lot."

Lassiter looked dazed. "Hullo."

Laura said, "Good morning, Francie."

It was as if Laura didn't exist, and Lassiter had just uttered a great truth for the ages. Francie hung on his word, and his arm too, for that matter. "Aaron! Are you all right?"

Lassiter, to Laura's infinite disgust, seemed even more spellbound. "Uh...sure. Why shouldn't I be?"

"I haven't seen...or heard from...you in so long," Francie murmured, beautiful azure eyes fluttering. "And I know how dangerous your line of work can be. When I think sometimes of how heroic it is for gallant men like you to be...*out there*...standing between us and the violent, criminal element...well"—Francie wriggled all over—"I just get goose bumps, really!"

"It's not like we do so much," Lassiter mumbled.

Laura intervened. "You were going to make a call, Aaron?"

He turned stupefied eyes her way. "Huh?"

Laura held on with some difficulty. "To call for a photographer?"

"Oh!" He shook himself back to reality. "Right." Scowl. "I'd better do that right away."

Francie still clung, beautiful tapered fingers making little pink ridges in his forearm. "We can talk more later, okay?"

"Sure," he said, dazed.

Laura cut in, "Telephone or your radio, Aaron?"

He looked at her but he wasn't quite seeing her. "What?"

"Your call, your call."

"Oh. Yes. Um...phone, I think."

Francie burbled, "You can use the phone in my office, if you want."

Laura cut in, "He'll use my line, Francie. You have too much to do."

"I do? Willikers! I'm such a *silly!* I thought my calendar was almost clear!"

"You've got to draw up an events menu for the Happy Days party."

"I didn't know we were going to have a Happy Days party."

"Well, you do now."

"And I'm supposed to plan it? I didn't know that, either."

"Well, you do now."

Francie's pretty face dropped. Laura pried her fingers off Lassiter's forearm and steered him toward the office area.

THEY WENT IN. Lassiter dialed for an outside line and started talking to the office in the courthouse in Norman. Steaming, Laura looked at the new batch of memos on her desk, all from Mrs. Epperman. The latest was hot off the presses and urged all hands to discourage the old darlings from using the JiffyGrub path until the exact nature of the accident could be ascertained. There was hardly evidence enough to suggest locking the back gate, Mrs. Epperman wrote. But staff could use their powers of suggestion to obtain compliance with the no-use-of-path edict. Laura's copy had a handscrawled note on the bottom: "Dear: You can be esp. helpful in this regard, using your little gab group." It was signed with a flourish, "JE" for Judith Epperman.

Lassiter finished on the phone and looked at Laura. "He'll be out in a while. No need for me to hang around, though. I'll call you later today, okay?"

"If you're not too busy reassuring Francie," Laura said under her breath.

"What?"

She instantly felt like a shrew and a bitch. "Nothing. I'll walk you to your car."

They left Laura's office and turned right, heading down the narrow corridor to the reception desk area. Mrs. Epperman was back in her office now, lights blazing.

"Laura!" she called sharply as Laura started past.

"Go ahead," Laura told Lassiter. "I'll just be a sec." She ducked into Mrs. Epperman's office, expecting more emergency management talk.

Mrs. Epperman sat behind her desk, the morning's crossword from USA Today atop the pile of unopened mail on the work surface. She glowered at Laura from over the top of her pince-nez.

"Laura. The clue is 'hunts.' Five letters. Fourth letter may be a 'y'."

Laura thought a moment. "Preys."

Mrs. Epperman glared. "That's a little farfetched."

"Yes it is," Laura agreed.

Mrs. Epperman labored over the puzzle. "Wait a minute, wait a minute. That might be it after all. That would make 'grab hold of' be 'grasp.' Thank you, dear girl."

Laura left the office and hurried to the atrium. She was just in time to see Lassiter going out through the double glass front doors with golden-legged Francie grafted to his arm. She was looking up at him adoringly, and talking a mile a minute, prettily gesturing with the hand that wasn't occupied with clutching him. He looked stupefied again.

"Dammit," Laura whispered, and went back to her office.

An hour later, Kay Svendsen brought Violet back from the hospital emergency room and life began to get more complicated.

THREE

VIOLET CAME INTO the atrium looking like death warmed over. Kay Svendsen hung on to her right arm, steadying her.

"Well," Violet told Laura, "I hope you're satisfied."

"If you had your X ray, I am," Laura told her.

"I had it, and it was negative. So I'm just fine."

"You're grumpy," Laura observed with a smile.

Violet did not respond with her usual gentle good humor. "Well, if you had fallen down and cracked your skull and hadn't had a cigarette since yesterday at noon, maybe you would be grumpy, too."

Laura had been wondering how she might gracefully try to interrogate the old woman a bit more as Lassiter had urged. Now she thought she had an inspiration: A pack of cigarettes in her desk that had been there ever since she decided to quit smoking, except for three or four momentary failures of willpower, resulting in clandestine trips out behind the Dumpster unit for a few guilty puffs.

She asked carefully, "You didn't stop on the way back and get a pack, Violet?"

"With this storm trooper beside me?" Violet snapped, glaring resentment at Kay Svendsen. "Fat chance!"

"You shouldn't smoke," Svendsen said serenely.

"You shouldn't fart, either," Violet shot back.

"I didn't—"

"Well, if you didn't, there's sure something dead in your car."

Laura intervened, "How about if I walk you upstairs,

Violet?'' She winked at the old woman. ''I've got something to discuss with you.''

Violet cocked her head with suspicion. ''What?''

''Hang on just a minute. I need to get something out of my office.''

Moments later, with Kay Svendsen gone and Violet hanging heavily on her arm, Laura led the way to the elevator and upstairs. Violet was unaccountably silent.

They got off on her floor and started slowly down the hall.

''Terrific headache,'' Violet mumbled.

Laura said nothing. They reached the apartment door. Violet fumbled with her keys and got the door to swing open. Laura helped her inside and to the recliner in front of the TV, then went around the fringed floor lamp and opened the draperies to let some sunshine in.

''You wanted to talk about something?'' Violet demanded.

Laura took the pack of Marlboros out of her skirt pocket. ''I thought maybe you'd like one of these.''

Violet's eyes lit up with the unholy joy of a confirmed addict. ''Regulars! Super!'' She pointed. ''There are matches in that end table, unless my meddlesome son took them away, too.''

The matches were there. Laura gave Violet a cigarette and lit it for her. Then, telling herself she was just using good psychology, she lit one for herself and inhaled like a drunk too long off the sauce.

''Sit down,'' Violet said softly through the layer of gray smoke wafting between them. ''You're a very nice girl. Did I ever tell you that?''

''I don't think you ever did,'' Laura said. ''Thanks.''

''I didn't know you smoked.''

''I don't, really.''

Violet chuckled and blew two perfect smoke rings. ''Me neither.''

"Feel better?"

"Some."

"Still got the headache?"

"Yes, and it's a bad one."

"I could go dig up some Tylenol."

"Maybe later. I'll tough it for now. You said you wanted to talk, Laura?"

"I just wondered," Laura said carefully, "if you had remembered anything more about what happened down on the path this morning."

"Not really. Just that funny red light, bobbing up and down, moving this way and that. And then feeling this terrific blow on the head."

"How far down the path were you when you first saw the light?"

Violet frowned. "I don't remember, actually. Isn't that odd."

"You had your change purse. How much did you have in it?"

The frown deepened. "Must have been a few bucks. But I don't remember." Violet moved her shoulders with apparent discomfort. "Laura. I don't remember much of anything from the time I left my room until I woke up with you and Still Bill hovering over me. You say I signed out?"

"Yes, and you said you would be back inside thirty minutes."

"I don't remember that, either." Violet grimaced. "Laura. Am I losing my mind all of a sudden?"

"No, I'm sure not. What you've got, I would guess, is a touch of post-traumatic amnesia. It's pretty common after a blow on the head."

"When will it go away?"

"The memory loss? Nobody could predict. Maybe this evening. Maybe tomorrow. Maybe never."

Violet tapped ash into the big brass ashtray at her side,

then inhaled again. Her frown deepened. "I have this funny feeling like you get sometimes when you know a person's name, and it's right there on the tip of your tongue only you can't remember it."

"You mean," Laura probed gently, "like there's more to remember?"

"Maybe. I don't know."

"When you've finished your cigarette, possibly I can jog your memory a little."

Violet looked suspicious. "How?"

"Just a little relaxation technique I know."

Violet snorted. "I saw you practice your so-called relaxation technique on Helen Smith in group one day. It's hypnosis, is what it is. Let's call a spade a spade."

Laura had to smile. "Ouch. Caught."

The old woman stabbed the short stub of her cigarette into the ashtray with a little explosion of sparks and smoke. "Well, hell, I'm game. What do I have to do?"

Laura was almost caught off guard by the quick acceptance, but recovered smoothly. She put her own cigarette out and mirrored Violet's posture—legs crossed, arms loose on lap, head cocked slightly to the right. "Nothing to it," she replied, lapsing at once into the quieter tone of voice, which carried both authority and sufficient word slurring to force the listener to strain to make out what was being said. "You can just relax, Violet, and be glad you're here in your apartment where it's nice and warm and safe. And it was a nice cigarette, wasn't it?" Violet smiled and Laura paced with a smile of her own. Violet blinked and Laura blinked in response, then began pacing along with the old woman's involuntary eye movements and her breathing, as well.

"I remember when I went to my own apartment one time not so long ago," Laura went on slowly, "and it was a day like this, where you can be relaxed and easy, and I don't know how you might relax more, Violet, but you'll find a way to slip gently into deeper softness, and when I relax more and more, sometimes I find it's like you have a third eye inside your mind somewhere, and as you drift, sometimes you listen to my words and sometimes you don't, it doesn't matter, and as you allow yourself to drift, and maybe you can get feeling softer and warmer and more relaxed, that third eye inside your mind, your mind's eye, can slowly close. And if you want, you can even close your other eyes, your regular eyes, too, and go deeper into a soft and lovely and relaxing trance.''

The tone of voice, physical pacing, and embedded suggestions all began to work almost at once. Violet was a good subject. Her eyes closed on cue and her breathing became slower, deeper, and steadier. Laura saw the pulse in her throat slow, too, and kept pace with that rhythm while continuing to talk. Then she took charge of the pace, leading rather than reflecting, slowing things still more.

"Now while you're completely relaxed and you're completely safe and comfy," Laura went on, "you can go back to this morning, back to the trip to the Jiffy-Grub."

"Didn't get there," Violet said in the curiously flattened, uncadenced voice of the hypnotic.

"You didn't get there," Laura repeated. "Are you remembering it now, Violet? Are you on the path again?"

The old woman heaved a sigh. "Yes."

"Tell me what's happening, Violet, if that would be all right with you."

"I'm going down the path.... See a blue jay fly across the path. Some bees. Just starting to have a false dawn...once your eyes adjust, you can see a little stuff...."

"Do you have your change purse, Violet?"

"Yes."

"How much did you have in your change purse?"

"Eight dollars, forty-four cents."

"And…"

"It's in my left hand, flashlight in my right, going down the path. Then—look!—over there—a weird red light."

"Tell me about the weird red light, Violet."

"Bobbing up and down. Kind of like you would see years ago…kids out in the park where I lived, after a rain…."

Puzzled, Laura pursued it. "After a rain?"

"Yes…. Worms come out of the ground…kids put red cellophane over flashlight, worms can't see red light… catch worms…fishing."

"Did this red light come from a flashlight with cellophane, Violet?"

"Don't think so. Just looks a bit like that."

"Where exactly is the red light, Violet?"

"Down by…pond. Can't see it now. Just saw it for a sec."

"Do you want to remember anything else?"

"Yes." The old woman's breathing suddenly sped. "Looking out there…almost make out…shadowy figure."

Laura got chills on her arms. "Shadowy figure?"

"Yes…."

"Tell me about it, if you want to, Violet."

"Shadow. *Big*. Scary. Man, maybe. With a Weed Eater."

"With a what?"

"Weed Eater. You know. String trimmer. You move it along and trim weeds around bushes and stuff?"

"Yes. I know. The shadowy figure had one of those?"

"Yes…."

"Then what happened, Violet? If you want to remember and tell me."

"I go off the path now. I'm trying to see better. But the shadow is gone. No red light, either. Dark. Everything gone—quiet. I'm starting to get scared. I'm going to turn around—run back. But then something is behind—I hear something. Someone. Then—oh, something hits me on the head and it hurts so!"

"You're all right, Violet. You're safe now. Okay?"

Violet's chest heaved and Laura saw the pulse in her carotid suddenly become more rapid. "Thought I was dead. Thought I had been a real fool. Wanted to run— got it—"

"Okay, okay," Laura said quickly, gently. "That's okay, Violet. It's all in the past. You're in your own apartment and we had a nice smoke and you're safe and warm and nice, remember? All right, now. I think you've done a really wonderful piece of work here. When you awake, you may remember this conversation and what happened on the path, or you may not. It doesn't matter. Whatever the wisdom of your unconscious mind says is best, that's what you'll do…taking good care of yourself. You'll feel fine and relaxed when you open your eyes. So you can open your eyes whenever you want, Violet, and come back here to me in the room."

Laura waited. The air-conditioning whispered in the vents, and somewhere in another apartment, distantly, someone slammed a door. Violet sat quiet, head down, eyes closed.

Then her breathing began to quicken and her hands stirred. Slowly she raised her head, opened her eyes, and smiled. "Oh, my. That was very relaxing."

"Are you feeling okay?" Laura asked.

"Yes." Violet rubbed the base of her skull. "I've still got this miserable, pulsing headache, though. Do you think we ought to have another cigarette?"

FOUR

BY THE TIME the Breakfast Club held its regular meeting the following day, curiosity about Violet Mayberry's "accident" had already begun to subside, overshadowed by varying degrees of outrage about Mrs. Epperman's latest memo, this one to all hands about JiffyGrub.

As usual she had communicated with all the subtlety of a grenade. Violet's injury showed how dangerous it was to use the back path for trips to the store, she wrote. She did not believe it had been a mugging, but the possibility did exist. Perhaps teenagers had done it and might come back. Therefore, out of an overabundance of caution, the Timberdale management was putting some new rules into effect: Everyone should abstain from use of the back path unless the following rules were observed: (a) travel in pairs or larger groups; (b) use the path only during daylight hours; (c) always be sure to sign out at the desk; (d) report any unusual events or circumstances observed in the vicinity; (e) use the path only in dry weather; (f) don't hurry on uneven terrain; and (g) wear sturdy shoes with nonslip soles.

Any deviation from these commonsense rules could result in locking of the back gate and cancellation of the lease of the resident in question.

"The woman is a monster," Col. Roger Rodgers snapped, so agitated that he couldn't stay in his folding chair but strode back and forth across the back width of the activity room, doing a perfect To the Rear, March! at each end. "One of *us* is injured in an accident, and *she* decides that all of us must be punished."

Stoney Castle, diminutive former political speechwriter, nodded agreement to his wife, seated beside him. "See? The colonel feels the same way I do. It's an outrage."

Artist Ellen Smith, wearing a paint-daubed white canvas smock over her sweetheart of the rodeo buckskin skirt and blouse, gestured with a soft tintinnabulation of her multiple silver Indian bracelets. "Where am I supposed to go to paint my nature scenes? I can't always take a companion along when I go down to the pond."

"How are we supposed to get to JiffyGrub at odd hours if we can't use the shortcut as we please?" Davilla Rose, Timberdale's resident poet, added plaintively. "I can't walk all the way around. I'm not strong enough. The path is my only hope." Davilla was very large. The wonder was not that she had already become one of the convenience store's best customers, continually hauling back large numbers of Twinkies and Hostess cupcakes, but that she could get down the narrow path between the trees at all.

At this point Laura tried to calm things down. "Well, look guys. Let me speak to Mrs. Epperman about it. I'm sure she didn't intend to curtail your trips to the store. She's just concerned about your safety."

"Safety shmafety," Ellen Smith rapped.

Massive old Judge Emil Young, ninety-three, stirred. "While consternation and resentment appear highly appropriate, given the insulting tone and content of this latest front-office effusion, Laura's suggestion that she carry our discontent to Mrs. Epperman seems to me to be a salubrious one. I suggest we move on to other matters of import."

Youthful-looking Ken Keen, sixty-two, got to his feet, a splendid figure in his crimson-and-white leisure suit. "Second the motion!"

"There isn't any motion," Ellen Smith snapped.

"Well, I second it anyway," Ken Keen retorted.

Julius Pfeister, seventy-one, raised a hand. Laura nodded recognition. Pfeister did not stand, but straightened in his chair as he turned to aim his remarks at Laura. A bear of a man, he wore a white linen suit and white shoes, and a red ascot. He looked very pink and very bald, as usual. When he spoke, it was with a measured dignity.

"Please try to make her understand, Laura," he said with stately calm. "We appreciate her concern for our safety. But there are too many occasions already when our own kids come in and treat us like children. We aren't children. We don't need someone to lecture us like children. We're capable of taking care of ourselves. Has she no sense whatsoever of our need for personal dignity? What do most of us have left if we are condescended to by fools a fourth our age, patted on the head and called senior citizens, treated like mental cripples? We are *not* feebleminded just because the hair is gone. We are *not* incapable of making our own judgments just because our knees are worn out. We are *not* senior citizens, either; the term reeks of condescension. We are old. It's as simple as that. But we still have our pride. In the name of heaven, will you try to find *some* way to make the woman understand that?"

"Mr. Pfeister," Laura said gravely, "I'll do my very best."

"Of course Violet did act pretty stupid," Stoney Castle observed. "Carrying all that money around all the time."

No one said anything, although Laura saw a couple of heads nod in agreement. She was puzzled. "Stoney, what do you mean? Violet just had some change in a little purse."

"If you believe that," Stoney Castle retorted, "I got a bridge I want to sell you."

"What do you mean?"

"Violet always carried big bucks in that little purse. All wadded up—fifties and hundreds, bunches of them.

Everybody knew about it. Everybody told her she was cuckoo to do that, but she said you never knew when you might have an emergency. If you ask me, somebody bad got wind of all that dough and creamed her to get it. She brought it on herself.''

TWO HOURS LATER, Aaron Lassiter showed up in response to Laura's call.

"You're shitting me!" he said after she told him what Castle had said.

"I'm afraid not. I asked around, and some other residents verified it."

"Lots of residents knew?"

"Yes."

Lassiter's face darkened.

"What?" Laura asked.

"Then maybe some resident attacked her, knowing the money was there for the taking."

"God, Aaron! On this trip she had only a few dollars."

He took a deep breath. "I don't suppose she said anything about usually carrying a lot more?"

"No. Of course I didn't know to ask her, either."

"And you didn't get anything else out of her?"

"No, I told you everything last night—the Weed Eater thing, the shadowy figure, the works."

"And you're sure she said the shadowy figure was big?"

"She was definite about that, Aaron. Hey. What's the deal?"

"I went over to the JiffyGrub and checked some things out. One of the clerks over there is named Henry Spurington. Twenty-two. A punk. Record for assault, grand theft auto, and second-degree burglary. Just the kind of guy you'd expect to mug an old lady for eight bucks."

"Great!" Laura breathed. "That's a relief. Good work, Aaron. I—"

"The trouble is," Lassiter cut in glumly, "the punk is five feet, four, and weighs about a hundred and ten. There's no way he could throw a big shadow unless he was on a horse."

"Damn."

"I'm going to talk to him some more, if for no other reason than to scare him and everybody else who works over there. If they're scared, they'll want to help me in order to keep me off their backs. They'll do a lot better job of watching that thicket across the road from them down there. Maybe they'll even see our mugger and get a good ID on him for us."

"I hope it works," Laura said.

"One other thing, though," he said reluctantly.

"Yes?"

"Is it possible that memories uncovered under hypnosis can be wrong?"

"Sure, it's possible if the hypnotist leads the subject and plants imaginary things in her head. But I didn't do that, Aaron."

"So if she remembers a big, shadowy person, it's probably an accurate memory."

"Probably. But the mind is strange. You have things like false memories, and screen memories. Whatever really happened...at some time...gets recalled later in some other form. So like a person who was in a bad car wreck as a child might later remember being hit by a train, when nothing like that ever really happened. Or more commonly a person will have been abused as a child, but remember it as being chased by a burglar, something like that that's a little easier to live with."

Lassiter frowned, unhappy. "Then the Weed Eater thing could be a screen memory or something."

"It could be. It certainly isn't a hundred percent accurate. You're not going to have somebody down there in the predawn hours with a Weed Eater, are you?"

"And the red light?"

"I think there was one, yes."

"But you're not even a hundred percent sure of that."

"I think there was a red light, yes. But it hardly makes sense, Aaron. How do you square a mysterious red light with a crummy mugging of an old lady with a change purse that had less than ten dollars in it?"

Lassiter's washboard forehead wrinkled further. "Damn. Well, maybe it was just a random mugging. Maybe it was something else—God knows what. But it happened once and it could happen again, so I intend to check out the JiffyGrub a little more in whatever time the sheriff allows me for it."

He paused and thought about it, scowling. "And now I can start trying to find out if any of your residents have financial troubles of the magnitude that they might risk a mugging to get quick cash."

"Aaron, I just can't believe that."

"Talk to Mrs. Mayberry again. You've got her confidence. Find out how much she *really* lost down there."

"She's in the late-day group. I'll try to talk to her afterward."

"Good."

IN HER ROOM, Violet Mayberry took two more extra-strength Tylenol. Her headache, bad last night and worse this morning during group, wasn't being touched by the nonprescription painkiller. It hurt—God, how it *hurt!*—and now she felt dizzy, nauseated.

Violet looked at the picture of her son and his children in the silver frame on her chairside table. Little Jason and Andrew smirked at the photographer, imps ready to do mischief the minute they were given a chance. How Violet loved those tykes. And how she wished her son weren't quite such an officious dodo about everything from national politics to her smoking habit. He would have trouble with those two fine ornery boys one day, she thought. Already he held the leash too tight. Babs, his wife, cowered and let him run over her, too.

One day these little boys would be big enough to break loose and run free, and the years of overrestraint would make them far crazier and more rebellious than they might have been with a gentler, more loving parental hand. Violet wanted to live forever, or at least for another ten years. But she hoped she would be gone before the lads staged their rebellion. It would not be a nice thing to see.

A fresh pulse of pain lanced into her brain, making her cry out in agony. She started to reach for another Tylenol, but her hand did not seem willing to obey her commands. Her vision began to turn pink and blur.

Her fumbling hand rattled against the telephone, knocking it loudly off the table and to the floor. She managed to get to her feet, staggering, badly frightened now.

In the hallway leading to the bedroom—the apartment's most central location—a wall box held a large round button painted red. It sent a direct signal to both the front desk and the clinic: *Medical emergency, I need help right away.* Violet's vision was so blurred now that she had to feel frantically along the wall with both hands in order to find the box and the button.

She pressed it with all her remaining strength and collapsed to the floor.

AFTER LEAVING TIMBERDALE, Aaron Lassiter drove around on the narrow gravel road that went past the JiffyGrub. Two battered pickups and three dusty Harley hogs were parked in front of the store. Lassiter pulled in past them and parked on the far side of the shiny metal building.

Inside, clerk Henry Spurington stood behind the

counter by the cash register, a cigarette dangling from his mouth. Two workman-types lounged on the far side, sucking on Budweisers. The three bikers—black leather jackets, ugly boots, crummy jeans, and hair to there—stood nearer the door, thumbing girlie magazines off the rack. They had all been talking and laughing when Lassiter entered, but he wasn't one step inside the door before a total silence dropped, leaving the store funereal.

Hostility simmered like the smell of bacon grease as Lassiter walked easily to the counter. Spurington squinted at him through smoke issuing from the cigarette in his mouth, and if looks could have killed, et cetera.

"Think I'll have a Coke," Lassiter said.

Spurington reached under the counter and opened a cooler. He produced a half-frozen can of regular Coca-Cola and plunked it on the counter.

"Diet," Lassiter said.

With a contemptuous grimace, the man grabbed back the regular Coke and put it back in the cooler with considerable impatient racket. He handed over a diet can.

"Ninety cents."

Lassiter produced a dollar and got his dime back. The *pfft!* made by opening the can sounded loud in the continuing dead silence.

Lassiter kept Spurington impaled with his eyes. "Appreciate your cooperation on the questions I had earlier."

Spurington's thin lips twisted in a sarcastic grin. "Anything I can do to uphold the law, Deputy. You know that."

The bikers sniggered. The two workmen stood impassive, watching, and then one of them dug in his pocket for a packet of snuff. He dipped some and inserted it into his mouth.

Lassiter half-turned from the counter to eye the bikers. One of them looked the size of a moose, and appeared to have about the same good humor.

"You guys regulars here?" Lassiter asked politely.

"What if we are?" the moose grunted.

Lassiter smiled and shrugged. "No big deal. See, we had a mugging across the street in that little thicket the other night. I'm asking everyone who's around here with any regularity to sort of keep an eye out for anybody or anything that might look suspicious. I hope I can count on your cooperation."

Moose stared at him and said nothing. It was calculatedly the most arrogant and insulting response possible.

They would cooperate, he thought, about like IRA terrorists with the British army. But word would spread about his little conversation. Maybe somebody would know or suspect something, and come forward. Maybe the perpetrator himself would hear, and get a message that he'd better clear out and not try anything like it again anywhere close. It never hurt to spread the word you were looking.

Lassiter turned to the workmen. "And you guys? Doing construction on those new houses going up about three miles north, I guess?"

"That's right," the swarthier of the two said. He had plaster spatters all over his overalls. "But we don't come down here regular."

"Will later, though," his companion volunteered, "if our boss gets the nursing home contract."

Lassiter's antenna went up a little. "Nursing home?"

"Sure." The workman pointed out through the window at the woods across the road. "Going to build a new nursing home right over there, on that ground where you said somebody got mugged. Big deal, from what I hear. Then you'll have the retirement deal up the road and this nursing home for when they start getting too old and sick to hack it on their own." He stopped and a small, choking laugh burst out of his throat. "All we'd need then is a cemetery, right? You could cycle them all the way from middle age to the tombstone.''

"I didn't know about that," Lassiter admitted. Not that he thought it meant anything.

The gabby workman nodded. "Sure hope our man gets the bid. Ought to keep us in business for most of a year."

Lassiter pushed himself away from the counter. "Well, I'll ask you guys to do the same as I've asked these others. If you do happen to notice anything, let me have a call." He pulled some sheriff's business cards out of his tunic pocket. "Here's the number. My name is written on the back."

They took the cards, the bikers doing so with hostile sarcasm. Lassiter turned toward the door. "Thanks again, gentlemen. Thanks, Henry. I'll be around."

He went outside to his Ford cruiser, got in, reached for the microphone, and called in to the courthouse.

The radio squawked back instantly, dispatcher Vergie Woods's voice conveying urgency. "Unit Four, this is headquarters. Ten-twenty?"

Lassiter thumbed the Motorola microphone. "Convenience store just north and east of Timberdale, over."

"Unit Four, report back to Timberdale at once, ten-four?"

"Ten-four." Lassiter slammed the mike on its clip, started the engine, and backed out fast. His tires spun as he accelerated up the gravel road toward the curve that led back to the retirement center.

Everything looked normal when he pulled into the long, curving driveway. As he parked under the entrance canopy, however, the front doors swung open and Laura rushed out. Her eyes glistened with tears.

Lassiter caught her in her arms. "What? What?"

"Violet," Laura choked. "She's dead."

FIVE

SHERIFF BUCKY DAVIDSON leaned back in the swivel chair behind his battered metal desk. The chair complained loudly.

So did the sheriff. "This," he said, disgustedly tossing the coroner's report onto the littered top of the desk, "is just what we need. A routine mugging turns into a homicide. And for evidence or leads we've got shit."

Aaron Lassiter stood silent and unhappy.

The sheriff glared up at him from beneath a shelf of shaggy eyebrows. "You didn't have to find that change purse empty, you know. You didn't have to put an 'Assault and Robbery' header on your incident report. That old lady could just as easily have slipped and bonked her head by accident."

"That's not what happened," Lassiter said, quiet and stubborn.

"Yeah," Davidson grunted. "But now we've got the newspapers writing it up as a—quote—mystery murder—unquote—and of course Channel Four is going ape as usual whenever there's blood or violence to be had. How natural can one case be for the press, Lassiter? Here's an innocent old lady doddering down the path to get a pack of smokes and somebody bashes her skull in."

"The hospital exam didn't show her skull bashed in," Lassiter pointed out glumly.

"Right." Davidson's voice dripped sarcasm. "And that makes everything all right, right?"

"No. Of course not. The doctor is pretty clear that she suffered an aneurysm as a result of the blow to the head, and it finally leaked enough blood that she stroked out. The cause and effect is unquestionable.''

''I only wish,'' Davidson shot back, ''that we had some evidence that was unquestionable. Look, Lassiter. Those TV people will be snorting and farting about this for days, at least. I've even got a call from one of the stations in Tulsa. It seems they want in on the damned thing, too. Is there *anything* else you know about that I might give them to make it look like we're not complete incompetents around this office?''

''I don't know of anything,'' Lassiter admitted.

''Can we say anything more than 'investigation continues'?''

''I can't think of anything,'' Lassiter repeated.

The sheriff's thick elbows crashed onto the pile of papers on his desk. ''Well, I want something else, goddammit, and I want it now. I want you to go out there and interview everybody that knew that old woman, see if you can at least eliminate that Channel Nine rumor that it wasn't a mugging but some kind of revenge thing perpetrated by somebody else in the home. I want you to go back over the attack scene again with a fine-tooth comb. I want you to go back to the JiffyGrub and lay some heat on that peckerwood Spurington. I want his ass real puckered, so if he knows anything at all he'll be begging you to let him talk about it. I want two investigation reports a day, one in the morning and another by six at night, and I want them to show we're working our butts off on this one and doing all kinds of neat stuff toward identifying the perpetrator. If you need more help, you can have Johnson and Hames. If you really come up with anything decent, I want to be notified personally, at once, day or night. Is that clear?''

''It's clear.''

''All right, then. Get your ass in gear. Go out the back

way. I think those dildos from Channel Five are still camped in the front hallway.''

DRIVING BACK OUT toward Timberdale, Lassiter wiped sweat from his forehead and tried to plan out his attack. The cruiser's air-conditioning wasn't working very well and it was almost a hundred degrees today, one full day after Violet Mayberry had been found dead on the floor of her apartment. But the stuffy interior of the car was not the only reason Lassiter was sweating.

Looking at it objectively, he had to admit that the death was made to order for TV news, and they were making the most of it. They had already shot footage out in front of Timberdale, in the atrium, with Mrs. Epperman in her office, and in the activity room with several of the residents. The Channel Four bulldog had gotten his teeth into a couple of old-timers who went on at great length about how terrified they were. Their comments made Mrs. Epperman's reassurances sound hollow and even desperate. The tape shot out on the path last night, with a ''dramatic re-creation'' from the station art department making a little red light dance in the bushes, had been dynamite stuff, enough to scare anybody and sell a hell of a lot more furniture store ads.

But there were always losers in a situation like this, and Timberdale and the sheriff's department were the obvious ones. In most of the reports, both were looking inept or incompetent. Timberdale shouldn't have allowed its residents to wander off into danger, the reports implied. And if the sheriff's department had been on the ball, then (a) there wouldn't have been a mugging in the first place and/or (b) the perpetrator would be behind bars by this time.

Lassiter wanted badly to make some progress on this one. He had a couple of ideas.

STRIDING BACK and forth across the front of the small activity room, Mrs. Judith Epperman kept whacking her thigh with a thin plastic pointer. Seated in front of her for the staff meeting were Laura, nurse Kay Svendsen, maintenance chief Still Bill Mills, social director Francie Blake, Dr. Fred Which, day receptionist Paula Burwell, and chef Pierre Motard.

"What we have to keep in mind, people," Mrs. Epperman said, whacking her thigh with the pointer, "is that we have the makings of a full-fledged public relations disaster here. Now what I want you to do is look at this chart I've drawn up. See? Here's the building and here's the back paved area, and here's the fence." *Whack!* "We have to present a united front by saying we've never had any trouble out in back before, and no one could have predicted this. We need to *(whack!)* be strong and clear about that. We need to *(whack!)* impress on every resident that the back path area is off-limits."

Mrs. Epperman stopped pacing and stared at them like a carnivore eyeing prey. "No official announcement on what I'm about to tell you is to be made for at least another month. But perhaps you'll understand, after I do tell you, why it's even more vital than normal to maintain a calm exterior and emphasize the safety and security of Timberdale.

"Our parent company, Timber Rest, Inc., plans to announce soon the beginning of construction on a major adjunct to our present facility, a full-care nursing home to be built behind us, here, on the land where the path now runs. Needless to say, bad publicity about a dangerous neighborhood could set back patient recruiting for months at least. *(Whack!)* It's *vital* for all of us to make sure this unfortunate incident with Violet isn't allowed to become a black eye for the entire operation."

Mrs. Epperman resumed pacing. "Each of us has a role to play in the damage control here. *(Whack!)* Laura, we'll start with you. You need to emphasize caution, but with optimism, in your little gab groups. You need to *(whack!)* radiate calm and confidence. Francie, I want a memo from you by this afternoon, suggesting a special fun party or outing we can set up right away to get people's minds off this situation. Paula! Make sure *everyone* signs in and out at the desk, and that includes every guest, I don't care who they are or how much money we know they have. Pierre, I want a special dessert tonight. Something gooshy and filled with butter and sugar—tarts or something like that. A nice dessert always cheers them up and distracts them from their complaints. Bill, flowers on the tables tonight. Kay, some of them will be whining and worrying in the clinic. You and Fred need to keep a stiff upper lip. Be cheerful, upbeat, reassuring. And Fred, if the situation warrants, I don't think handing out a few extra Valiums would be so far out of line at this juncture.

"Okay. *(Whack!)* Are there any questions? Good. Let's go out there and do a great job for Timberdale, gang. Remember: Good PR is vital, and every one of you is a crucial part of that PR."

STAFF MEMBERS drifted out of the activity room. Laura thought she had never seen most of them look anywhere near this depressed. Francie Blake was the only one who appeared perfectly normal.

"Gosh, Laura!" she gasped, falling in step. "This is a big assignment, planning a special event on a moment's notice. You've got to help me with it."

Laura hurried. "Isn't that your department, Francie? I mean, you're the expert."

"Maybe so, but you're the shrink, right? Give me some thoughts on the subject. Should the event be a party? A dinner? A trip? Should it be in costume of some kind? What sort of theme would be the most fun?"

Laura was about to reply when Francie's little gasp

made her turn to examine the pretty blond's face. Francie had the mute, wondering expression of someone who had just seen a supernatural vision. She was staring in the direction of the front entrance.

Laura looked in the direction of her stare, and saw Aaron Lassiter just coming through the doors.

Without a word, Francie broke off from Laura and rushed across the carpeted atrium, killer legs twinkling. She had a hand on Lassiter's forearm and an adoring look all over her face before he had a chance. She started talking softly, a mile a minute.

Trying to control herself and not grit her teeth into fine white powder, Laura went over after her.

"So all of us are upset," Francie was saying breathlessly. "And my job is to find things to divert their interest, make it all easier to bear, don't you know. As a law enforcement officer, I'm sure you understand human nature far, far better than most people. So do you have any ideas you might offer me?"

Lassiter appeared paralyzed by this vision of fluffy pink loveliness. "I guess," he said thickly, "you really ought to get Laura's opinion. She's got the training, you know, and I would like to help, but——"

"Oh, that's so sweet of you!" Francie gushed. "Look, I know you must be here on official business now, and you're such a busy person. But I was thinking, maybe it would be good if we got together sometime real soon away from all this hustle and bustle." Putting a crimson nail to her soft wet lips, she frowned for an instant. "I know. Maybe you could just come by my apartment in the next night or two. I could make iced tea. We could have a real good talk about the whole situation."

Lassiter cast a despairing glance at Laura. "I'm not sure I could be of any help, really. Hullo, Laura."

"Hello," Laura replied, so mad she felt like crying. "What—?"

"Oh," Francie cut in breathlessly, "I'm *sure* we would find lots to talk about...you know...brainstorming."

"Uh..."

Laura asked icily, "Shall I leave the two of you alone to discuss it?"

"No!" Lassiter said. "Hey. I came by to talk to you. Official business."

"I'll be in my office," Laura told him, "when you can tear yourself away."

She was in her office and throwing the morning newspaper at the wastebasket by the time he caught up with her.

"Hey." He frowned. "What's going on?"

"Nothing," Laura snapped.

"Are you mad about something?"

"Of course not. Why should I be mad about something? Do I have anything to be mad about?"

Lassiter stared at her, his eyes sagging, looking for all the world like he might cry. "I guess I should have called first. Is that it?"

"You wanted something?"

"What *is* it, babe?"

"Don't call me babe. I'm not a babe. You wanted something?"

His puzzled frown became an angry scowl. "Okay. Yes. I want to get a list of the residents you know about who had begun using the back path to the JiffyGrub since it opened."

"It's hardly the kind of information we put in their files, Aaron."

"But you know who a lot of them are, right off the top of your head," he snapped back. "And your sign-out register ought to show the names of people who went out that way."

Laura forgot to be angry. "I don't understand why you need such information."

"I intend to interview as many of them as are willing to talk to me."

"Why?"

"It doesn't look to me like our mugger just happened by one time only. Maybe someone else who lives here saw him at some other time. Or saw something else that might be helpful to us."

"Don't you think they would have come forward by now if they knew anything helpful?"

Lassiter's forehead furrowed. "Sometimes people don't know that they know. I'm going to prepare a list of questions that will touch all the bases—make them remember if they saw anybody unusual or suspicious."

Laura studied his handsome, troubled face. "You're really upset, aren't you?"

He glared. "Aren't you?"

"Sure. But I knew her. Why should you care?"

He stiffened. "Why should I care? Why should I care? Well, I didn't know her, of course. But when some damned petty thief hits and kills a little old lady who never did anybody any harm, I have this stupid impulse to take it personally whether I knew the victim or not."

The sudden intensity of his answer cut through Laura's pique. "I'm sorry," she groaned. "Of course you care. I was being a bitch."

He was in high dudgeon now. "Will you provide me with a list and a place where I can conduct some interviews?"

"Of course, Aaron. I'm sorry."

"Do you want to tell me what you're mad about?"

"I guess I just reacted when I saw Francie sinking her fangs into you, and you reacting like you had just been bitten by a vampire, and loving it."

His face fell. "Damn! What am I supposed to do? Pull

my revolver on the woman? I didn't encourage her, did I?''

"No, of course you didn't," Laura said with a wince. "I can get that list made up for you real quick, okay? Why don't you sit down while I check with Paula at the desk."

Still fuming, he plopped down onto the straight chair facing her desk. She resisted the impulse to hug and kiss him and apologize to him for being such a dumb-dumb. Instead she hurried past him and into the hall.

It was not just his dumbstruck reaction to Francie's wiles that had gotten her, she thought. Violet Mayberry's death had come as a tremendous shock, especially after the hypnosis session when everything had seemed all right.

But Violet had complained repeatedly about a headache, Laura remembered. God, that had been the first symptom of the aneurysm, busily leaking away inside her skull, creating pressure on brain centers, ready to kill her. *And I wasn't smart enough to tumble to the fact that the headache might be serious. If I had, maybe she could have had surgery. Maybe she would be alive right now.*

It was a ghastly line of thinking. She had been telling herself for hours already that it was silly, egocentric, and fruitless. But the thought would not go away. *I am partly to blame. I am partly guilty.*

Another thought had also been eating at her memory: that of the first day someone mentioned construction of the new JiffyGrub, and Violet had told the group how glad she would be to have a place nearby where she could buy cigarettes. Everyone had agreed it would be nifty. It had been the colonel who first suggested that they could use the frog pond path as a shortcut, and Laura had not so much as considered trying to discourage the idea.

Maybe she could have discouraged it at that early stage. Maybe nobody would have ever used the shortcut if she had been intelligent enough to see potential danger. So maybe she had allowed the killing situation to develop, and maybe she had missed clues that could have saved Violet's life, and maybe she—*no, no, no, you're thinking like a crazy person, it isn't your fault.*

Or was it?

She reached the desk. Paula Burwell looked up expectantly. "Paula, we need to copy some names out of the register. Everybody who signed out for JiffyGrub since it opened. Deputy Lassiter needs it."

Mrs. Burwell reached for the book. She had a dubious expression on her face. "I'm afraid it's going to be a long list."

"So much the better," Laura told her. "He wants to talk to everyone who's been down that way. He's hoping someone else might have noticed something or someone out of the ordinary on a different occasion."

Mrs. Burwell tapped a few keys on her computer keyboard, clearing the screen for a new text file. She began typing names at high speed, her eyes never leaving the register book on the counter.

"I, FOR ONE, plan to follow Mrs. Epperman's suggestions," resident Davidson Bell said.

"Well, of course you would," Helen Smith said waspishly. "You're new here."

Bell, a tall, lean man with a full head of gray hair and the profile of an old movie star, looked down his nose at Smith. Someone had once told him that he resembled the late Stewart Granger (God rest his soul!), and he had since seldom missed a chance to stare with Granger's once-famous disdainful hauteur.

"I believe," Bell said with great precision, "the warnings are justified."

"Oh yeah?" Helen studied him with narrowed eyes. "You believed all that crap poor Violet put out about a dancing red light and somebody with a twine trimmer, right?''

"Her injury was not an accident," Bell replied.

"Which gives wimps like you a good excuse not to go out in the dark where the booger man might get you," Smith snapped.

"Madam, I am as brave as the next man."

"Baloney. I heard what you said behind my back about my new Durango painting the minute I hung it in the dining room. You didn't even have the nerve to say it to my face, did you?''

"Ah. The truth behind your hatefulness comes out! To attack a man like me, as brave as any man here—"

"You're as scared as poor, cracked Maude Thuringer, is what you are," Smith said. "Seeing ghosts and red lights in the dark, oh my!"

Her heavy sarcasm still dripping in the air, she whirled off down the hallway.

Davidson Bell, hearing his pulse thick in his own ears, watched her go. She was wrong, he thought, and there had to be a way to prove it.

One way, obviously, would be to demonstrate that there really was a red light—actually was a someone down there.

Bell wondered. His room faced the back of the complex. On many nights since his arrival here he had sat at his bedroom window late into the night, looking out at the black sky and denuded prairie landscape so alien in the night, so unlike his beloved mountains. He had never seen a red light down in the pond area, nor had he spotted any movement down there after dark.

But he hadn't been looking for such things, either. Perhaps, if he looked...

SIX

AARON LASSITER was still in the small activity room, doggedly conducting resident interviews, when Laura left at 6:15 p.m.

She felt like a shrew and an idiot, among other bad things.

Violet Mayberry's death had affected him as sharply as it had her, Laura thought. And he could hardly have been expected to shoot Francie full of holes with his .357 Magnum. Actually he hadn't done *anything* to Francie; he had just stood there in shock. If somebody should be hated, it was sloe-eyed, golden-tanned, Miss America Francie, not poor Aaron.

Francie was so transparent she shouldn't be a threat, Laura thought. Any man with a shred of intelligence and taste would see through her at once, possibly laugh at the Southern belle act, and go about his business.

The trouble with that line of reasoning, however, was that it was demonstrably wrong. In the two years Laura had known Francie, the blond had gone through (and devastated) a wealthy young attorney, a middle-aged stockbroker, a doctor with a growing private practice, and a graying writer whose undying affection now survived as a pitiful, abject dedication in the front of a just-published novel. No, men did *not* see through Francie's transparent tricks and enticements. They stared into her vivid baby blues, inhaled her exotic perfume, went goggle-eyed with every tiny wriggle of that fantastic young body, and would have swallowed not only her act but strychnine if she had just been willing to smile as she administered it. ("Here, drink this, you sweet boy. It's a love potion. Doesn't it taste nice? Hello? Hello? Oh, dear.'')

A man killer. Laura had heard the quaint expression used now and again in reference to a femme fatale ever since childhood. She had never understood until Francie. Francie gave dimension to the terminology.

But none of that was Lassiter's fault. He had done nothing to warrant her jealousy or nasty anger, Laura told herself abjectly.

All the way home she alternated between worry about ways to make it up to him and worries about what had happened to Violet and what such nearby violence implied for all the other people she loved at Timberdale.

She wasn't functioning normally, she realized. Grief did that to people—screwed up their emotional functioning and cognition in all aspects of their life—and she would grieve for Violet for perhaps a long time.

At her apartment complex in Norman she carried notebooks and social work texts from car to apartment, hurrying through the dense dry heat of late day. Then she went across the courtyard and collected her daughter, Trissie, there with the sitter since school. The two of them trooped home together and closed the door rapidly to save as much cool air as possible and make life no more profitable for Oklahoma Gas & Electric than absolutely necessary.

Trissie rushed to the TV set in a corner and grabbed the remote control, bringing the picture tube to life. "You should have been here to see the news, Mom. It was great."

"What was?" Laura asked, afraid she knew.

"All the stuff they had on about Timberdale! They interviewed a whole bunch of the people that live there. Most of them said they were terrified and traumatized."

"Somebody used those words?"

"Yeah! Junetta Jones, the anchor on Channel Four!

And then their crime reporter, John Garvey, got on there
and said there's a theory that maybe the attack on that
old lady wasn't random, but some kind of put-up job.''

Laura turned to stare at her daughter. ''Put-up job?
What does that mean?''

''Well, like it wasn't a stranger or a mugger, but somebody else who lives at Timberdale, and they were mad
at her about something, and this was revenge.''

''Great,'' Laura groaned.

''They interviewed what's-her-name? The old lady
with a magnifying glass in her purse?''

''Maude Thuringer?''

''Yeah! She said she can't discount the inside-job
theory.''

''Lovely.''

''Maybe you can watch tomorrow night. It ought to be
real good. They said they're going to start a five-part
series, 'Shock for Senior Citizens,' and they'll have a lot
more on the terror at Timberdale.''

''Somebody is really into alliteration.''

''A little what?''

The telephone rang.

''Nothing,'' Laura told her daughter. ''I'll get that. I
have an idea it might be Mrs. Epperman.''

She was right. ''Laura?'' Timberdale's manager
sounded extremely agitated. ''Did you see it?''

''No,'' Laura said. ''I just got in the door.''

''I mean that dreadful TV news report?''

''No.''

''It was horrible! I don't know how I can trust you
with anything anymore. Where *were* you when they were
carrying their cameras all over the place, getting the old
fools to say they're scared out of their minds, and we
don't provide enough security, and the murderer will be
right inside the atrium next?''

''I knew they were taping,'' Laura said. ''I didn't

know it was that extensive. We're a pretty public place, Mrs. Epperman. We can't just lock the media out.''

"The hell we can't. That's exactly what I intend to do, starting immediately.''

Laura felt dismay. "They'll go crazy, Mrs. Epperman. You know how they are about the people's right to know.''

"That's balderdash. That's what those terrible tabloids say, and do you remember that hideous lying story in one of those rags that I showed you just a few weeks ago? They'll say anything to get attention—anything. It just makes me sick. Don't talk to me about the people's right to know. They don't have any right to know balderdash.''

Laura hesitated, trying to figure how to respond. The story Mrs. Epperman was referring to had been a long piece on psychics and channeling to the spirits of the dead. Centered on a commercial channeling group in Florida whose members claimed they could predict the future, it implied that claims of spirit-communications were usually false. Mrs. Epperman, who regularly channeled to Cleopatra and another woman who she thought might be Queen Victoria, had gone ballistic.

"Well?" Mrs. Epperman said now over the telephone. "Well?''

"Please?" Laura said, confused.

"I've told you what I intend to do in the morning, you dreadful girl. Now tell me what *you* plan to do to help enforce my orders.''

"I hadn't thought about it," Laura stammered. "It's a complete shock to me. I have to think—''

"Then think! Think! I want action! This is all your fault, you know. If you had been paying attention to business instead of mooning around after that brainless muscular hunk in a sheriff suit, none of this would have happened.''

"Are you sure you want to keep the TV people out?" Laura asked. "Because—"

"Yes, and you need to reassign staff to help guard the doors. You also need to use your little talk groups to convince everyone not to go outside and talk to the cameras in the driveway. I don't suppose there's any good way to keep them entirely off the property, short of armed guards. Furthermore, I want some input on the entire security question. I intend to lock that back gate to the pond path in the morning. I also intend to hire a new security guard to patrol outside at night. I've already put in a couple of calls about that, and one man is coming by for you to interview at eight tomorrow morning. What else should we do? I can't think of everything by myself."

Laura forced herself to speak despite her galloping despair. "This thing will quiet down all by itself in a few days unless we—"

"Quiet down by itself? We can't wait for it to quiet down by itself. I've already had two calls tonight from members of the board of directors. They're fit to be tied. They want action. I intend to give them action."

"I just don't want to go too far too fast," Laura said lamely.

"Baloney! I was in communication with Cleo not thirty minutes ago, and she said that stern action is the only alternative. As a matter of fact, she was the one who suggested hiring an additional security man."

"Cleo," Laura repeated, further discouraged.

"You know who I mean. Don't pretend you don't. Now listen to me. I want a complete report and list of additional suggestions on my desk by eight o'clock tomorrow morning. This crap has to *stop*. Do you understand me?"

Laura gave up. "Yes, Mrs. Epperman."

Mrs. Epperman moderated her tone, the martyred

leader showing heroic patience with an underling. "We
have to work together on this, darling girl. We have to
give it all priority. I know you'll do your part. I have to
have somebody in your job who will take decisive action
and not let bad things happen, and I know you would
like to keep the position, so you'll do everything in your
power to do the right thing. Am I correct? Can I count
on your cooperation?"

"I'll do everything I can, Mrs. Epperman."

Mrs. Epperman hung up.

IT WAS LONG after dark when Aaron Lassiter called it
quits for the day on his interviews with residents who
had used the back path to the JiffyGrub. It had been one
of the most discouraging experiences of his life, possibly
the worst since he had gone oh-for-seventeen in one
stretch at Tulsa and finally realized he would never be
able to hit a curve ball.

There didn't seem to be anything helpful in his notes
so far. The Andersons had seen two small boys catching
frogs at the pond. Stoney Castle had found a golf ball
down there, but it was a very old one and not playable
anymore. Sada Hoff had spotted a hiker once, and Julius
and Dot Pfeister had liked to take a lunch and thermos
down there from time to time and sit under a tree and
have a picnic, but no one had ever bothered them. Maude
Thuringer had a theory, either one theory in several parts
or maybe a number of theories clustered close. She believed someone inside Timberdale had been angry with
Violet, and followed her down the path to yell boo and
scare her, just out of meanness. She also believed that
the JiffyGrub had attracted a bad element into the neighborhood, and teenage criminals liked to hang around over
there. She also believed no one was safe here now because the publicity would bring in more of the criminal
element. She also believed that she had begun to dope

out exactly what had happened to Violet, and why she had remembered a dancing red light. The red light was marsh gas from the pond.

Discouraged, Lassiter walked through the dark of the parking lot to his cruiser, climbed inside, started the engine, and made a routine call to the courthouse. There was nothing new for him there. He backed out and drove down to the gravel road at the end of the long entry and turned right to cruise down past the JiffyGrub once just to have a look-see and show the flag to any bad element that might see him.

The JiffyGrub sat quiet in a blaze of mercury vapor lights, and a pickup was parked at the gas pumps, an elderly farmer pouring in the unleaded. Two small Japanese cars had angle-parked beside the store. A Honda motorcycle leaned over on its kickstand around to the side. Lassiter could see a young woman looking at the magazines and a middle-aged man paying for a couple of items at the counter. The clerk was a slender blond girl who looked sad and down on her luck. As Lassiter passed, he caught a glimpse of a long-haired young man coming out of the rest room area, his motorcycle helmet in hand.

Lassiter drove on down the road a quarter of a mile or so, peering intently at the pitch-black woods off to the right. He couldn't see a thing. Where another rural road—this one dirt—intersected, he pulled in and backed around to reverse direction. It was lonely and dark, with a sprinkling of faint gray stars in the haze, and no moon.

Hurrying back the way he had come, he again started past the convenience store. The pickup was gone from the pumps and one of the cars had gone, too. As he started past, the young woman customer came out and strode to the remaining car. She got in and a few seconds later her headlights flared against the front windows of the store. The long-haired biker was still inside, talking intently to the girl behind the counter.

Lassiter drove forty yards or so and wheeled his cruiser onto the narrow shoulder. Cutting the engine and dousing his lights, he leaned back and observed the store through his rearview mirror. He needed some time to get the layout indelibly fixed in his mind. More important, he needed some time to think.

He didn't get it.

He had been parked there only about five minutes, maximum, when a movement back at the store drew his attention. The long-haired boy came out, pulled on his helmet, straddled his bike, and fired it up. The big front headlight came on with the ignition. The boy backed the Honda away from the side of the building where it had been nosed in. The headlight flared brighter as he fed the engine some gas. He pulled away, angling across the parking area to the side of the road.

Lassiter decided to take down the bike's license plate number when it passed him. He pulled a small sheet of paper off his windshield-mounted scratch pad and waited.

To his surprise, the cycle didn't come onto the road and head his way. What it did was pull onto the gravel, then tilt sharply as the rider turned it sharply into the roadway, heading it back east. But as Lassiter watched, it went only a few paces and slowed, the brake light going bright, and then the driver steered it onto the far shoulder near the lower end of the woods, cut the engine and the lights, and essentially vanished in the dark.

Lassiter felt a sharp pulse. Maybe, by blind luck, he was onto something here. He flicked the switch that prevented the cruiser's dome light from flashing when a door opened. Then he cracked his door and stepped out onto the tarry gravel. He crossed the road quickly, moving into the deeper darkness of the scant borrow ditch that separated road from thicket. He unsnapped the flap of his leather holster and pulled out his .357 before slipping ahead.

After a few dozen short strides he was able again to make out the shape of the motorcycle, pulled well off the road and parked beside a big bush of some kind. He had no sight of the long-hair, who evidently had moved on into the woods.

The slightest night wind riffled Lassiter's hair and pressed his uniform shirt against his rib cage. The light-weight material felt harsh and scratchy against his bare skin, which had quite suddenly gotten damp with sweat. His big hand, closed around the grips of the .357, had gotten slippery.

There were probably lots of reasons why a teenage cyclist would park beside the road in the dark and slip into the woods, Lassiter thought. Probably lots of reasons, but he couldn't think of any. Not unless he assumed that the kid's business was petty theft, and he was looking for another easy score from the retirement center.

Peering in through the brush, he saw a brief flash of bright white light, then darkness again. The flash repeated itself moments later. It wasn't a nice red light like Violet Mayberry had reported, but it was good enough. Lassiter dropped to one knee in the damp earth at the bottom of the ditch and waited.

Minutes passed. He saw the momentary flash of white light several more times. He waited.

Finally he was rewarded. The young man came back through the dry brush with all the quiet grace of a rogue elephant going through a thatched-roof hut. Lassiter watched him approach the bike; he had a small flashlight in one hand and a sandwich-size plastic bag in the other.

He reached the cycle and swung a leg over the saddle. That was when Lassiter moved.

"Hold it there! Sheriff's deputy. Don't move and no one will get hurt."

The skinny figure froze. Something—the flashlight—fell and clattered against the rubbed sides of the motor, making a very great racket. Lassiter hurried over and shoved the barrel of his revolver into the man's face. "Get off the bike. Very slow. You're under arrest."

"What did I do, Sheriff?" the man choked. He was badly scared and already starting to shake. "I didn't do anything."

Lassiter didn't want to continue standing here in the dark, and the convenience store across the road was considerably closer than his car. He nudged the young man with his revolver, prodding him out across the gravel.

The sad girl behind the counter started badly when Lassiter walked in, the young man in front of him with the .357 poking him in the back.

"Gosh!" she cried. "You're already back? My lord, what have you been doing?" Her dazed glance swung to Lassiter. "What do *you* want?"

"You know this man?" Lassiter demanded.

"Gosh, yes, we're pals. What did he do?"

Lassiter noticed the plastic bag still in the youth's right hand. "Put that on the counter. What is it?"

"Mushrooms," the young man choked.

"What?"

"Mushrooms."

The girl intervened. "He was telling me he knew where there were some wonderful wild mushrooms over there, officer, and I—well, I guess I teased him. He said he'd prove it to me. About the mushrooms, I mean." She put her hands on her hips and glared. "Danny, that was really dumb, going over there in the middle of the night like that! I told you it's private property." Her eyes swung back to Lassiter. "Are you going to arrest him, officer?"

Lassiter began to have the dread, drab feeling of having made a really stupid mistake. He glared at Danny and made a brave attempt to recoup. "How did you know about the mushrooms? Do you spend a lot of time over there, or what?"

"I fish over there in the pond sometimes," Danny said. He had begun to shake again. "I didn't know it was against the law to pick mushrooms. I really didn't! I'm sorry."

Lassiter drew in a long, regretful breath and shoved his revolver into its holster. "Show me some ID, please."

The young man tremblingly dug out a battered wallet and started searching through its grimy interior for a driver's license. Lassiter waited, glaring and pretending he hadn't just made a fool of himself.

IT WAS A little past 3 a.m. when Davidson Bell got out of bed and started for the bathroom and saw the red light through the third-floor window of his apartment. He forgot about nature's call and crouched by the window, fumbling around in the dark for the binoculars he sometimes used to look at birds, and sometimes at resident women strolling out back.

This, thought Davidson Bell, was too good to be true. He had daydreamed about seeing the red light, investigating it, and solving the whole mystery, but the last thing he had anticipated was wish fulfillment.

But there it was, vague and seeming to blink constantly in the dim field of his binoculars—a red light, unquestionably.

Seen at a downhill distance of a thousand yards or more, and partly obscured by tree leaves and vegetation, the light was never visible for more than a few seconds at a time. But there was no doubt about its reality, or the fact that it seemed to be moving around at ground level. Bell realized that it was the moving around, going in and out of blocking vegetation, that created the illusion of a flicker.

His breathing, never all that great due to a touch of emphysema, came faster as he watched. He imagined himself telling Laura Michaels about this in the morning, or calling the little boob on the desk right now to report it, or doing something that would let him get a lot more credit on his own while at the same time putting that snotty Ellen Smith in her place once and for all.

The thought of showing up Ellen Smith decided him before he had much time to think about alternatives.

Banging his knee against an end table in the dark, he fumbled around in his closet and found a pair of work pants to put on. A T-shirt followed. Afraid he would mess around so long the light would vanish, he crammed his bare feet straight into the cool, hard, slippery interior of a pair of dress shoes, pausing only long enough to tie the laces.

He put his keys in his pocket and grabbed his flashlight. Going to the apartment door, he let himself out without a sound. The hallway stood vacant, silent. His footsteps made only the slightest whispering sound as he hurried to the back elevator.

Down on the first floor, the tile-floored corridor leading to the kitchen was also deserted at this hour. Bell tried to walk silently, but his heels made slight clicking sounds as he walked to the back security door. Of the kind that automatically locked to the outside world, it had to allow quick exit in order to satisfy the fire code. A press on the horizontal bar was all it took to open the lock from inside.

Bell pushed on the bar and swung the door open onto a warm, humid night. He went out onto the tiny concrete pad and let the door close behind him with a soft whoosh. He could walk around and get the little boob's attention at the front doors when he was finished.

At ground level he could no longer see the blinking red light down the hill somewhere in the thicket. If he was going to find out what caused the light, he was going to have to go out through the gate and slip down the path.

He felt an enormous sense of danger, thinking about it. But he never stopped moving across the bare tarmac. Violet hadn't known what to expect, he told himself. She had been surprised. He was going to be a lot more cautious and clever. Nobody was going to get the drop on him.

Thinking of somebody getting the drop on somebody made Bell wish he had thought of bringing the .22 caliber pistol he always kept in his bedroom. Well, it was far too late now. He reached the metal gate in the back fence, depressed the locking mechanism, and stepped through onto the dirt path.

This could turn out to be very dumb if I get caught.

It was harder than he had anticipated to move down the path without making a racket. There were dried leaves on the dirt, and decaying vegetation. He went very slowly, putting one foot deliberately ahead of the other. Not enough noise to alert someone, he decided. Still, apprehension made his breath more painful in his throat. Sweat stung his eyes. *You are an old fool to be doing this.*

More than halfway down the hill, the path curved slightly to the left. That was where he could look on down through the brush and get another glimpse of the red light. It was gone as quickly as it had blinked. So maybe it really was being turned on and off.

He continued downward, moving even more slowly. The farther he got into the woods, the less secure and sure he felt about everything. But it was very quiet and he knew he hadn't been spotted and if he just continued to be very, very careful, he might be able to solve this thing once and for all. He could just imagine what a hero that would make him. Even insufferable Colonel Rodgers would have to salute him.

A night bug came out of nowhere and crashed into his face—fluttery bunch of fuzzy stuff and stingy little feet or wings—and he involuntarily dashed at it with his free hand, making a slight racket. His pulse hammered in his skull as he froze, scared he might have given himself away. The mystery person was right out there somewhere close, and this was serious.

An eternity—at least a minute—went by. His pulse began to get back toward normal. Not to worry, he consoled himself; he was still undetected.

He moved forward along the path again, crouching a bit now, looking all around. More minutes slipped by and he saw and heard nothing. He began to think the mystery person or thing had vanished and was almost ready to feel disappointed.

Then, almost straight off to his right, in the direction of the little clearing and the frog pond, the red light winked on and off again. It was very, very close.

Bell went to one knee and peered through the weeds, trying to get a better look. He began to hear something— a very faint, high-pitched whine. It was getting even closer and he could hear someone out there breathing now...could hear feet crunching vegetation.

Maybe, he thought, this hadn't been such a good idea after all. But now he couldn't run because he would be discovered if he moved a muscle.

The red light twinkled again, very quickly on and off. But in the second or two it was on, illuminating everything in reflected pink, Bell registered the whole scene. He was astounded, and a lot of things began to fall into place at the same time new questions arose. So *that* was the Weed Eater, he thought. And of course the red light would be the least likely kind to be spotted. And—

His knee, planted in the dirt of the path, suddenly slipped, pitching him sideways. He tried desperately to catch himself but it was too late. He fell heavily onto his side, making a most dreadful racket.

Panic flooding through him, he scrambled to get to his feet and run. But he wasn't fast enough. He heard the thrashing of brush right on top of him and then saw the legs, and the long dark tube.

"No!" he pleaded hoarsely, throwing up one hand to try to defend himself.

That was too late, too. The shadow-figure moved and something crashed into Bell's head with paralyzing impact, and he fell deeper and deeper, darker and darker, until the last scintilla of light went out.

SEVEN

WHEN LAURA ARRIVED shortly after dawn there was an ambulance, lights flashing, in the side driveway leading to the center's back service area. As she parked, she could already see yellow crime scene tape strung everywhere back there, cordoning off the entire area. She spotted two sheriff's cruisers, a covey of Norman city police cars, and enough TV crews to cover a small war. Mrs. Epperman's silver Cadillac was parked behind one of the TV vans, which had a pop-up tower in place. In front of the van, a young female news reader in a pretty blue dress was talking earnestly to a camera held by a fat man in shorts and T-shirt. Bracing herself—continuation of a process she had been working on since receiving the telephone call at five-fifteen—Laura hopped out and hurried down the driveway toward the back.

"—And so still another shock is added to the mounting terror at Timberdale," the news reader was saying breathlessly as Laura walked past her. "No official word has yet been given on the exact time of death...." Laura got out of earshot and hurried on.

One of the three Norman policemen standing behind the yellow tape politely stopped her. "Sorry, ma'am. Investigation in progress."

"I'm Laura Michaels. The assistant manager at Timberdale. They called me here."

The policeman frowned. "Please wait." Unbelting a handheld radio, he pressed the button and said something Laura couldn't quite understand. He held the radio to his ear to hear the reply, issued a few more monosyllables, listened again, rebelted the radio. "You can go back, ma'am."

Laura started past him. Behind her a shrill voice started calling her in a frantic tone. She turned to see Maude Thuringer approaching across the pavement with all the speed she could muster in her long floral bathrobe and floppy-eared bunny slippers. Not wanting to, Laura waited for her.

"My good God," Maude panted, reaching her side, "why didn't somebody notify me? I slept in this morning and then I didn't have the radio or the TV on and I didn't know diddly about any of this until I went downstairs to get my prunes." The little woman clutched at Laura's arm. "Is it true? Is it Mr. Bell? Has the murderer struck again?"

Laura gently but firmly disengaged herself from Maude's grip. "Maude, I don't know a thing yet. I just got here. I'm going back now."

"Great! I'll go with you." Maude took a step toward the tape.

The policeman moved in front of her.

"Maude," Laura said, "you can't go."

"I got to go! I've got to see the clues!"

Laura patted her on the shoulder and ducked under the tape.

"It isn't fair!" Maude cried after her. "I'm the expert!"

On the far side, behind another police car, Laura encountered another policeman. He nodded and pointed wordlessly in the general direction she was already walking. She went around the corner of the building and across the tarmac, and ran headlong into two paramedics and two more policemen coming fast, pushing a gurney. The blanket-shrouded figure on it was strapped down and completely covered, head included. Laura's stomach lurched.

"Coming through," one of the paramedics panted. "Coming through."

She got out of the way. They went on, staggering as they hurried the gurney along on wobbly wheels not made for pavement. Grabbing a deep breath, she headed on back in the direction from which they had come.

Near the back gate that led down into the woods, more yellow tape had been strung in all directions. A strobe light flashed in the shade as a photographer moved around. Laura saw the sheriff and Aaron Lassiter and another policeman and Mrs. Epperman.

Mrs. Epperman spied her at the same time and rushed over. "There you are at last. This is terrible. Terrible!"

Lassiter came over and joined them before Laura could reply. He gave her a brief hug. He looked drained and tense.

"Mr. Bell?" Laura asked, already sure.

Lassiter pointed, and for the first time she noticed the ugly dark puddle on the pavement near the gate. "He was found here. Looks like he had been dead a few hours, probably middle of the night sometime."

Laura hugged herself. "Killed?"

"Skull smashed. Yes."

"Who found him. How?"

"In spite of everything we said yesterday, one of your people came out here this morning, on the way to the JiffyGrub to get some Twinkies for breakfast. It wasn't light yet. She stumbled right over his body, then went screaming bloody murder back into the building."

"Who was it, for heaven's sake?"

Lassiter frowned and flipped the pages in his notebook.

Mrs. Epperman growled, "Sada Hoff. I'm going to kill her."

"Sada! She's the last person I would have expected to disobey instructions."

"Well, she did, and now unless I miss my guess she's

either up at the front entrance, regaling the TV people with blood and gore, or else she's in the atrium, holding everybody spellbound with details about how hideous it all was. It's horrible, Laura, *horrible*. What are you going to do about it?''

''What am *I* going to do about it?'' Laura said, hearing her voice come out a squeak.

One of the Norman policemen who had gone up with the gurney now returned and said something to the sheriff, who plodded morosely over. ''I've got to go make a statement.'' He paused a moment and scowled at Lassiter. ''What am I supposed to say?''

Lassiter looked dumbfounded. ''You're asking me?''

''Have you got any theories? Hey, you're the college graduate here. I can't just say we've got a raving maniac roving around these woods, knocking people off at random.'' The sheriff stopped abruptly, his face going slack, then tight. He turned to Mrs. Epperman. ''What do you think? Is there a chance in hell that one of your old codgers has gone berserk and might be luring other residents down here to do them in?''

''Of course not!'' Mrs. Epperman gasped. ''It's out of the question.'' She paused and swallowed hard, turning Laura's way. ''It's impossible, dear girl—right? Tell them it's impossible. Laura? Laura?''

Laura felt the breath chill in her throat. ''My God,'' she whispered, staring at Lassiter. ''I never really thought seriously about that possibility until this minute.''

Lassiter nodded grimly. ''Come with me, okay? There's something else that needs checking out.''

He turned and opened the back gate. Laura followed him as he went through and started down the dirt path under the trees, striding hard.

Over his shoulder he told her, ''One of our deputies is down here. I think we've found the spot where the old geezer was actually attacked.''

"But his body was up—"

"I know," Lassiter interrupted. "But there's grass trampled down here, and a little more blood. Might be that whoever killed him did it down here and then dragged his body up above to be found."

"But my God, Aaron, why would anybody do something like that?"

"If you get a clue, babe, let me in on it.

"I DON'T THINK there's any question the deed was done in the woods," Lassiter said later, behind the closed door of Laura's office. "Do you agree?"

Laura shuddered, remembering the bloody weeds. "Yes. Of course."

"But hell's bells. None of your old codgers could have hauled a body that far, right?"

"Right."

"But maybe one of them could fool us."

Laura rubbed her aching head. "But what would the motive be? Robbery?"

"Not this time, I think."

"Revenge?"

"For what?"

"I have no idea. I do know that an early symptom of Alzheimer's sometimes is hostility, even threat of violence. What if someone here has started to slip over the edge?"

"Have you seen any sign of that?"

"No. We've got people who are kind of shaky mentally, and a lot more who are eccentric. But dammit, when you're seventy-five years old you've earned the right to be eccentric if you want."

"But you haven't," he persisted in that bulldog tone he got sometimes, "actually suspected anybody of getting violent."

Laura almost felt a pulse of irritation with him. "No.

But maybe there could be such a person who's not in either of my groups. Or maybe they're good at hiding it. I mean, why should I see something that no one else can?"

"Because you're the damn therapist, that's why!"

"Oh, lord," Laura whispered. "Look, honey, I'm *in training* to be a therapist. And even when I'm finished I'm not going to be trained to deal with homicidal maniacs, which is what this person would have to be. That's why I think there could be someone in Timberdale who's capable of this, but I don't believe so. That's the best I can do."

Lassiter paced the few feet between desk and wall. "To make an attack like that, I would need considerable physical strength. A lot of the old folks simply couldn't handle it on that basis."

"Yes, but a surprising number could. A lot of them are far from feeble."

"Now you're talking like it *could* be some resident!"

"Aaron, I just don't know, period."

His chest heaved in frustration. "But you don't think so."

"I don't think so."

"You'll watch for possible signs?"

"Yes."

Someone tapped insistently on the door. Lassiter, standing right beside it, got an okay nod from Laura and opened it. Francie Blake, a vision in a mauve sundress and matching heels, burst in.

"Oh, there you are," she told Lassiter, breathless. "I'm so glad I found you! I got in a little late this morning and just heard all the dreadful news! I know a lot of people are going to be asking me this morning—do you think it's wise for me to go ahead and plan this luau for the weekend, in view of all the turmoil and all?"

Her hand went to his forearm. Jewels glittered. Francie

was one of the world's great touchers, and always perfectly innocent, of course.

Lassiter frowned. "Looks like Laura, here, would be the one to give an opinion on that."

"Well, yes," Francie said, pretty lower lip pouting. "But you're a law officer, Aaron. You're more experienced than Laura is with the reactions of people after a violent episode of some kind. Tell me, do you think you might want to think about it, and then call me back later today? We could get together for coffee or something after I get off work and go over all the angles."

Lassiter gently disengaged himself from her hand. "You'd better discuss it with Laura, ma'am. I'm real busy right now."

Francie looked a bit crestfallen, but tried to muster a bright smile. "You naughty man! I've told you before, call me Francie."

"Yes, ma'am," Lassiter grunted, and shoved out of the office.

Despite everything else, Laura felt a small twinge of satisfaction when she saw Francie's expression.

"Heck!" the golden blond murmured. Then she escalated to her strongest expression: "Fudge!"

Mrs. Epperman appeared in the doorway Lassiter had just vacated. "What are the two of you doing, standing around?" she demanded in her best drill sergeant's tone. "Francie! Get out there and start talking up the luau. Figure out some things you need volunteers for. I've got Still Bill starting on the wall decorations early—at once—in order to create something else for them to think about. You must do the same thing. I also want some kind of musical entertainment in the atrium this afternoon. Call that banjo player. Well? Move, child! Move!"

Francie fled, gorgeous legs twinkling.

Mrs. Epperman whirled on Laura. "You, too. Get out there and mingle. Do something to shut Maude Thuringer up. She's rushing around with that damned notebook of hers, getting everybody even more stirred up. Have an extra group session or something. Anything. We need all the diversions we can come up with. Hurry!''

Laura obeyed, going out through the reception desk area. She got a soft surprise when she looked around and realized how early it still was. Paula Burwell hadn't come in yet, and Stacy was still on the desk, eating a Dunkin' Donuts cream-filled. Although a handful of residents stood around the atrium talking in hushed tones, the dining room had just opened and most of them were in there, going through the breakfast buffet line. The grandfather clock in the far corner showed exactly eight o'clock.

Still Bill Mills appeared, trailed by a wimpy little custodian who seemed to spend most of his time reading Westerns behind the boilers in the basement. Still Bill had a tall stepladder in hand, and his aide was carrying big bunches of dusty, wilted-looking fake palm tree leaves. As Laura watched, Still Bill set up the stepladder on the far side, produced a big roll of masking tape from a pocket of his overalls, and signaled the custodian to dump the imitation leaves in a pile nearby.

Laura walked over. ''Bill, I don't think you need to hurry with this. Mrs. Epperman just wants some activity to take people's minds off...things.''

''I know,'' Still Bill said. ''But I tell you what, I might's well just go ahead and tape them up, Miz Michaels. I've never been one to prognosticate. It's not my style. You know what they always say, a thief in time saves nine.''

Dr. Fred Which came in through the front doors, spied Laura, and made a beeline. ''I imagine we'll have a lot of extra customers with anxiety reactions of some kind this morning, Laura. Maybe you could spend some time around the clinic?''

"I will," Laura promised, "after I attend to some other things."

Which scowled. "We need to consult on this issue. What say we have dinner at my place tonight? We should be able to come up with a plan of attack designed to maximize the efficacy of whatever therapeutic interventions we might find are required over the next few days."

Laura knew from past experience what kind of attack the good bachelor doctor would mount if she got anywhere near his apartment. "Gee, Fred, it's a great idea. But I've got to go to a school function with Trissie tonight."

He brightened. "Afterward. Doesn't matter how late."

"I'm sorry. It sounds nice, but I really can't."

Coming across a corner of the atrium in their direction were gigantic Davilla Rose and tiny Sada Hoff. Seeing their approach, Which sighed and walked away.

"Laura?" Davilla Rose said. "Do you suppose we could have a word, the three of us?"

Overhead, Still Bill Mills dropped a palm frond and muttered what might have been an obscenity. "Sure," Laura said, pointing to the couch and armchair arrangement nearby. "Over there?"

They went over. Sada perched on the edge of the chair, so small and light she seemed not to make an impression in the soft pillows. Davilla sank into one end of the couch like a whale hitting the beach; springs creaked, cushions whooshed, and wood frame groaned. Timberdale's resident poet, Laura noticed with interest, did not have her usual notebook to record any random bursts of poetic inspiration.

Laura sat on the remaining end of the couch between the two women.

"I just hope we're doing the right thing," Sada murmured fretfully.

"We are, Sada," Davilla said. "We agreed."

"What's going on?" Laura asked.

Davilla heaved an enormous sigh. "Laura. We're worried about Ken Keen."

Sada nodded. "Deeply worried."

"Why?" Laura asked.

Davilla heaved a tidal sigh. "He isn't himself."

Sada frowned with worry, then suddenly tittered. "Of course he never has been."

Laura wondered if this was more of the grumpy paranoia she was so familiar with among some of the residents. But Davilla Rose and Sada Hoff had never been part of the group of chronic complainers. So she said carefully, "Suppose you guys tell me what's going on."

Davilla's enormous bosom heaved again. "For one thing, he's been more secretive lately."

"And staying to himself," Sada put in.

Davilla nodded. "Standoffish."

"Almost, you would say, reclusive," Sada added.

"And we think he's been worried about money," Davilla said.

"I hadn't noticed any of that in the group," Laura told them.

"Oh, he can put on a good act when he wants to," Davilla said.

"That's right," the tiny Sada agreed. "A good act."

"But he doesn't sit with anyone in the dining room these days if he can help it," Davilla went on.

Sada's head bounced up and down in vigorous agreement. "That's right. He sits alone if he can."

"And if he has to sit at a table with other people, he hardly says a word."

"Hardly a word."

"And you know what a terrible letch he is, Laura. Well, he hasn't tried anything naughty with any of the ladies that we know about for a long, long time."

"Months," Sada explained.

"Maybe he's just not feeling well," Laura suggested. "We all—"

"Then how," Davilla cut in, "would you explain the way he blew up at Ellen the other night at the bridge table?"

"Yes. Explain that."

"And the way he yelled and cursed at Still Bill last week, for no reason at all?"

Laura glanced across the atrium to Still Bill, perched atop his tall, shaky ladder. "Bill hasn't said anything about it."

"We think there's something seriously wrong," Davilla said.

"Seriously wrong," Sada echoed.

"We are deeply worried."

"Yes. Deeply."

Davilla shifted her great bulk, making the couch complain. "What if we haven't seen the worst of it?"

"Yes," Sada agreed. "What if?"

Laura had begun to get an uncomfortable feeling. "Meaning?"

"Meaning what if these two deaths out on the path are not accidental incidents—robberies? What if somebody from inside Timberdale is responsible?"

Sada added quickly. "We aren't accusing anyone, you understand. But we definitely believe management should be aware of all this. And you, Laura, as head of our groups, you above all should know about it so you can be alert...possibly say or do something to check the accuracy of our observations."

Davilla nodded. "My brother, rest his soul, got Alzheimer's while he was only in his fifties. He made life miserable for his wife, poor thing. He went from agitation to being practically a hermit to shouting and throwing things, and finally she had to have him put in a nursing home. It can happen. It could happen to any of us."

"To any of us," Sada chimed in.

"I'll certainly look into the matter," Laura told them, being as guarded as possible.

Davilla grunted satisfaction and heaved herself up off the couch. Observing her effort was a little like watching a circus tent being struck. "We'll report if we notice anything more that's specific," she promised.

"Yes," Sada said. "At once."

"It must have been a terrible shock for you, Sada," Laura put in, "finding the body that way this morning."

The little woman shuddered. "I'll never forget it."

"What were you doing on the path so early?"

"I was on the way to JiffyGrub for some cupcakes."

"Yes, that's what someone told me. But hadn't you heard the notice suggesting that no one should go down there alone until we had this straightened out?"

Sada's face wrinkled in a frown. "Well, yes, of course. But I didn't think it applied to me. I'm not one of those doddery old fools who can't take care of themselves."

Laura took a slow breath. "Of course. Well, thanks to both of you for giving me this information about Ken. You can be sure I'll look into the matter. In the meantime, I know you both understand how vital it is that you not talk about this with anyone else. The last thing we need is another rumor added to the mill."

Davilla blinked. "Of course." Her voice sounded weak.

"Maybe we shouldn't have told Maude," Sada said.

"Oh, I'm sure little Maude will be the soul of discretion!"

"Yes," Sada murmured, dubious.

The two old women moved across the atrium. Laura watched them go. She didn't know whether to be sad or dismayed or suspicious.

Her first thought was that if Maude Thuringer had heard about Ken Keen's "suspicious" behavior, poor

Keen was in for surveillance that might drive anybody crazy. And Maude would talk. To think Maude wouldn't talk was like thinking you could have a thunderstorm without thunder.

Probably, Laura thought, the women's suspicions of Ken Keen were based on nothing of significance. Everyone was likely to come up with suspects and theories now that there had been a second death; hysteria was sometimes deceptively quiet, feeding itself like this.

On the other hand, she felt chagrined that Keen had apparently shown *some* signs of uncharacteristic behavior, and she hadn't picked up on them at all. She prided herself on being observant. But she hadn't noticed anything. And surely it wasn't true, the rumor about his needing money; his bills were always paid early.

Did that mean there was nothing at all to the two women's observations? Laura remembered one thing they had said that she could check out at once.

EIGHT

STILL BILL MILLS looked down with sharp alarm as Laura put her hand on the side of his teetery ladder. "Watch out, Miz Michaels," he said a little shrilly. "This ladder is real presumptuous, and with me up here on top it's overbearing."

"Bill, could we talk a minute?"

He paused, fists full of fake palm frond. "Now?"

"Yes, Bill, please."

He stowed the fronds over the top of the ladder, balancing their clumsy length on the platform. They shook but didn't fall. He came down with surprising agility and grace for such an ungainly, elderly man, and mopped his forehead with a red bandanna as he faced Laura.

"Bill, did you have some kind of tiff with Ken Keen last week?"

Still Bill's long lantern jaw swung. "Heck, I knew he'd complain to somebody sooner or earlier."

"You *did* have a fuss?"

"Well, you might call it that, Miz Michaels, but it didn't really amount to a hill of jeans. He just got sort of crabby with me. Maybe some people would have really taken offense at what he said, but for me it was no big deal. I've got a thick head, stuff just rolls off me like off a pig's back."

"What happened?"

Still Bill's good eye looked south and his weak one turned a bit toward the southeast as he remembered. "Nothing much, really. I was working in the side flowerbeds, see. And he's got this gardenia he's wintered over in the inside second-floor hallway, by one of the north

windows, for two years now. I'd carried it back outside
for him this spring. The pot weighs about a ton. So there
it was, and I had the hose in my hand, and it looked kind
of dry, so I irritated it some.''

"You mean irrigated it? Watered it?"

"That's what I said, yes."

"And?"

"I guess Mr. Keen was out in the garden not far away,
or in the vicissitude. Because I hadn't gone more than a
few feet on by with the hose when he come up ahint me,
crazier than a hunningbird.''

Laura couldn't get a picture. "How crazy? In what
way?"

Still Bill grimaced. "I'm not trying to get anybody in
trouble.''

"Nobody's in trouble, Bill. Just tell me."

"Well, he was red as a tomato in the face and his
mouth was all quivery and his eyes looked...I
dunno...wild and crazy. And he started telling me he was
the only one that knew how to water the gardenia, and I
probably washed the acid right on through, and I was a
dolt, and so on.''

"And that's it?"

"Well...no."

"What else?"

"He grabbed my rake out of my hand and tried to
brain me with it.''

"He *what?*"

"He didn't even get close," Still Bill added quickly.
"It was no big deal. And by that time he was screaming
and cussing so, I had plenty of warning. I just ducked
and took the rake back from him, and he just sort of beat
a tasty retreat back inside again.''

Laura began to get a black feeling in the pit of her
stomach. Ken Keen had been the center's resident letch
ever since his arrival, and he worked out every day in

the exercise room. To an outsider he looked even younger than his sixties, and in the prime of health. Only his mind showed signs of Alzheimer's—loss of short-term memory and slight confusion at times—and those symptoms had been benign up to this point. Now could his illness have taken a terrible new turn?

It didn't seem possible. But Laura didn't know as much about Alzheimer's as she wished she did. She groped.

"Bill, have you seen or heard Ken getting into it with anyone else?"

"Well, just what they said he did at the card game a week ago, when he went down a couple and slung his cards clean across the activity room."

"Didn't he used to be a fisherman?"

"Yes, I'd call him an invertebrate fisherman, actual. But he sure hasn't been out there at the pond in a long time, judging by my observations."

"Thanks, Bill," Laura murmured, and started away.

"I don't want to get him in trouble," Still Bill called after her. "He's a good old boy, if you want my opinion."

"Okay, Bill. Thanks again."

She had to check this out. But she didn't want to because she knew it could lead to a necessary—but terrible—discovery.

At least she had every excuse to go slowly, she thought. In some circumstances it might have been best simply to walk up to a resident and ask what was going on with them. But if Ken Keen really was experiencing serious troubles, alerting him with a confrontation might be the worst thing she could do. She would have to watch, but be careful how she did it.

She walked back toward the reception desk. Paula Burwell had come in to start her workday there. She looked pale and a bit nervous.

"Hi, Paula," Laura said. "Mess, isn't it?"

"You have a man waiting to see you," Burwell said, inclining her head in the direction of a small sitting room up near the front doors. Usually used for new visitors, it had a couch and three chairs, a coffee table, and a nice floorlamp. It also, Laura saw now, had a visitor in it. The man was wiry, middle-aged, and almost bald, sitting at one end of the couch and staring at one of the year-old magazines kept in there.

"Not a reporter," she groaned.

"No." Burwell's pretty dark eyes scanned a note on the desk. "He says his name is Aikman. James Aikman. He told me Mrs. Epperman left word at his office for him to report here to you about some kind of security job."

"Oh, hell, I forgot. Okay, Paula. Thanks."

James Aikman got to his feet as she entered the sitting room. Her first impression of him was of his stature, his extraordinarily lean and muscular build, and the flat, emotionless chill of his expression. He had eyes like pale gray marbles. A thin attaché case rested on the floor near his loafer-clad feet.

She put her instinctive aversion on the back burner and smiled as she extended her hand. "Mr. Aikman? Hi. So sorry you had to wait. I'm Laura Michaels."

Aikman's handshake was every bit as cold and lifeless as she might have expected. "Glad to meet you, Mrs. Michaels. I talked to your Mrs. Epperman about a security position."

"Yes. Won't you come with me to my office?"

He nodded, picked up his attaché case, and followed her.

"We've had quite a bit of excitement around here, as you know," she told him as they neared the reception counter.

He didn't comment.

"And we can certainly use some additional help."

Again he said nothing, and his face had the flat featurelessness of a statue. Most people in this situation would have made small talk, but he made none whatsoever. Leading him around the counter and into the hallway leading to her office, Laura began to feel spooky.

Once in her office, however, she had no more than sat down when Aikman came at her from all sides at once.

His cold face not changing expression in the slightest, he opened his attaché case on his knees and produced a thin manila folder. He handed it across the desk. "Here is an up-to-date résumé along with three recent letters of reference. You'll see I have background in the military as well as law enforcement. I've operated my own security and detective agency for almost ten years. That fourth sheet represents my fee schedule."

Laura glanced through the heavy, ivory-colored sheets. Produced on a laser printer, they were crisp, efficient, and coldly well organized. She noticed some of the special schools he claimed to have attended and a list of some other current clients—businesses only, no private individuals' names revealed. She came to the last sheet, the rate structure.

"For this position," the expressionless Aikman told her, "those fees are not applicable."

Laura met his eyes. "Oh?"

"Correct. Those fees reflect hourly rates for short-term jobs. I have no other full-time corporate-type clients at this time. I assume that your utilization of my services would require at least six ten-hour nights on my part. I have here"—he handed over an additional crisp sheet of paper—"my bid to perform that kind of contract security work."

Laura glanced at the figures, comparing them. "A lot lower."

"I can afford to offer such a rate due to the extended nature of the work schedule."

"I see." She looked back at the pages. She knew he was watching her with intense, frozen interest. She felt uneasy, almost like shivering. Maybe a lot of people on the fringes of law enforcement were like this, she thought.

"Assuming we wished to retain you, Mr. Aikman, when could you start?"

He didn't blink. "Tonight."

"And you would…"

"Primarily patrol the outer perimeter at night, on foot. Also I will require a master key to an outside entrance and information on turning off the alarm system whenever I wish to enter or exit the building. It may be that I will need to establish some mode of surveillance within the structure, you see, if it appears that certain individuals are attempting to circumvent my observation and use the path despite warnings."

"And will you work alone, Mr. Aikman?"

His eyes looked like a snake's. "I need no assistance."

"What is likely to happen if you encounter a mugger?"

"I will apprehend him, of course."

"But if he struggles or attempts to escape?"

For the first time, a chill smile fleeted across Aikman's face. "There will be no struggle."

"Will it be perfectly safe for you?"

"As safe as I can design the surveillance to be. I will have a cellular telephone on my person as well as a flashlight and a weapon."

"A weapon?"

"A revolver."

"I see. A weapon is standard in cases such as this?"

"It is for me, Mrs. Michaels. That's why I'm still alive."

Laura hesitated. She didn't like the man. But Mrs. Epperman had been clear enough. "Thank you, Mr. Aikman." She stood and extended her hand. "Will there be anything else you require?"

"I think not."

"Who on our staff shall I introduce you to at this time?"

"No one. I'll introduce myself to the people I need to know."

"Fine." She took a deep breath. "And you can start tonight, you said?"

Aikman took a step toward the door and looked back at her with the same expressionless face. "Actually, in order to establish certain criteria, I'll start this first day now. At once."

Laura tried once more to be friendly. "Good luck, Mr. Aikman. We really need your help."

He left without replying.

BY TEN-THIRTY, when Laura managed to assemble a special session of the Breakfast Club, all sign of the media had vanished, and so had police and sheriff's department people. A stranger walking into the atrium might have detected no sign at all of anything amiss. Francie Blake was scurrying about, trying to get volunteers for a talent show as part of the luau party, and Still Bill Mills had several of the fake palm trees already installed. Mrs. Epperman, after rushing around in all directions and having a loud argument with a TV reporter who had gotten into the dining room, had suddenly vanished, and her car was not in the parking lot. In Laura's experience, she had a tendency to do this when things became too hectic.

By this time, however, even the therapy group members, although unusually reserved as they trooped into the activity room, did not appear exceptionally agitated.

It was a smaller gathering than normal, although the meeting had been announced twice over the public address system. Laura was not surprised. Some people needed time alone after a shock to get themselves sorted out emotionally.

Stoney Castle and his wife were in the front row. So was Ellen Smith, wearing a white painter's smock over her leather skirt and vest. Julius and Dot Pfeister completed the first row. Judge Emily Young dozed in the second row of chairs, with Col. Roger Rodgers and the Buckinghams beside him. Ken Keen was not in attendance. Just as Laura was about to begin, Maude Thuringer came in late, hectic and overstimulated, skirt flapping with her hurry.

Then, to Laura's considerable surprise, a newcomer entered and quietly took a chair in the last row: tall, painfully skinny, always formal in a shapeless dark suit, old Mr. Whitnaur was one of Timberdale's charter residents. But he took no part in any organized activity that Laura was aware of, spending most of his time alone in his room smoking a pipe and reading obscure academic journals. Laura didn't know much about him except that he had been an English professor at the university long ago, was a widower, and stayed to himself. To see him coming into a meeting of the Breakfast Club startled her.

All the regulars were staring mutely at her, waiting.

"I'm glad we could get this nice a gathering on short notice," she began. "It's been a rough morning for all of us. I know everybody feels terrible about Mr. Bell. I just want you to know that Timberdale has just hired a new, additional security man. He'll be patrolling outside at night. We intend to make sure there won't be any more tragedies around this place."

She paused and looked around again. "Stoney, good morning. Good morning, Judge. Maude, I hope you're feeling well. Mr. Whitnaur, it's really nice to see you here with us this morning. If at any time you have something you want to say, just feel free to break in. We don't have many rules in this group except a ban on punching each other.'' She grinned to show it was a joke.

Whitnaur, however, did not smile. To the contrary, his deeply inset eyes instantly glistened with tears. She saw his big, bony hands clench into fists on his knees. His shoulders began to shake silently.

''Let's talk about Mr. Bell a minute,'' she told the group, hurrying ahead to prevent undue attention being put on the old newcomer. ''Boy, I'll tell you what. He was a stubborn old gentleman, wasn't he? Colonel, I think you and he used to partner in bridge sometimes, didn't you?''

IT WAS A short session, and one that Laura left feeling inept and frustrated. Clearly everybody had come for some kind of reassurance or help with their shock about the latest death. But it was too fresh, apparently, and no one had much to say. Even Maude Thuringer was uncharacteristically quiet. At eleven-ten, Laura gently closed it down.

''There won't be any more accidents,'' she told them. ''We've got more security now and we're going to find out who did these things. If it's someone messing around outside, waiting to take advantage of one of us and steal our money, our new security man is going to catch them.'' Then she planted her thought-out threat: ''If it's someone closer to us here—one of our own—we'll spot them and root them out. I've already begun to construct a profile, if it should be somebody we all know.''

No one responded.

''So let's call it a day,'' she said, giving them a much brighter smile than she felt.

Most of the members silently left the room. Maude Thuringer scurried up, breathless with excitement. ''So you do think it could be an inside job,'' she whispered.

"I saw you talking with Sada and Davilla. Is that what decided you? Do you think they're right about—"

Laura shushed her. "I just wanted to make sure everybody understood, Maude, that we'll leave nothing undone to get to the bottom of this."

Maude's eyes glittered with excitement. "Yeah, but you realize what you did, kiddo, when you talked about constructing a profile."

"That was just more reassurance. And if—"

"Right! If these deals *have* been an inside job, you just put yourself squarely in the middle of the target."

"Oh, Maude, I think you're being a bit—"

"I can't wait to hear what people are saying about that!" Maude said, and rushed out of the room.

Laura sighed and bent over to retrieve her notebooks. She felt a slight, uneasy chill. It had never occurred to her that mentioning a "profile" would do more than make people feel better. After all, she knew nothing about constructing a profile of a killer.

Gathering up her papers and stowing them in her briefcase, she thought everyone had gone when she turned and saw old Mr. Whitnaur still sitting in his chair. His big, sad eyes never left her face. He slumped like a man who had just been given a physical beating.

She went back and plopped down on the chair beside him. "Thanks for coming today."

He licked liverish lips, started to speak, failed, tried again. His voice rasped huskily, on the edge of tears. "I don't know how to cope with it. Maybe you can't help, but people say you're good."

"What is it?" Laura asked quietly.

"It's grief. A man my age ought to know how to deal with grief. At some point in your life you ought to be able to come up with some damned wisdom. You ought to know *something* about *something*."

"I can tell how sad you are. You feel kind of lost."

He nodded almost violently. "Now I've got no one left."

"Tell me."

The old man made a sudden, slashing motion with his hand. "I'm just being a damned old idiot. I shouldn't have come here. Nothing can help. A man my age ought to keep his problems to himself—at least try to have some dignity."

"Not many of us are as strong as we would like to be," Laura told him. She was puzzled and going on instinct, with no idea of what was at issue here. "I know I beat up on myself sometimes for getting sad or scared or something—"

"After fifteen years of being alone!" he burst out with soft rage.

"What?"

"Fifteen years! My wife died fifteen years ago! All that time I managed on my own. Then, instead of just going on, I had to be a damned old fool and think there could be someone again. And then, just as sure as I opened the door to her...and she opened it to me...she goes off like this and they find her dead."

Laura still didn't get it. "They find her dead?"

He turned reddened eyes to her. "Violet! Who did you think I was talking about? Minnie Mouse?"

"Violet," Laura repeated, stunned.

"Oh, we were discreet," the old man raged. "You can't get married at our age. Lose some of your retirement benefits. Can't be open about it, either. Old fools around here would cackle and giggle behind our backs. She would...come down to my room. Late. Or I would go up there. She was a beautiful lady. I never thought I would love anybody again. Then she came along. We had—what we had—was beautiful. So beautiful. Now she's gone." Big tears began to course down his rutted cheeks, dripping onto the big, wrinkled hands he had folded impotently in his lap.

The truth finally thundered into Laura's consciousness, and she felt so stupid and so sorry for him that she leaned over and hugged his shoulders. "I'm so sorry, Mr. Whitnaur. I didn't know."

He shuddered again. "I'm going to find out who killed her, you know. I'm no detective and I'm not real smart, but I'm going to watch everybody all the time, and I don't care how many security people you put out, I'm going to get down that path real regular—I've got a gun—and I'm going to find that man one way or another and I'm going to kill him for what he did to her."

"Mr. Whitnaur, I know how sad you are. I know how hard it is for you. But you mustn't talk like that. The sheriff's department is working on the case, and we've got this new security man. We'll catch that person. You have to keep yourself safe."

The lank old man shrugged her off and got unsteadily to his feet. "I've already heard the rumors about Ken Keen. I don't think they're right, but I'm already watching him. I've got another idea, too. You can't stop me. I'm going to keep on."

"Mr. Whitnaur, let's talk a little more. Let me—"

"No! I thought maybe you could help, but you can't. I see that now. Nobody can help. Just leave me alone. Leave an old fool be."

"Mr. Whitnaur..."

Ignoring her, he limped to the door of the activity room and went outside.

NINE

MRS. EPPERMAN was back after lunch.

"I've had a terrible migraine," she told Laura in her office. "Have you followed my instructions while I was gone? Have steps been taken to keep those dreadful TV people off our property?"

"I've asked Still Bill and our other custodial people to keep an eye out," Laura said. "If we have anyone intruding, I'll be ready to ask them to leave."

"That isn't enough, you terrible girl! What's the matter with you? I told you I want all access barred. I want them arrested if they so much as poke their noses in the front door."

"Mrs. Epperman, we can't do that."

"Of course we can do that! Why can't we do that? This is private property, isn't it?"

"Well," Laura said lamely, remembering her telephone conversation with a friend who was a faculty member in the university's law school, "it is and it isn't."

"Oh! Do I have to do everything myself? You go ahead and work on those cost analysis figures I gave you days ago. You should have finished them long ago. I'll take care of this press thing myself, if I must."

Mrs. Epperman stormed out. Laura tried to pay attention to the pages of computer spreadsheet materials showing a slight but continuing stream of red ink on Timberdale's operating budget. Mrs. Epperman wanted to raise rentals or cut costs by reducing the quality of food served in the dining room or by cutting heating and air-conditioning costs, or by firing some of the women who cleaned rooms once a week and did laundry chores. It didn't appear to Laura like any of those options would get the job done without raising the hackles of everyone involved, and she went through the columns of figures with mounting anxiety, trying to find another alternative.

By three in the afternoon she had a splendid headache. After taking some Tylenol she went back to the sheets briefly, but Timberdale's other troubles kept gnawing at her. Finally, a little before four, she gave up and went out into the atrium.

It was quiet. A half-dozen residents sat around one of the conversational areas, quietly visiting. Judge Young dozed over one of his jigsaw puzzles. Laura went by the art room, where she found Ellen Smith angrily scraping oil paint off a desert scene in order to start over on it. In the lab, Kay Svendsen was alone, reading a magazine.

Laura thought about her idea as she moved around, and finally just gave in to it.

When Ken Keen opened the door of his apartment in response to her tapping, he looked half-asleep and rumpled in his red-and-white sweats. But his eyes widened when he recognized her. "Hey! Come on in!"

Laura entered with some sense of trepidation. Ken Keen might or might not be entirely harmless where his sexual preoccupations were concerned. She thought she could beat him off if it came to that; she had done it before, in the elevator, in the hallway, and in the dining room. But being in his apartment with him made her a bit more uneasy.

The apartment was unlike any other in the complex in the way Keen had furnished it. As nearly as Laura or anyone could figure, he wanted something resembling the interior of a sheik's desert tent. On the walls he had colorful tapestries, and on the floor—over the Timberdale gray carpet—Oriental throws. His couch looked like an explosion of fat red and green pillows, and his two easy chairs had yellow and red blankets tossed over them. An incense burner smoked on the big bronze-topped coffee table, filling the room with a scent that resembled Turkish tobacco. The draperies were drawn and two ruby-shaded floorlamps cast an eerie light. The stereo in the corner was on, playing some kind of exotic reed music.

Keen got an arm around Laura's waist before she took three steps inside. "I knew you'd come sooner or later, babe. I could tell you're hot."

Laura spun out of his grasp and held him at arms' length. "Ken, behave yourself."

He waggled his eyebrows. "Want a drink? I'm sorry, but I don't have any dope."

"You weren't at the group this morning."

He frowned. "Naw."

"You're one of our regulars, Ken."

He grunted, frowned, and looked glum. "Don't feel good."

"I haven't seen you around the building as much as usual either," Laura told him. "You missed the string quartet the other night. Is something wrong?"

"Maybe I just want to have some time to myself," he snapped in an uncharacteristic angry tone.

"The quartet was wonderful, and I know how you like chamber music."

He studied her with hostile, suspicious eyes. "What quartet?"

"The string quartet that played in the atrium. I just mentioned it."

"Why don't you just get out of here?" he demanded, his voice harsh. "I've got things to do."

"Ken, have you been having any money problems? Someone might be able to help, if that's the case—"

"Dammit! Who gave you the right to ask me a question like that?"

She felt she had to persist, as quietly as possible. "If you do have any problems like that, Ken—"

She broke off as he moved with astonishing—frightening—speed. He grabbed both her arms and whirled her toward the door. He had grabbed her on other occasions, but with nothing like this power. She felt a surge of panic.

"Ken! Let go. You're hurting me!"

"Just lemme alone," he growled, propelling her toward the door. "Is that asking too much, goddamn you? I told you, I don't feel good! Now get out! And don't come back!"

As he spoke, he grabbed the door open with one hand and thrust her out into the hall with the other. She stumbled and almost fell. He slammed the door in her face. She had just one last glimpse of him as the door closed. His eyes, red with anger, looked capable of anything. She had never seen his face twisted with such a boiling anger.

AARON LASSITER, back for still another Timberdale visit, dug into an inside pocket of his tunic. "I thought you'd like to know we got a report back on that kid who works the register nights over there at the JiffyGrub."

"I thought you already knew about his past."

"I knew the charges that had been filed in the past. I didn't know any details on the cases, or their disposition."

Laura watched him unfold several sheets of thin printout paper. "And now you do?"

He unfolded the flimsies and scanned them, reading from here and there: "Spurington, Henry, age twenty-two, weight, height, et cetera. Okay, here we go…June 1989, arrested and charged with grand theft auto, dismissed for insufficient evidence; July 1990, charged with simple assault on a store clerk, copped a plea of disturbing the peace, sentenced to thirty days in the county jail and five hundred dollar fine, served the time, and paid up; May 1991, arrested on suspicion of second-degree burglary, dismissed, insufficient evidence; August 1992, burglary again, convicted, sentenced to seven years at McAlester, released after a year under the federal court overcrowding order; December 1993, speeding and drunk driving, reduced to speeding, fine of ninety bucks.'' Lassiter stopped reading, refolded the sheets, and looked thoughtfully at Laura. ''A badass thief and burglar, and so far he's beaten most of the charges.''

''But he would be crazy, with that record, to be mugging people right across the street from where he works!''

''Yes, he would.''

''So how do you explain that, Aaron?''

''I don't.'' He hesitated, scowling. ''But on the other hand I can't ignore his record and proximity to these attacks. Maybe nobody in his right mind would mug somebody so close to the job. But maybe this punk isn't quite in his right mind, either. I've got to keep an eye on him. He's all we've got as a suspect right now anyway.''

''What can you do, exactly?''

''Hassle his a—rear end a little. Go back and ask more questions. Find out where he lives and talk to people in the area to see if he's been flashing any extra money or anything lately—if he has any pressing debts that might make him desperate enough to risk some penny-ante change purse robberies. Maybe establish that it isn't him, but he's got a pal who hangs around over there at the store, and the friend is doing it.'' Lassiter's forehead wrinkled. ''Hell! I don't know. Like I said, he's all I've got.''

Laura hesitated, then knew she had to mention the Ken Keen incident. ''There are some people at Timberdale who think one of our residents has been acting strangely lately.''

His head shot up. ''Yeah? Who?''

"One of our youngest residents. Ken Keen. He—"

"I remember the jerk. Isn't he the one that wears OU sweats a lot, and looks about forty, and goes off to hit golf balls and forgets to come back half the time, and tried to rip your clothes off in the elevator once?"

Laura had to smile. "You've got him pegged."

Lassiter leaned forward, his intensity radiating. "What's he been doing? How has he been different?"

She told him what Sada Hoff and Davilla Rose had told her, and then about her own visit to Keen's apartment.

"Well that old bastard!" Lassiter grunted. "I ought to just go over there and whip his butt for him!"

His quick, protective anger made her flush with pleasure. "He didn't hurt me, Aaron."

"I don't have to like it anyhow. Wow. Jesus." He frowned again. "I've got to think about this. Maybe interrogate him. No, not unless I had something tangible. No sense starting more wild rumors out there, creating even more problems for you. And it would just tip him off anyway, if there's anything to this."

"I don't think there is. I really don't, after mulling it over."

"You can't be sure though. Listen. Make damned sure *you* don't go out there in that little woods without an escort. Especially at night. I know how often you have to be here after dark. Watch it. I mean it. If something happened to you, I'd—I don't know what."

She squeezed his hand. "Hey, I'll be careful."

"You'd better be, dammit. If I had my way, nobody from Timberdale would go over to that JiffyGrub at all."

Laura studied his worried expression, eyebrows knit and mouth turned down. "I don't imagine many will, after this."

"It isn't just this peckerwood Spurington. You've got bikers cruising the back roads all the time, and most of them are just fine. But there's a rough element in that group, too, and they love to stop at places like that JiffyGrub out in the boondocks and swig a few beers and stand around and intimidate the normal folks who happen by. Then you've got workers from that construction project up the road. Good guys, mostly. But, again, you don't know about some of them. Of course it could be none of those. But somebody is out there, and none of this happened before the JiffyGrub went in, so there's some kind of connection.''

Laura nodded agreement. ''Not much chance it could be anyone inside our place, including Ken Keen.''

''No, we can't overlook anything if we can help it. I'll expect you to be keeping a sharp eye on him and letting me know if you notice anything else weird. But I'm still betting it's somebody connected with that store in some way. I mean—it opens and somebody gets attacked; cause and effect, somehow.''

''We're beefing up security,'' Laura told him. ''We hired a new guard today and he's already on the job. I think that will help a lot.''

Lassiter looked interested. ''What will he do, exactly?''

''Patrol outside at night, mainly. Especially in back.''

''Good. Mrs. Epperman said she was going to look for somebody. She worked fast.''

''Yes. She made some calls, and then this company called her first. She liked that kind of initiative. And he seems okay.''

Paula from the front desk rapped urgently on the office doorframe. ''Maude Thuringer is on TV in the atrium.''

''God,'' Laura groaned, and hurried out.

A dozen or so residents were clustered around the big console. There on the screen a fluffy pink news reader stood in front of Timberdale, sticking a microphone into

Maude Thuringer's face. Maude looked excited enough to take off vertically and hover.

"—which is much like the classic situation in *The Hound of the Baskervilles*," Maude panted. "Goodness! A suspect is out there, and all we have to do is nail him!"

The girl pulled the microphone back long enough to ask, "Is there terror inside the retirement center? Are the rumors we hear true, that residents fear the next attack may come inside the building?"

Maude's false eyelashes batted up and down like hummingbird wings. "Oh, my yes! There's lots of terror. Lots! We must apprehend this culprit at the earliest possible opportunity. It's like that Ed McBain story—"

The girl jerked the microphone back. "Thank you, Mrs. Terwiliger."

"Thuringer!" Maude yelled, almost inaudible away from the mike.

"Thuringer," the girl repeated with her most radiant Miss Tulsa University smile. "Thank you, Mrs. Thuringer. Reporting from Timberdale Retirement Center, this is Melissa Morgan. And now back to Bob at the news desk."

Walking back to Laura's office, Lassiter growled, "I didn't see anybody acting all that scared out there. Worried and upset, sure. But terrified? Isn't that a little much?"

"Hang on a sec," Laura said.

"What?"

"Just checking a theory." She counted, "A thousand and one, a thousand and two, a thousand and three—"

The door to Mrs. Epperman's office burst open. Mrs. Epperman came out like an NFL fullback running the draw. "Laura! Did you *see* it? Did you *see* that dreadful old biddy? I thought I told you to hush them all up, you awful girl! Now what are we going to do? Don't you know how badly publicity like this can hurt someone?

Don't you remember the Food Lion stories and what happened to *them*?''

"I saw it, Mrs. Epperman," Laura replied, hanging on to her fraying nerves. "I'll speak to Maude again."

"Laura! I *told* you before. Timberdale simply cannot afford any more unfavorable pub. I've trusted you to put a better spin on all of this. Why don't you get out a press release about our new hot tub, for example? Or why don't you point out that we've got almost two hundred residents and nothing like this wave of attacks has ever happened before?''

Laura felt her self-control beginning to crumble. "I'll get right on it, Mrs. Epperman. I—"

"Well, see that you do! Laura, I never thought I would have to say this *seriously,* but if you can't handle the requirements of this job, I'm sure I can find someone who can. Do I make myself clear?''

"Yes, Mrs. Epperman."

Mrs. Epperman turned and stormed back into her office. Lassiter watched Laura with his dear, worried, corrugated-forehead expression.

Without knowing exactly why or how, she began crying.

Lassiter enveloped her in his strong arms. "Hey! It's all right, babe."

"I feel like it's my fault," Laura choked. "First Violet. Now Mr. Bell. And I don't have a clue about who might be responsible, and Maude is running all over the place with her *Pit and the Pendulum* stories, and Mrs. Epperman keeps threatening me, and I've got that damned test Saturday and I'm not *nearly* ready for it—" Which was when she really broke down, and Lassiter held her while she wept.

"It's not your fault," he told her. "None of it is your fault. We'll catch this guy and then everything will be fine again. Believe me. You aren't to blame here. You've got to believe that.''

But she didn't believe that. She knew she was not being entirely rational. But she loved the people at Timberdale. In some ways she felt she had cast her future with them. They needed her, and she needed them. Their troubles were hers.

And she was scared to death for them right now. The fear clung after Lassiter departed. She felt she had a million routine chores to do, but she had to satisfy her curiosity, at least, about the boy who worked at the JiffyGrub. Maybe—she knew it was a slender hope—she could observe something about him, or he might say something, that wouldn't have come up in a more guarded conversation with Lassiter.

She kept telling herself her idea was silly, but it kept returning to her mind, making other work impossible. Finally giving in, she left her office in a mess and went out to the parking lot. She was not about to walk down that path to the convenience store, daylight or not.

No other cars were in sight when she pulled off the narrow road and into an angled parking place in front of the JiffyGrub. She hurried inside, grateful to get back into chilly air-conditioning. A short, slender, gray-skinned boy with stringy hair, a fuzzy mustache, and an earring peered out at her from behind the counter. His narrow eyes looked mildly hostile. His nametag said SPURINGTON.

"Hi!" Laura said brightly, giving him her biggest smile. "Pack of Marlboros, please?"

Expressionless, he flicked a pack off the rack and put it on the counter. Laura handed him a five-dollar bill. "I'm sure glad you guys opened here," she told him. "We'll all be coming in a lot, I imagine."

He made change without a word, but she had gotten his attention. Handing the money back to her, he studied her without hostility for the first time. "You work around here?"

She pointed over her shoulder. "At Timberdale."

"Oh, yeah. We've had some of the old farts in already. Make sure they know we're open twenty-four hours a day. I'm the usual night man. Jeannie is sick today, so I'm filling in an extra shift. You send 'em over and we'll take good care of 'em. We aim to make this the best JiffyGrub in the country."

Laura looked around, pretending to be impressed. "You've got it looking nice already."

He flushed and nodded. "Damn right we have."

She hesitated, wanting to keep him engaged while she formed further impressions, but she couldn't think of anything useful to say. She heard another car pulling up outside. With a wave, she headed for the door.

He couldn't be their attacker, she thought as she climbed into her Toyota. Dirty, yes. Not very smart, yes. But she hadn't gotten any intuitive feeling of violence in him.

As she backed out, however, she glanced back toward the store. She saw that Spurington had come around his counter to stand near the front glass. He was watching her, and his eyes had a bright, watchful malevolence that she hadn't seen inside the store with him.

She shivered. She remembered that no one could judge character with a great deal of accuracy most of the time. In this last glimpse, she had seen another part of his personality. It was the kind that could do violence.

She pulled out onto the narrow country road and headed back up the hill toward the Timberdale driveway.

TEN

EXCEPT FOR STACY at the desk, the atrium appeared deserted when Laura walked in at 6:30 a.m., an hour earlier than usual. The handsome high banks of white railings stood empty, as did the conversation areas on the first floor. The grandfather clock was just striking the half hour.

Laura started across toward the desk.

A sharp movement from the visitors' sitting room startled her badly. She started to turn, nerves jangling.

"Laura! Laura! Wait till you get a load of this!"

Maude Thuringer, wearing dirty overalls, workman's boots that looked several sizes too large for her, and a filthy baseball cap, clomped across the carpet, strewing dirt clods from the boot treads. She had a big, rusty chunk of jagged metal in her hands. "Look at this!" she panted.

Laura looked. The object appeared to have been a steel box, or possibly a piece off some kind of heavy equipment, at one time. But it had been crushed into an irregular blob. Chunks of red Oklahoma earth clung to its rust-pitted surface, and a few shaggy weed or grass roots stuck out of the dirt here and there.

"What is it?" Laura asked.

"I don't have any idea," Maude said. "Isn't it neat?"

"Where did it come from?"

"I just found it. I dug it up down in the gully not far from the frog pond."

"You—"

"Or maybe," Maude interrupted breathlessly, "I should say I re-dug it up. See, that's how I knew it was there in the first place. When I was down there yesterday

I noticed where an area under one of the oaks had been dug up recently, so I slipped down there this morning just as soon as it started to get daylight.''

"Maude! You went down there right after dawn this morning after all the warnings you've had?''

"Well, I had to wait until that new security guard got in his pickup and went home. Boy, he was all over the place out there all night last night. But he left when it got daylight, so that was when I could go down and investigate this.''

"You could have been killed.''

"Nah!'' Maude shook her head, almost losing her Detroit Tigers cap. "I was extremely vigilant at all times, and besides that I had my CS gas canister with me. If anybody had messed with me—pow!—right in the eyeballs.''

"Maude,'' Laura groaned.

The old woman shifted the heavy crushed object in her filthy hands, dusting the carpet with dirt and chunks of rust. "See, I knew somebody had dug around for something real recently, since the last rain. So I went down with my garden spade and gas canister and I found the spot and I dug and here it was. This is what I found only about six or eight inches down.''

"But you don't have any idea what it is.''

"No, but it's got to be a clue of some kind.''

Laura stared at the ugly mess in Maude's hands and wondered how it could be a clue to anything except the location of a junkyard. "What,'' she asked finally in despair, "do you propose to do with it?''

"I want you to call that cute deputy of yours. Tell him what I've dug up. Have him come and get it.''

"Get it?''

"Sure! He can take it to the forensics lab. They can x-ray it and analyze its composition and probably tell what it was used for once. There might even be some

recoverable fingerprints on it. I'm being careful to hold
it only by these two jagged edges, see? My guess is that
this is why somebody was lurking around down there,
and conked Violet and Mr. Bell. Somebody was burying
this."

"Recently?" Laura demanded. "On two different
nights?"

Maude grimaced. "Well, I can't explain everything
yet. Just call your deputy."

"IT'S PART OF a muffler," Aaron Lassiter said disgustedly, putting the rusty object on the corner of Laura's
desk.

"But why would somebody murder to hide that?"
Maude Thuringer piped up.

"They wouldn't," Lassiter told her.

"But—"

"Mrs. Thuringer," he exploded, "goddammit—pardon me, but goddammit—who said you could sneak
down there at the crack of dawn? Don't you know people
are getting killed down there?"

"I didn't," Maude snapped. "Are you taking it downtown to the forensics lab now?"

"I suppose so, yes. But I can tell you right now it's
not going to get us anywhere."

"Yeah, that's what Adrian thought in that novel—
which one was it?—maybe *The Savage Day,* by Jack
Higgins."

Lassiter turned to Laura. "Let's go down there and
take a look at where she dug this up."

Maude jumped up and down. "Great! I'll show you
the exact—"

"You're staying here," Lassiter said sharply.

Maude stuck her chin out. "You can't make me. I'm
a United States citizen. I have rights."

Lassiter pointed a blunt index finger at her. "You try

to go down there with us, lady, and I'll have your rear end in the county jail.''

"On what trumped-up charge, if I may ask?''

"Let's try obstruction of justice.''

Maude's frown vanished, chased by a broadening grin. "Hey, great! A chance for me to do some firsthand research on the criminal mind. Let's go, kids.''

"You're not going,'' Lassiter repeated.

To Laura's considerable surprise, Maude deflated and said nothing beyond some formulary complaints as Lassiter led the way out of the office wing and across the atrium toward the back doors. Breakfast was being served and the dining room was packed, but no one was around to stop them or ask where they were going.

At the dining room doors, Lassiter stopped and pointed. "In there.''

Maude set her jaw. "No.''

"In there,'' Lassiter repeated in a tone of voice that almost gave Laura chills. "Now.''

Maude made an awful face and went into the dining room, dirty overalls and all.

"Come on,'' Lassiter muttered to Laura, and led her to the doors.

It was going to be a clear day, and very hot, with a brisk south breeze. The wind was already up enough to pluck at their clothes as they hurried out past the Dumpster units, across the pavement, and to the gate that led through the back fence to the path and the thicket beyond. There Laura saw a fresh new sign, neatly painted black on white, about a foot square. It read:

NO ADMITTANCE
DO NOT USE PATH
USE ROAD ONLY
                    J. Epperman, Mgr.

"Maybe Maude didn't see it," Laura observed weakly.

Lassiter's lip curled down. "Oh, sure. Right." He held the gate open and let Laura precede him down the path.

It was still shady and moderate under the overhanging tree limbs, but the dense humidity made it clear how hot the air would be down here later in the day. Wasps and bees buzzed around on obscure errands, and a handful of mourning doves bolted out of the grass as Laura and Lassiter approached. Smaller birds twitted in the treetops. Even with Lassiter beside her, Laura felt small chills of apprehension. But the little woods seemed to have no other people in it.

Lassiter walked well down the path, then, looking right and left as the path neared the pond, grunted suddenly with recognition and veered off to his right. Laura followed through ankle-deep weeds. He walked unerringly to a spot where freshly dug dirt was piled up around a small, shallow hole.

"Here's where she dug it up," he said, crouching to examine the area. "Hey, that's strange."

"What is?" Laura asked.

He pointed. "Look here. She was right about one thing. Somebody else had dug around here not long before she did. See here? You can see where she dug clearly enough, but somebody else dug a bigger hole first; the larger bare area is where the earlier digging had been done, and then the hole filled back in and tamped down."

"What does that mean? Somebody buried something?"

"Maybe." Lassiter probed around the soft dirt with his fingers. "Nothing else in here." He stood, looked around, and strode off farther north, staying in the brush but roughly paralleling the path. Laura stood watching him, wondering what next. After five or ten minutes he stopped abruptly and dropped to his knees at a spot in higher weeds about forty feet from where Laura stood.

She went over. He was poking into an irregular patch of loose earth about three feet in diameter.

"Here's another one," he said unnecessarily. He gave up probing the loose dirt with his hands and began scooping it out, double handfuls at a time, and tossing it aside. In a minute or two he encountered something and carefully dug it free: a very old, very rusty tin can. Shards of the label said it had once contained tomatoes.

"More buried treasure," he said ironically.

"I don't get it," Laura said.

He made a little snorting sound. "I wish I did."

He got to his feet again and resumed pacing back and forth, scanning the weeds and dirt. Laura again waited. After what seemed a very long time, he came back to join her. He was sweaty and slightly out of breath and grim. "We're wasting our time. Come on. I'll walk you back to the center."

He led the way back to the spot where he had left the tin can on the ground, picked it up, and turned toward the path. Laura fell into step with him.

"It doesn't compute," he said, frowning.

"Why would anyone bury rusty old trash?" Laura asked.

"Exactly." He took an audible deep breath. "I'll have the lab boys look at this thing and that piece of a muffler Maude found. But—" He paused, stiffening slightly as he moved, and Laura saw his head cock to one side with intensified attention to…what?

With his free hand he signaled her to keep walking. He resumed loudly, "We'll just have to wait and see what develops. I hope nobody uses this path without really needing to. I would hate to see anybody else—" At that point, with startling quickness, he dropped the tin

can and darted off the path to his right, plunging headlong into brush that totally obscured what was beyond.

Somebody—not Lassiter—let out a squeaking shout.
The bushes shook. Lassiter called out sharply and then
there was a sound of bodies hitting the dirt and rolling
around. Laura rushed through the hole in the bushes that
Lassiter had made and saw him sprawled on the ground
a few feet beyond, hanging on to another person, who
twisted and struggled helplessly in his grasp. She hurried
nearer.

"Hold still, dammit!" Lassiter growled, and managed
to hang on to his prey at the same time he scrambled to
his feet. Then he hauled his prisoner up and held him at
arm's length.

"Oh, no," Laura said in dismay.

The elderly man held easily by Lassiter was tall and
painfully skinny, wearing an old-fashioned dark suit now
filthy from rolling in the red dirt. He had half-lost his
eyeglasses, and struggled to right them. He was shaking
from head to foot like a man with palsy.

"Mr. Whitnaur," Laura said, "what are you doing
down here, spying on us?"

"You know him?" Lassiter asked sharply.

"Yes. He's August Whitnaur, and he's one of ours."

Lassiter held Whitnaur out like a ventriloquist's
dummy. "Don't try to run, bozo." He let go abruptly
and Whitnaur almost fell. "Answer the lady's question.
What were you doing, spooking along there and eaves-
dropping on us? What did you have in mind?"

Whitnaur feebly brushed at his suit, which looked like
it would never entirely clean up. He shot Laura a re-
sentful look. "I told you I plan to conduct my own investigation. I told you I won't rest until Violet's murderer
has been found."

"And I told *you* to let us handle it," Laura retorted
hotly. She was getting awfully tired of being ignored.

"Don't you know how you could have just gotten hurt? What if Deputy Lassiter had just shot you through those bushes?"

"You won't stop me," Whitnaur said sullenly. "You won't."

"Go on back up to the building," Lassiter told him. "If I see you down here again, I'm going to arrest you."

"What for, if I may be so bold as to ask?"

"I'll think of something. Now haul ass."

The old man turned and stumbled up the path. Shaking his head in disgust, Lassiter again retrieved the tin can they had found below. He led the way up the path and Laura followed, feeling embarrassed because she couldn't keep any of her people in line.

FROM A HALL window on the second floor of Timberdale, Ken Keen watched the two of them follow old Whitnaur up the path to the back gate. Keen felt a pulse in his temple—felt almost nauseated.

They suspected him now, all of them. It had come as a great shock to him when Laura Michaels visited, with her pointed questions, and it became clear that she was acting out of suspicion.

They didn't understand his problems. He had to be very careful not to arouse additional suspicion. Things would improve. His head would stop hurting, and then he would stop being crabby.

In the meantime, however, he must really try to be more cheerful. But that was going to be very difficult when he knew that the people he had considered his friends were now watching him.

He had expected to live out his life here, at least until the damned sickness in his head got so bad they had to take him away to a nursing home and strap him in a wheelchair in the hall each day. That would come; he

knew it sometimes, when his mind was clearest. But until
then he had thought he was among friends.

He watched old Whitnaur come through the back gate,
and then Laura and her deputy not far behind. He felt a
pulse of resentment. They would never solve this case,
he thought, any more than crazy old Maude Thuringer
would solve it. It was up to him to make the next move.

He didn't know what it should be. He felt sick and
scared. He hoped no one else would die.

ELEVEN

WEDNESDAY WAS Errand Day at Timberdale. Still Bill Mills would bring the Ford bus around to the front canopy at ten o'clock sharp, and residents without cars could come out, climb on board, and be taken to virtually any destination in Norman for an hour or two of shopping, the beauty parlor, lunch, or visiting with in-town friends.

Usually one or two residents had the bus drop them off at the public library on Gray Street, but Maude Thuringer had seldom done that. She liked to buy books, not feel like she was walking her fingers through pages previously thumbed by God only knew how many strangers. Books were too important—too intimate and serious—to be passed around like hot dogs at a baseball game.

Maude's favorite activity on Errand Day was far different. She liked to have the bus drop her along Boyd Street west of the campus and walk southwest from there into the old neighborhood where she and her husband had lived for more than forty years before he died and the big house was too much for her physically to care for...too much, too, in its burden of memories.

But she knew the family to whom she had sold the house—dear people, not a lot younger than she was—and she liked to visit them. Ordinarily she could sit with Mrs. Smatheson on the wraparound wooden front porch and look out past the tall spirea and locusts, down the slope of the old yard, to the sidewalk and the street and, across the street, the little park. She liked that. She liked sitting in the backyard, too, in the gazebo, under the sweet gums.

Today, however, was different. Today Maude got off

the bus at the library along with the usual group of in-
sensitive oafs who didn't mind paging through books
smeared by the dirty thumbprints of people who probably
moved their lips when they read.

Once inside, the small group split up, the Buckinghams
drifting into "New Releases," Stoney Castle into "Westerns," others elsewhere. Maude headed straight for the
newspaper archives and the cross-indexed microfilms
provided by the state press association and the historical
society.

Seated alone at a library table in the stacks, she took
out her notes and consulted the short list of names she
intended to check out today. Then, turning to a micro-
fiche reader, she started to work.

It was slow, aggravating work. Much of the local in-
dexing had not yet been done, so there was no assurance
that the lack of a name in a particular year meant that
the person really had not been in the news. The only way
to be sure—if you could maintain your patience and sanity that long—was to start back in the earliest possible
year of your intended search, crank in the first roll of
microfilm, and start laboriously scanning headlines.

Maude scanned. An hour passed, then another. She realized it was almost time for the bus to come back.
Glancing around a corner of the stacks, she spied the
Castles and Buckinghams already seated in the outer
lobby near the sun-blasted glass doors, books in their
laps, waiting for Still Bill to drive up.

Maude hurried.

She was just ready to give it up for the day when she
stumbled upon the entry that sent her rushing to the newspaper microfilm.

"Hurry up, hurry up," she muttered nervously to herself, finding the right yellow box of film, hurrying back
to a reader, spooling it into place. The staging device

clicked down into place and she started spinning the crank so fast it made her head swim dizzily.

Then, suddenly, she stopped cranking and stared with disbelief at the front page on the screen in front of her.

"My cow," she whispered. "I never expected *this*."

Just as she turned the crank to advance to the second page, a voice startled her so badly she almost fell off the stool: "Maude, come *on!* Still Bill is waiting in the bus and we're already late."

Maude turned to see Stoney Castle standing there, frowning.

"What are you reading, anyhow?" he demanded, leaning closer and squinting.

"Nothing!" Maude chirped, and hit the light switch on the machine.

"Well, hurry up, then," Castle grumbled.

Maude cranked the machine as fast as it would go. The end of the microfilm roll snapped out of the staging mechanism and flapped free. Hurriedly she extracted the reel from the machine, stuffed it back into its storage box, and carried the box back to its filing cabinet.

This one, she thought triumphantly, was too big for her. She wondered what Laura's deputy friend, Mr. Lassiter, would think when she dropped *this* bombshell on him.

Outside, the bus horn tooted. Still Bill Mills was getting impatient. Maude ran for it.

LATE THURSDAY morning, Aaron Lassiter sat in Sheriff Bucky Davidson's office while the sheriff growled and scowled his way through Lassiter's thin sheaf of notes.

"The old lady brought this to your attention?" the sheriff asked at last.

"Maude, yes," Lassiter said.

"How the hell did *she* uncover anything?"

Lassiter's face got warm. "For one thing, she was

smart enough to get his name. I wasn't. I just figured it was Acme or Confidential, one of the regular security outfits.''

"But there aren't that many people around today who know his name anyway.''

"She checked it out at the library. Old newspapers.''

"Maybe we ought to deputize the old gal. Sometimes she seems to think of stuff you don't.''

"You want my resignation?''

The sheriff looked up sharply. "Take it easy, take it easy. For God's sake, man. It was just a little joke.''

Lassiter felt his shoulders slump. "Sorry.''

"You're too edgy, man.''

"I know.''

"You couldn't know to check him out.''

"The hell I couldn't!''

"Well, we know now.''

"You feel sure it is the same man?''

"Oh, I don't think there can be any doubt about that. It's the same feller, all right. He went to Texas for a while but he's been back a long time, doing piddly-ass security stuff.''

"How can he get anybody to trust him?''

The sheriff's eyes looked like slate. "The same way he got Timberdale to trust him: ignorance.''

Lassiter got to his feet. "I need to tell Laura right away.''

Davidson held up a warning finger.

Lassiter paused. "What?''

"He was never charged with anything, Salt. Never.''

"Dammit, I need to read up on the case.''

"I imagine there's a pretty big file up on Four, in the storage room.''

IT WAS THURSDAY afternoon before Maude Thuringer perfected her plan and confronted fellow resident August Whitnaur with it.

Whitnaur had been sitting in a mauve easy chair at the south end of the atrium, alone and staring into space. He looked unusually thin and old and sad, Maude thought as she hurried up and plopped down into the chair next to his.

"Gussie," she chirped, "we need to talk."

Whitnaur turned to look at her. His eyes were dark and bitter. "We have nothing to talk about, Maude. Never did."

Before replying, Maude glanced around to reassure herself that they would not be overheard. There was no one else at this end of the atrium. Colonel Rodgers sat far toward the other side, scowling at a book. Other residents, the Davises and Pfeisters, occupied facing couches even farther up front, toward the desk, and seemed lost in their own quiet conversation, oblivious to everything else.

It was safe.

Maude leaned closer to Whitnaur anyway, keeping her voice low. "I know you have a special reason for wanting to find our killer."

Whitnaur did a nice job of looking puzzled. "Me?"

Maude had no time to be roundabout. "Yes. Because of Violet. Now don't bother with your gentlemanly denials, Gussie. It's very sweet of you to want to protect her reputation and all, but she's dead. Reputation doesn't matter very much when you're dead, and I won't tell anyone anyhow."

Whitnaur's rheumy eyes narrowed with pain. "You... know about us?"

"Sure."

"How?"

"I make it my business to know all I can, Gussie."

"But, how?"

"I was out in the hall one night, late, and saw you walking."

Whitnaur frowned. "I remember that. But I told you I was just restless."

Maude smiled. "Yes, but a man that's just restless doesn't reek of English Leather the way you did. He hasn't just shaved and brushed his hair the way you had."

"But—"

"Oh, hell, don't deny it, Gussie. I followed you that night. I saw you go into Violet's room. You didn't come out until almost five the next morning."

Whitnaur's jaw trembled. "How did you know that?"

"I camped out behind the sofa in the hall waiting area and waited for you to come out, that's how."

The old man really began to shake. "How dare you! You had no right to spy on people that way! What do you want now? To gloat over my sorrow? Get a verification so you can spread the dirty gossip all over—"

"Grow up," Maude cut in.

"I'll get you for this if—"

"I've got information, Gussie, that might shed a lot of light on Violet's death. But I need help keeping watch. That's why I'm here. You've got a motive to want to help me. Now do you want to help me try to catch Violet's killer or not?"

Whitnaur studied her with narrowed eyes. His anger subsided as quickly as it had arisen. He said with grave dignity, "You know how much I want her attacker apprehended. Of course I will do whatever I can."

"There's going to be some spook work involved, and it might get dangerous if you're not very careful," Maude warned.

"Tell me."

Maude did.

IT WAS FIVE o'clock when Aaron Lassiter arrived. In response to his telephone request for a meeting, Laura and Francie Blake had been summoned to Mrs. Epperman's office to wait for him.

Frazzled after individual therapy sessions with three residents, a set-to with temperamental chef Pierre Motard and a long session at the computer working on resident billing changes, Laura felt frumpish and rumpled. Francie, who had spent most of the day composing a cheerful memo outlining the festivities planned for the weekend luau party, looked dazzling: not a golden hair out of place, makeup perfect, expression serene. Today she had decided to wear her hair back, tied with a pink ribbon in a frilly ponytail, and the style made her look even younger and more piquant than usual. Her dress—pale ivory, with pink cabbage roses—was matched by hot pink pumps. Laura thought the pumps were tacky, but had to admit they did great things for Francie's long, tan, bare legs. Her own light gray dress and flats looked old maidish by comparison, she thought. But she hadn't known she was going to get called into a meeting like this.

Lassiter came in looking like a summer thunderstorm. Mrs. Epperman, frowning, leaned over her littered desk to shake his hand. "Come in, Deputy. Sit down. You know my staff members, of course."

Lassiter smiled and nodded. It didn't ease the tension that stuck out all over him.

"Oh, Aaron," Francie gushed, reaching out to touch his arm. "You look so tired!"

Lassiter stared at her, surely aware that her movement had hiked the hem of her dress halfway to the north pole. "It's getting to be a long day," he told her. "But—"

"I just hope nothing else has gone wrong! You poor man, they give you far too much responsibility. Wouldn't you agree, Laura?"

Staring into Francie's innocent eyes, Laura felt her fillings begin to pulverize. "Yes, Francie, I'm sure you're right."

Mrs. Epperman found her eyeglasses and perched them on the end of her nose. "Now, Deputy Lassiter, suppose you tell us what it is you wanted to talk with us about. You haven't found the murderer, I assume?"

"No, ma'am," Lassiter said. "But some other information has turned up that we thought you ought to know about."

"What would that be?"

He scowled. "It's about your new security man."

"Mr. Aikman? Yes. I handpicked him, you know. He showed real initiative in seeking the position. I like that. He seems very efficient and businesslike—"

"In 1974," Lassiter cut in, "he was the primary suspect in a double murder in this county."

Mrs. Epperman scarcely blinked, and kept right on talking as if he hadn't interrupted. "Although, on the other hand, I must say I have had some serious doubts about him, and probably would never have hired him if Laura, here, hadn't interviewed him and given him a glowing report."

"What's this about a double murder?" Laura asked, chilling.

Lassiter locked his big, capable hands together over his knees and stared down at them with the look of a deeply worried man. "Aikman was a deputy sheriff here from 1971 to late 1974. Before that he was a police officer in Tulsa and an MP in the army for two years."

"How did he get charged with murder?" Mrs. Epperman demanded. "Laura, my heavens! How could you be so stupid as to miss something like this?"

"There was nothing in his résumé—"

"Do you think he would put 'murderer' on his résumé,

you awful girl? I knew I should have interviewed him myself!''

Lassiter intervened. ''He was never convicted. He was never actually charged. I said he was a prime suspect.''

''But they found that someone else actually did the crime?'' Mrs. Epperman prompted hopefully. ''Well, then—''

''The murders were not solved,'' Lassiter said grimly. ''They remain unsolved to this day.''

Francie hugged herself and shivered, making her big silver earrings bobble and sway. ''This is scary! Oh, Aaron, we're so lucky to have a man of action like you to protect us.''

Lassiter stared at her, then returned his gaze to Mrs. Epperman. ''As soon as we learned who you had hired, we thought you ought to know about his background.''

With a growing sense of dread, Laura cut in, ''Tell us the story, Aaron. Okay?''

''Aikman joined the sheriff's department after Vietnam. He was a little flaky, according to reports, but a hard worker. Nobody liked him much. He seemed to be a loner. Bucky—Sheriff Davidson—wasn't here then. Nobody presently on the force was on duty during that time, so we don't have a lot of firsthand knowledge to draw on.

''Apparently Aikman served his warrants and did his other routine work faster and better than anybody had done them before. He also spent more time out in the boonies, cruising, than most deputies ever had. He brought in some wanteds, and broke up a couple of penny-ante rural burglary rings. People didn't like him, but everybody thought he was a good officer.''

Lassiter paused, then resumed. ''After a few months on the force, complaints started coming in now and then about how he would cruise some of the lovers' lanes at night, evidently on his own time, and hassle kids out necking. There were five or six of those complaints documented in the files. It looks like there might have been a lot more than that.''

Laura said, ''You said he hassled them. What does that mean?''

''From what I can piece together, he would pull in behind a parked car, shine a handheld spotlight on the kids inside, sometimes order them out, ask questions, take ID, generally scare the hell out of them.''

''And charge them with what?'' Laura asked.

''Nothing.''

''Nothing?''

''If what I can get out of the files is accurate, what he liked to do, apparently, is ask them what they were doing, how they were doing it, how the girl, especially, felt about sex. Then he would stand the boy up against the car, spread-eagled, pat him down, maybe rough him up just the slightest little bit, and tell them he was letting them go this time, but not to be back around the area again.''

''How awful!'' Francie gasped. ''Imagine, out in a car, having a little innocent fun, and along comes this dreadful, frightening man—a law officer, to boot—who acts like you're criminals. Did he have a gun, Aaron? Did he make them put their hands up?''

''Ah, Francie,'' Laura breathed sympathetically.

''Actually,'' Lassiter said, ''he did. On a number of occasions he pointed a service revolver in through a car window. The sheriff at that time, Wick Willingham, had him in the office to discuss complaints about behavior like that on at least five occasions. There was one official reprimand after he pointed his gun at a boy who happened to be a city councilman's son.''

''But,'' Mrs. Epperman growled, ''none of that amounts to murder.''

Lassiter's chest heaved. ''On August twentieth, 1974,

out on a little country road east of here—a couple from the university, Richard Twaine and Nancy Bartholomew, drove out and parked. The next morning, a farmer going by noticed their car alongside the road. He stopped to investigate and found both of them. They had been shot—murdered.''

"Oh, no," Francie mooed, twisting crimson talons in her string of pearls.

"There were signs the boy had been out of the car at some point," Lassiter went on grimly. "The girl had been raped."

Lassiter straightened up, taking another labored breath. "No murder weapon was found. Some tire tracks in the dirt on the shoulder a few yards away checked out to be the same brand of tire on the small personal car driven by Aikman on his own time. But there were no tracks close-by.

"Aikman had been off duty the night of the twentieth. He said he had been home alone. None of the neighbors could corroborate or disprove his story. Nobody had ever seen him with a gun as small as a .22.

"His record for bullying kids in lovers' lanes, plus his being off duty that night, plus his having no alibi, led the sheriff to question him four different times about his activities on the night of the murders. Aikman was even suspended for more than a month while certain other charges—there's no record of what they might have been—were investigated, considered, and then dropped.

"No other suspects ever turned up. It was quite a celebrated case at the time, the 'lovers' lane murders,' that sort of thing. The sheriff dearly wanted to file charges against Aikman, but the DA said there wasn't a chance of winning on the thin circumstantial evidence they had. At almost the same time, fingerprint records and some photographs of the crime scene vanished from the sheriff's office, leaving the case even weaker.

"It was never filed. Aikman quit and vanished for a while. He turned up in Texas a year later, but then returned to this area, going into business for himself as a security man and sometimes-PI. As far as anyone can tell, he's kept his nose clean."

"But," Mrs. Epperman rumbled, "he was never really cleared—the murders were never solved."

"I'm afraid that's right."

"And no murder weapon?"

"Was ever found. Aikman owned a .22 pistol at the time, incidentally, but he said it was stolen only a few days before the shootings, and there was no way to disprove that."

A profound silence fell over the office. Francie even forgot to maintain her cutest pose, actually letting her shoulders slump. Laura felt numbed by the recital and couldn't believe it had any relevance.

Mrs. Epperman said, "None of this means Mr. Aikman is guilty."

"That's right," Lassiter said, his eyes bleak.

Timberdale's manager had begun to look more cheerful. "It appears to me, then, that we have no grounds on which to suspect anything about him at this time."

"But what if he was the murderer?" Laura blurted. "What if he's a real crazy of some kind?"

"My dear, the Timberdale deaths took place before the man appeared on the scene. No, no. We can't dismiss him over an old case like that. We would be opening ourselves to a terrible lawsuit, actually. Not to mention the added bad pub we would reap if we fired him and the TV people found out."

"What if we keep him on and the TV people find out?" Laura countered, alarmed.

"Discovery is less likely from keeping him on than from firing him," Mrs. Epperman said. "Maintain the status quo. They haven't noticed yet, I don't think they will.''

"I agree," Francie chirped.

Laura turned to Lassiter. "Your opinion? You must have one, or you wouldn't have brought this information out to us.''

Lassiter's forehead wrinkled. "I would fire him. I don't care what the legal situation was more than twenty years back. Reading those old files and old reports, I think the son of a—the so-and-so was a murderer.''

"You don't think he committed the murders here!''

"Well, he wasn't on your payroll yet. But I think he's a showboat and a pathological something-or-other. I just wish there was more evidence to prove something on him. As it is—''

"As it is," Mrs. Epperman boomed, "we don't have a legal leg to stand on. Mr. Aikman will have to stay on board. It's the safest way all around. He hasn't done any harm here, and surely he won't.''

Lassiter stared. "So you're not going to get rid of him.''

"How can we, dear boy? We would open ourselves up to terrible pub, a lawsuit, goodness only knows what all!''

Scowling, Lassiter reached for his hat. "Thanks for the meeting. I'll be on my way.''

Mrs. Epperman stood, letting her glasses fall to her bosom. "I assume we'll all maintain silence about this, Deputy? After all, whatever happened was more than twenty years ago. Let sleeping dogs lie, eh? Maintain Timberdale's reputation and calm insofar as possible.''

Lassiter nodded curtly and left the office. The door closed softly behind him.

"Well," Mrs. Epperman sighed, "see no evil, speak no evil, and so on, eh?''

Laura got to her feet.

"Where are you going, dear girl?"

"I'll be back in a minute," Laura said, and hurried out the door.

She caught Lassiter outside, already halfway to his cruiser. His face strained dark with suppressed anger.

"The woman is crazy," he fumed. "She should fire his butt."

"Aaron, maybe she's right. Maybe—"

"And maybe she's wrong. Listen. Everything in those old files cries out that Aikman was a bully who murdered two kids on a lovers' lane. It just couldn't be proved. Now how do you think it makes me feel, knowing you're out here close to that goddamned creep?"

"I'll be okay, Aaron. Really."

He glared down at her, gave her a quick peck on the cheek, climbed into his car, and drove away without another word.

Left standing on the sidewalk in the hot afternoon wind, she considered the new information with a combination of incredulity and dismay. What if James Aikman *had* been a killer? What if—incredible notion—he was here now, working at Timberdale, because he knew something about the deaths of Mayberry and Bell? How in the name of God could such diverse people and events relate to one another?

Was there some way, Laura thought suddenly, to try to investigate some of this on her own?

She shuddered and almost laughed aloud. She had been around Maude Thuringer too long.

But already her mind was darting over possibilities—actions she might take to try to clarify things.

TWELVE

LEAVING TIMBERDALE, Aaron Lassiter made a quick call to the courthouse and found there was nothing new for him. He was already a mile down the narrow asphalt road toward the highway by this time, but when he put the microphone back on the dashboard clip he decided to turn around.

Big storm clouds had trundled in from the southwest, and raindrops pelted the windshield of the cruiser as he approached the JiffyGrub. In the premature twilight the store's neon signs glowed brilliantly. The only vehicle in sight was a fancy late-model sports car parked well around toward the back. Lassiter swung wide in the parking lot, noted and jotted down the license number, and then parked near the front doors.

His man Spurington was alone in the store, standing behind the cash counter. Stubble-bearded, wearing a shapeless denim shirt and khaki pants that had never seen an iron, Spurington looked even more disheveled than usual. When he saw Lassiter enter, he visibly braced himself and his mouth became a pencil line.

Lassiter walked to the counter. "Evening."

Spurington's eyes bristled with hate. "What do you want?"

"Just in the neighborhood," Lassiter said easily. "Thought I'd say hello."

"Fuck you, Deputy."

"Henry, Henry. Is that any way to talk?"

"You've got nothing on me. I didn't have anything to do with that shit that came down across the road. You can come in here and hassle me a million times and you still won't get anything. Why ain't you out trying to find out what happened over there? Is all you got to do come in here and hassle an honest man?''

Lassiter maintained a glacial calm. ''Henry, what do they pay you for this job?''

''None of your business.''

''Minimum wage, right?''

''I said, none of your business!''

Lassiter leaned an elbow on the counter. ''You know, some of those old folks across the road have a considerable amount of money.''

Spurington glared silently.

''A man might hope he could catch one of them with a pocketful of cash—make a real score.''

''I don't know what you're talking about. You're crazy.''

''What time of night do you usually get off, Henry?''

''Sometimes two, sometimes four. So what?''

''People who were clobbered over there were attacked a lot later than that. Almost dawn in one case. You would have been off work.''

Spurington's face reddened. ''So was about ninety percent of the people in this county. Why don't you go talk to some of them?''

''Oh, I'm not saying you had anything to do with anything,'' Lassiter crooned.

''You're not?''

''No. Not at all. But it does occur to me that a man in your position here might be able to look outside…see if a car pulled up over there or something. Maybe see somebody walking around. Something like that.''

''I didn't see nothing.''

''Do the JiffyGrub people know about your prior record, Henry?''

''You sonofabitch! If you tell them anything about that, I'll—''

"I wouldn't do such a thing! Why should I do that? I've got nothing against you, Henry. I know, if you knew anything about the doings across the road, you would tell me immediately. Isn't that right? We're practically pals. Right?"

"I haven't done anything." Spurington's eyes were so bright with desperation and hate that they seemed to glow. "You got no right to bother me like this. I'm a law-abiding citizen."

Lassiter abruptly switched gears. "How do you get back and forth to work, Henry?"

Spurington's face went slack for an instant. "What?"

"I said—"

"I drive."

"Is that your fancy Mitsubishi parked around the back?"

"What if it is?"

"Real fancy car for a man making minimum wage. Must take just about everything you earn to make the payments."

Spurington's mouth turned in a sneer. "I don't eat much."

Lassiter smiled back at him. "Yeah. A few Twinkies here, a pack of Ding Dongs there, I guess a man could just about live off the store."

Spurington made a little snorting sound through his nose as if something had struck him funny. "I would never eat stuff off the shelf here."

"Oh?"

"No. That would be like stealing. Illegal. I don't break no laws."

"You must be a model employee, Henry."

"That's right. That's what I am. A fucking model employee."

"You say you're a fisherman, Henry?"

"I fish. So what? You want to see my fishing license?"

"Right time of year, a man could go to that frog pond over yonder and drag a buzz bait across the right spots, bring up some nice bass right up from where they're guarding the nest."

"I've never been over there. I wouldn't know."

"Never a single time?"

"Never a single time."

Lassiter pushed away from the counter. "Nice talking to you, Henry."

Spurington watched him with gimlet eyes.

"I'll be back, Henry. Take care."

Back outside, the storm had continued to gather. It was not raining at the moment, but a freshening wind tossed the trees in the woods across the road. Lassiter could not see the lights of Timberdale from here, although it was now storm-dark enough to require them.

Getting back into his car, he started the engine and switched on the headlights. Inside the JiffyGrub, Henry Spurington stood like a gaunt mannequin behind the counter. The lights around him shone brightly on colored plastic and tin and glass and steel, a calliope store of junk food and patent medicine. As Lassiter wheeled his cruiser away from the glass front, light-sensing devices turned on all the outside ramp and gas pump lights, making everything spring to brightness, an ocean of white in the dark.

He pulled onto the gravel road and shifted into second gear, headed back toward the Timberdale cutoff. He thought about Mrs. Epperman, refusing to fire Aikman because of her fear of bad publicity. He gritted his teeth. Maybe there was nothing to his suspicions anyway, he told himself.

As he drove toward the curve in the road that would bring Timberdale into view, his headlights glinted for a fraction of a second on something off the road. Braking sharply, he squinted through the gloom and made out a vehicle of some kind, pulled well off the road and into the high brush.

Doing a U-turn in the narrow road, he drove back the few dozen yards to the place where a glint had first caught his eye. From this angle he could not see the vehicle in the brush at all. He parked, cut engine and lights, and climbed out. Thunder rolled overhead, and lightning flashed to the southwest.

Crossing the shallow ditch, he walked through knee-high weeds and then into the stand of stunted scrub oak and willows that had almost entirely hidden the vehicle he had seen. Pushing his way through, he came upon a small Chevrolet pickup truck, rusty yellow, with a camper shell on the back. He saw at once how it had been pulled in through a natural opening in the trees and parked here where the chances were a hundred to one against its ever being seen.

The pickup was deserted, doors locked. The camper shell was locked, too. He couldn't see into the shell. The cab of the truck was filthy and littered with newspapers, hand tools, and the trash of what looked like the remains of dozens of fast-food meals. The back license plate carried a "VAK" prefix, one of several identifying a local county registration. With the exception of special tags such as vanity plates and those assigned to amateur radio operators, Oklahoma did not issue front plates. In the plastic holder on the front bumper was an OU Sooners sign.

Lassiter looked around again but still couldn't see the owner. He started across the small clearing to go deeper into the thicket. As he did so, lightning flickered and thunder again rolled, closer this time.

He moved in under bigger trees, looking for the path where they had found the bodies. He knew the pond was not far ahead.

The voice startled the hell out of him: "Can I help you?"

He spun. Standing there beside a tree that had hidden him from view was a small, wiry man wearing a plastic rain jacket, rain hat, Levi's, and heavy boots. Lassiter instantly registered the flashlight in a belt holster and a bulge under the left armpit that was either a very nasty tumor or a shoulder holster. The man had a bloodless face, narrow eyes, ugly little chin. And Lassiter knew who he was at once.

"Hello!" he called. "I saw your truck. Thought there might be trouble."

The man walked over, light on his feet despite the boots, his shoulders moving in that bound-up way weight lifters get when they work for bulk rather than real strength or endurance. This man was thin, but Lassiter could see that he was as strong as bridge cable.

"Nothing wrong, Deputy," he said, toneless. "Routine security patrol here."

Lassiter stuck out his hand. "Aaron Lassiter."

The man's hand felt like ice. "Aikman. James Aikman."

Lassiter played dumb. "Would you be the man Timberdale hired to provide some extra security down here?"

"That's right."

Lassiter made a thing of consulting his watch. "Mrs. Epperman told me you work the night. You're on early today."

Thunder drummed again. Aikman looked up at the dark sky, barely visible here and there through the canopy of trees. "Storm made it get dark early tonight."

"That's a longer night for you."

"I'm used to long nights."

It was the kind of quietly boastful, macho bullshit thing people said sometimes, and always drove Lassiter crazy. But he showed nothing. "No trouble, I assume?"

"Not so far."

"I think you're going to get wet if you stay out here."

"They're paying me for security, not comfort."

"Is that a shoulder holster under your jacket, Mr. Aikman?"

Aikman slid the zipper down on his jacket and peeled back the left side of the nylon. The butt of a big revolver stared out of a holster. "It's registered. I've got a permit."

"I never doubted it," Lassiter said with a smile. "Well, anything I can do for you before I get on my way?"

"It's under control."

"Nice meeting you."

Aikman's death-mask face had never changed expression in the slightest, and it didn't now. "Nice meeting you, too."

"I'll probably be around from time to time. This is my area. So I'll be seeing you again."

Aikman said nothing.

"Take care." Lassiter turned away.

Aikman stood in his tracks, hands on hips.

Trudging back to his cruiser, Lassiter had something new to think about. He had dealt with his share of rough characters in his brief tenure on the sheriff's force, but none had given him a chillier, creepier sensation than James Aikman. This was one strange man, a real weirdo. Lassiter felt sharply uneasy.

THE RAIN STARTED with a rush of wind, a loud crack of thunder, and water pelting the windows of Laura's apartment with frightening force. Leaving her textbooks and notes on the kitchen table, she hurried into Trissie's room to reassure her. But Trissie was sleeping right through it.

A quick check of other windows and doors showed everything shipshape. Outside, the storm seemed to gather force. Lightning crackled blue-white beyond the drawn draperies.

Going to the TV, Laura switched it on with the sound muted. The Channel Nine weatherman was on, standing in front of a radar presentation that showed yellow and red in the midst of the green rain band sweeping directly across Oklahoma City and Norman. Laura turned the sound up just enough to hear.

"Lots of noise and lightning, but nothing severe at this time," he was saying. "Stay with Nine, we'll keep you advised."

She muted it again and went back to the kitchen. But getting her mind back into her studies was not easy.

Nothing would be the same at Timberdale for a long time, she thought. James Aikman would continue to patrol outside, making things feel like a prison camp, making her flesh crawl with the spooky knowledge of his past. Maude would continue to launch wild investigations. Even Davilla Rose and Sada Hoff would continue their paranoid watch over Ken Keen's every action.

Far worse than any of that, however, was the knowledge that everyone in Timberdale would be almost a hostage for as long as they lived now. The murders had taken away an innocence, a feeling of safety and security. It was not likely to return.

And she would miss Violet. She would mourn Bell, but had never known him well. But Violet, with her bawdy wit and cigarettes and genius for driving her son crazy, had been a favorite.

Thinking about all of it, Laura came face-to-face with a conclusion that had been gathering in her mind, but one she had avoided facing. Both deaths had come under bizarre circumstances, and now they had begun to slip into the past. There were no real clues. The deaths were now likely to remain unsolved...forever.

Like the murders of the two college kids in a parked car so long ago.

It struck her that it was very strange, the way James Aikman had volunteered his services and never quibbled a bit about money. Penny-pinching Mrs. Epperman had loved it, of course. Laura felt sure that her refusal to consider dismissing Aikman now sprang as much from his low salary as from worry about new bad publicity. But Laura did not feel as good about it. She had felt uneasy with the man from the beginning. Now she detected a note of fear inside.

She had to find out more about him—reassure herself that he was safe to have around. Her mind had been turning over ways she might try to accomplish that. It was not a project she wanted to undertake. But she felt a growing awareness that there were steps she could take, and she would never rest easy until she had taken them.

Thunder hammered again, rattling the window beside the kitchen table. She shook herself and forced her thoughts back onto the book and notes in front of her. She had to concentrate. She had to. The effort felt like trying to shape Jell-O with a hammer.

IN AN UPSTAIRS hall window at Timberdale, Ken Keen stood near the glass, watching the storm pound sheets of rain onto the rear parking and delivery area. It was hard to remember why he was watching, but Keen was concentrating hard and doing a good job at it.

Through the intense rain, in the almost constant flickers of lightning, Keen could see him far down there in the woods. He was moving around, evidently oblivious to the pounding storm. The man had to be mad, Keen thought. But of course that was obvious.

Keen had no way of knowing it, but he, too, was being observed.

The rear window area he had chosen for his vigil was

only six doors down the hall from August Whitnaur's apartment. When Keen had gotten off the elevator earlier, Whitnaur had been prowling the corridor. He had ducked quickly into his own doorway. Now he remained there in the dark, the door barely cracked open, watching to see what Keen would do next.

Whitnaur heard the distant sound of laughter. He knew it was from a bridge table in the atrium, the Buckinghams and the Castles at their weekly game. He had covertly watched them for a little while from the pale balcony railing sixty feet above the floor, but that had been idle curiosity for the most part. It had been Ken Keen he was waiting for, and now he had him under observation, just as planned.

THIRTEEN

THE LUAU PARTY Saturday night started at 7:00 p.m. with a four-piece collegiate combo striking a gushy Hawaiian chord from the platform set up near the front doors. The band, in loud floral shirts, floppy straw hats, and cutoffs, consisted of a guitar player, an electric bass, a drummer, and a lead singer with a ukulele.

Their first number was "Blue Hawaii."

Still Bill Mills and his maintenance assistants had set up several rows of folding chairs in a rough semicircle around the bandstand. The rugs had been rolled back from the area directly in front of the musicians, leaving the oak parquet floor open for dancing. Nobody was dancing yet, but most of the residents had shown up and stood around the periphery, visiting a bit glumly and probably feeling foolish.

With chef Pierre Motard—white apron and two-foot white stovepipe hat—in the lead, the kitchen staff paraded out with bowls of punch, fruit trays, cookies, tarts, and cupcakes. The cupcakes had green leaves painted into their thick white icing, and little plastic grass skirts. Motard had bitterly protested the grass skirts to no avail, and Francie Blake had pronounced him simply precious for finally acceding to her wishes.

Mrs. Epperman, frighteningly large in a sunburst muu-muu, cellophane lei, and thonged sandals, rushed in from the parking lot and rumbled around the perimeter of the atrium, gaily greeting everyone and bearing down on Laura and Francie with all the subtlety of a moving van.

"There you two are!" she gushed, lei rustling loudly. "Isn't this all just divine! I wish I had been here sooner, but I knew the two of you would have everything well in hand. Channel Thirteen had a special on psychic events, and I couldn't bear to miss the end of it. Well! It looks like everyone has turned out, Francie. You've done a glorious job on short notice.''

Francie, her hair piled prettily atop her head with fresh-cut roses and dianthus entwined in it, beamed satisfaction. She was wearing a brazen pink swim top and a grass skirt cut only to the knee in the first place, and capable of revealing bare leg all the way to the top whenever she chose to move, which was often. ''I think everyone is having a wonderful time, Mrs. Epperman.''

Mrs. Epperman beamed. ''The punch and goodies look just right, Laura! I see you followed my instructions to the letter. But it would have been nice if you had at least made an effort to look festive.''

Laura looked down at her pale yellow dress and white thonged sandals. They were just about the most festive things she had in her thin wardrobe. ''I thought I looked okay, actually.''

''You look,'' Mrs. Epperman pronounced, ''like you're going to a funeral.''

Francie burst in, ''Oh, don't be too hard on Laura, Mrs. Epperman. She's worked so hard this week. It's no wonder she looks drab, poor thing.''

''Thanks, Francie,'' Laura murmured.

Mrs. Epperman glowered. ''I just hope and trust those terrible people from the TV station don't try to crash in. I told them in no uncertain terms that this is a private party, and we don't need them nib-nosing around, upsetting anyone.''

''Why would they want to come anyway?'' Laura asked. ''They've never covered one of our parties, and we've had many that were more elaborate than this.''

''Oh, they said something dumb about a feature on 'Life Returns to Normal at the Scene of the Tragedy,' something like that. I told them balderdash, I wouldn't hear of it." Mrs. Epperman turned her head, sweeping the atrium. "Is your deputy sheriff here, dear girl?"

"He'll be here later."

"But Mr. Aikman is on duty?"

"As far as I know, yes." Laura consulted her watch. "He was due to start five minutes ago."

"Well, I want you to find him, dear, and tell him to be ready to take swift and decisive action if we call for him on that beeper thing he carries. I intend to ask Still Bill to station himself out under the canopy all evening. If those dreadful TV people try to crash our party despite my orders, Bill must notify us at once, and we must hustle Mr. Aikman around there to block their way."

Before Laura could respond, Maude Thuringer rushed across the empty dance floor and joined them. Maude had picked out a bright blue sundress that showcased the age spots on her bare arms and shoulders. "Hi, everybody! Great party, Francie! Laura, can I have a word with you in private?"

Mrs. Epperman rumbled, "Maude, dear, I sincerely hope you're not still deluding yourself in the belief you can do a better job on our mystery than the police or sheriff."

"You might be surprised," Maude shot back, jaw jutting. "Careful observation often results in amazing deductions that the untrained eye and mind might miss altogether. Agatha Christie proved that time and again. I have a working hypothesis now."

Mrs. Epperman put a maternal hand to the little woman's forehead. "Do you have a fever, darling?"

Maude shook her off and glared at Laura. "Now or later?"

"Will you excuse us please?" Laura asked and walked toward the back of the room, around behind the seating area, with Maude in the lead. Up on the bandstand, the leader hit a few juicy chords on his ukulele and began singing, "I want to go back to my little grass shack...."

Maude turned on Laura with glowing ember eyes. "This is a perfect night for another crime, you know."

Laura's impulse was to groan in despair and run away. But she couldn't do that. "Why?" she asked, bracing herself.

Maude leaned closer, conspiratorial. "It's a beautiful evening out there. You know how people are. After a while the judge will teeter outside for his nightly cigar. Mr. Johnson will join him for a cigarette. Emily will be sneaking out to smooch with Mr. Andrews. Before the evening is over, I'd bet anything someone will scrunch down that path to get aspirin or Pepto or something at the JiffyGrub. There are going to be residents all over the place, a lot of them outside. I intend to watch closely because something is bound to happen."

Laura studied her excited expression with a feeling of dismay. "So you plan to be right out there, on watch?"

"Right! And I think you ought to help me, if you're half smart."

"Do you have an assignment in mind? A specific station for me?"

"Sure. Down by the back gate. You can hide behind the azaleas."

Laura tried to think of the gentlest way to discourage all this. "I'm surprised you don't want that hiding place, Maude. It might be the best."

"Maybe so, but I don't always have to have the best place, even if I'm the mastermind. Besides, if anything goes wrong, you're a lot younger than me. You can run a lot faster."

"I need to confer with Mr. Aikman," Laura told her. "I'll see what he thinks about your idea."

"Are you crazy?" Maude gasped. "You don't tell him a thing! He's one of our prime suspects!"

"Maude, there's not a shred of evidence to implicate him in anything."

"He wasn't suspected of those old lovers' lane murders because he's a nice guy, Laura."

"He wasn't formally charged, either."

"Yes, but he quit the sheriff's office and went off to Texas for a long time before finally coming back here."

"What does *that* prove?"

"Nothing! That's just the point!"

Laura's head reeled. "What's the point?"

"He's as good a suspect as anybody we've got, and a lot better than most."

"Maude, that doesn't make sense."

"Hon, you just don't understand criminal investigation."

"I guess I don't," Laura said glumly. "Look, Maude, just stay indoors and behave yourself. I've got to talk to him about watching out for the press. I'm sure he doesn't need surveillance."

Maude grimaced. "Okay. But only for now. You can't expect me to stick around the atrium when the situation is so perfect for more bad stuff to happen."

"Let me tour the room a little and make sure everything is going smoothly. Then I'll talk to Mr. Aikman and get back to you, okay?"

"Okay, but hurry it up, hurry it up."

Laura moved away from her and toward the thickening crowd around the snack and beverage tables along the far wall. The Castles had decided to dance now, she in a sunburst blouse and grass skirt and he in shorts and a loud Hawaiian shirt. The Buckinghams were out there too, although they were always a sedate couple and had refused to wear anything festive. Laura hoped more would unbend a little and start dancing soon, even though many of them were so unsteady that dancing represented tremendously strenuous exercise for them.

All she needed, she thought—moving around the chairs and toward the clustered residents—was Maude Thuringer stirring things up. The whole idea of the luau was to take people's minds off the trouble. Although she had first thought the idea ridiculous, she had seen in the past twenty-four hours how many of the residents had gotten into it. Maybe it was not a bad idea after all. But someone like Maude could scurry around with notebook and tape recorder and quickly remind everybody that bad things had happened recently.

And the last thing she wanted was for Maude to antagonize the dour James Aikman with her fussy spying. They did not need that man antagonistic on any grounds. And if by some wild chance he really was involved somehow in the awful violence...

Laura forced herself to break off that line of speculation. She had nothing on which to base it, she reminded herself.

Still, she didn't like him and she didn't know why. And it had been a serious shock, learning about his past. Maybe he was an honest working man, nothing more. Laura intended to continue believing so until proven wrong. She had to be rational instead of listening to the bad vibes she felt every time she was around him, she told herself.

So circulate a little, she thought, make sure everything is running smoothly. Then take Mrs. Epperman's darned assignment to go find the man and talk to him about keeping the press away, even though she was convinced that strategy was the worst they could adopt; she knew the TV and newspaper people a little, knew how they reacted. Parade a whole legislature full of thieves and opportunists by them and they would ignore the whole thing because it didn't make for dramatic prose or pictures. But tell them they couldn't come into a kindergarten picnic and they went crazy, screaming bloody murder about the First Amendment and the people's right to know, et cetera. The *worst* way to discourage coverage was to try to do so; it only made their knees jerk.

But first things first: Circulate, check the feeling around the atrium.

She walked up to a group that included Ellen Smith, Davilla Rose, Col. Roger Rodgers, and the Pfeisters, Julius and Dot.

Only the Pfeisters had bowed to the pleas for island costumes; at seventy-two years of age, the bulky Pfeister looked uncomfortable in his loud shirt and borrowed faded Levi's; his porcelain doll wife, in a scarlet sundress, had a flower in her gray hair and was smiling gamely, but also appeared uneasy. Usually they were the essence of propriety, he never appearing in public in less than slacks, natty sportcoat, and gleaming shoes, she in nothing more casual than a dress others would have saved for Sunday church. Pfeister's idea of informality was the substitution of an ascot for his usual four-in-hand. Events like the luau sorely tried his dignity.

"You look great," Laura told him. "I love the volcano shirt."

He winced. "One attempts to get into the spirit of things."

Dot Pfeister gave her a little maternal pat on the arm. "It's too bad you didn't have time to put on anything festive, dear."

"Yes, I was a little rushed."

"I wouldn't worry about it if I were you. You look very sweet in that old work dress. And my goodness, Francie looks cute enough for the entire staff, don't you think?"

"That's exactly what I was thinking," Laura told her.

Colonel Rodgers harrumphed. "Nonalcoholic punch tastes like toothpaste."

"Maybe," Ellen Smith snapped, "somebody's dentures fell in it."

Davilla Rose, sedate in a black dress, shuddered. "That paints a terrible picture in the mind, Ellen."

Smith ignored the comment, bright eyes fixed on Laura. "Have the authorities come up with any new evidence at all that might point to the killer we seem to have lurking around here somewhere?"

"I don't know of a thing," Laura admitted.

"No trace of a murder weapon?"

"Not that I'm aware of."

"And no other leads?"

"Not that I know about."

Ellen made a disgusted snorting sound through her nose. "I devoutly wished for hair spray this evening. In the days prior to these terrible events, I could have toddled down the path to the JiffyGrub and thought nothing about it. Now we're all practically prisoners in here."

The colonel stiffened his back and stuck out his jaw. "That won't last."

Ellen stared. "I'm glad to hear that, but why won't it last? Until they catch the attacker, we're hostages here."

"Indeed not, madam," the colonel retorted. "Short-term standard operating procedure may dictate some caution among the residents. However, it can't continue. This outfit is composed of the most disorganized and undisciplined personnel it has ever been my misfortune to know. If the ban on use of the back path is not lifted within a few days, I predict that many of our peers here will return to their previous ways and resume utilization of the path whether higher echelons approve or not."

"That would be foolish," Laura put in.

"Of course," the colonel said, nodding briskly. "That's why it's so certain, because foolishness is the order of the day around this establishment."

"Colonel, I hope you're wrong."

"Madam, I never have been."

Laura gave up. She scanned their faces. "Is everything all right? With the luau, I mean? Anybody need anything?" No one responded. "See you later. I've got a little errand to run."

She turned and escaped in the direction of the darkened dining room. What if the colonel was right? she asked herself. Good lord, what if they started sneaking down the path again, inviting another mugging? James Aikman couldn't be here all the time. Were they going to have to nail the back gate permanently shut?

Going down the back hallway behind the kitchen, she wished Lassiter were already here. She would have welcomed his reassuring bulk beside her right now as she went about Mrs. Epperman's cuckoo instructions. She realized that she wasn't looking forward to going out back in the dark, even if Aikman was supposed to be nearby and on alert.

She had thought and thought about it, many times when she should be studying for the big test tomorrow, and there was no explanation of the two deaths other than random violence—petty robbery that got out of hand. She had worried herself far into the night, thinking about Violet Mayberry's red light. That made no sense and could have been a false memory of some kind, caused by the concussion, she thought. Surely the hypnosis recollection of a figure with a Weed Eater was faulty; why not the red light, too?

In which case they had nothing whatsoever left in the way of a clue. Two deaths, no clues, no leads, no nothing. She hated it. She hated being scared the way she was right now as she opened the back security door and stepped out into the humid evening.

At least it wasn't dark yet. Late-day sunlight shafted around the far corner of the building, lighting the stand of scrub oak and willows beyond the back fence. Birds sang. It was absurd to feel afraid on an evening like this.

She hurried across the pavement to the back gate, slipped the latch upward, and pulled the wood apparatus back. She stepped through the opening, hoping she would locate Aikman easily.

The voice made her jump. "Can I help you?"

She whirled, heart clamoring in her throat. Standing just inside the fence, hidden by shrubs until he chose to step into view on the path, James Aikman studied her with the cold, surgical intensity of an assassin.

"You scared me!"

Aikman did not smile. He did not move, even his unblinking eyes. "Is there something I can do for you?"

Laura briefly explained about Mrs. Epperman's worries concerning TV crews. Aikman listened with no expression.

"How," he bit off, "am I supposed to provide security out here in back and patrol the front for possible reporters?"

"I'm sure Still Bill will be vigilant out front. I just wanted you to know that he might come calling for you on short notice...and what Mrs. Epperman's instructions are."

He nodded, disgusted. "Understood."

Laura hesitated. She felt a strong urge to establish some kind of genuine human contact. She gave a little laugh. "It's no fun, being a security man, is it?"

His eyes widened slightly in genuine surprise. "Fun?"

"I mean, you have a lot to do. Heavy responsibility."

"I see." He looked away, then swiveled his ball-bearing eyes back to her face. "It's very rewarding, providing security measures for senior citizens such as inhabit Timberdale. They are good people. I only hope I can provide adequate safety for all concerned until the authorities apprehend the perpetrator of these crimes."

Then, quite astonishingly, he moved his facial muscles into what was supposed to be a smile. "As I'm sure you can understand."

"Yes," Laura replied, startled. "Well. I'd better get back inside."

"You can be sure I will be alert, Mrs. Michaels."

"Thank you."

She fled back across the pavement toward the security door. It had been a nice little speech about providing security for "good people" at Timberdale, she thought. It had been delivered with the dull rote tonal quality of something carefully memorized.

The smile, too, which had been meant to be reassuring, must have been planned. Realizing these things made her shrink further inside at the thought of Mr. James Aikman. Talking to him was like trying to converse with an android. She was struck more forcefully than ever by the intuition that there was something really weird and frightening about him.

She had to put these feelings to rest, she thought, shivering as she unlocked the aluminum-jacketed door and reentered. She had to find out more about Aikman—prove to herself that he was just an ordinary businessman in a spooky business, with odd mannerisms that meant nothing.

Going back up the rear hallway past the kitchen, she could hear Pierre Motard screaming French obscenities at his helpers. From the front came the distant sound of more ersatz Hawaiian music. Instead of going directly back to the atrium, however, she continued through the back corridor and took it to her right, where it intersected with another hallway leading to the office section up front.

In her office with the door closed, she pulled out the filing cabinet drawer with personnel records. The newest, brightest folder had Aikman's name on it. She took the folder out and quickly scanned the application form for his home address. Finding it—an apartment complex on Norman's near east side—she wrote the street and number on a small card, which she slipped into her purse.

After the test tomorrow she would have some weekend time she could invest in setting her fears at rest, she told herself. It was just because she knew so little about him that he seemed so threatening. It would be easy to check him out, and that was what she intended to do.

Turning out her office light, she proceeded up the inside corridor and emerged behind the reception desk. The combo was in full cry. More people were dancing. Aaron Lassiter had arrived. He was on the dance floor with Francie, and both of them looked like they were having a far better time than Laura liked to see.

FOURTEEN

THE LUAU IN the atrium ended promptly at midnight with the stately chiming of the big grandfather clock.

Actually it was ten-thirty.

The residents of Timberdale liked to stay up late for parties. The last thing their pride would have allowed was an event that broke up before the witching hour. But long experience had proved that parties lasting until midnight, or later, wound up with only a handful of bleary-eyed party-goers on the scene, and even fewer on their feet. The day following a real midnight party also inevitably saw a long line of headaches, sore bunions, upset stomachs, and back pains outside the clinic, awaiting treatment. So a subterfuge that everyone knew about but no one ever talked about had been in effect for major social events at Timberdale for more than three years.

The grandfather clock in a corner of the atrium was the official timepiece. During the height of festivities— ordinarily around nine o'clock—it usually fell to Laura to slip over to the clock, quietly open the front door, and advance the hands an hour and a half. If anyone ever saw her do this, they never commented. It was a benign deception: Residents could look up a few minutes later and exclaim about what a lovely party it was, and how time flew by, and would you look at that, it's already going on eleven. So the party could end gracefully before anyone almost dropped dead.

The Hawaiian band played a final piece, "Blue Hawaii" again, and left the stand to polite applause. Pierre Motard's staff came out and started cleaning up the food tables. Couples and singles drifted off toward their apartments. Still Bill Mills, sleepy after spending the night outside watching for TV crews that never showed up, came in and hopefully picked through the wreckage of the snacks, running a race with the kitchen crew.

Dr. Fred Which and Kay Svendsen came over to where Laura stood near the clock. Both had worn island getups, but by now both looked a bit worn. There had been a couple of cases of nausea, one fibrillation, and one strained back to contend with in the clinic during the evening.

"Another day, another dollar," Which observed cheerfully. "I guess it was a big success as usual."

"Mrs. Kallman is feeling better?" Laura asked.

"Nothing serious. Her heart fluttered for a few minutes there, but she does that all the time. A good night's rest and I think she'll be fine."

"I guess you noticed," Kay said, "that Ken was notable by his absence?"

Laura smiled. "I noticed you got through an entire evening without being chased three times around the desk."

Svendsen, long the major object of Ken Keen's amorous attacks, did not smile. "Fred went up and checked on him. He stayed in his room all evening."

Laura turned to Fred. "And?"

Which shrugged. "He said he's feeling all right. Nothing physical."

His expression made Laura's question a natural one. "But?"

"I think he's very seriously depressed."

"That doesn't sound like Ken."

"I know. I don't know what's going on. I've never seen him like that. He had no affect at all. I wanted to mention it to you. All of us need to keep an eye on him."

"I have that big test tomorrow," Laura said. "I won't be in."

Svendsen said, "I plan to give him a call in the morning. Whatever is going on with him, we just need to stay on top of it."

"I'll check by phone Sunday if I don't come in," Laura said. "And Francie is supposed to be here. I'll tip her off that something is wrong."

Which asked, "Has anything happened in his life that you know about?"

"That could cause a major depression? No."

Which's frown deepened. "Very unlike him. *Very* unlike him. Something has happened. Bears watching."

"Nothing happened in group," Laura told them. "But it's the kind of thing we might be able to check when we meet Monday."

"If he's like he is tonight when you meet on Monday, he isn't likely to say a word. That's how down he is."

They broke up, Which heading for the front doors, Svendsen back toward the clinic to turn out the lights and lock up. Laura stood where she was for a moment, remembering the suspicions voiced by Davilla Rose and Sada Hoff, and Keen's evident depression at that time. She felt a distinct chill. *What if something in him really had changed—a new phase of his dementia making him dangerous?*

No, she told herself, that was absurd.

Maude Thuringer scurried across the far end of the atrium, notebook in hand. The Pfeisters wearily made their way toward the elevator. Ellen Smith continued some kind of argument with Sada Hoff. Colonel Rodgers stood at attention against the far wall, grimly surveying everything with the rapt attention of a military commander watching troops go ashore. Francie Blake scampered around on her spike heels, shooing residents off to bed, laughing with delight, and generally being darling. Lassiter stood near the reception desk, watching her, his forehead mightily rumpled.

Laura started that way. Stoney Castle, his wife nowhere in view, crossed the atrium in front of her. He saw her and waited. He looked pale and a sickly film of sweat made his face glisten.

"Nice party," he told her.

"Yes, it was," she agreed. "Are you okay, Stoney?"

He stiffened defensively. "Sure. Why shouldn't I be?"

"You look a little under the weather."

He paused, seemed to wrestle with something, then let his right hand creep up to his chest, fingers light on the cloth of his ridiculous loud shirt. "Maybe a touch of indigestion."

"Or angina?" Laura asked quickly. She knew he had a history of two heart attacks. "Do you have chest pain?"

Castle's face twisted. "Well, maybe a little."

"Stoney, I can still catch Dr. Which—"

"No, you won't, no, you won't! I'm fit as a fiddle."

"You don't look fit as a fiddle."

His face regained a bit of color as his temper rose. "You can't send for a doctor to go to the emergency room every time you have a little pain when you're my age, Laura. You'd spend all your time doing that."

"But, Stoney, what if this is serious?"

"If it's serious, it's serious." He took a long, ragged breath. "Look, Laura. I've tried to explain this to you before. We're all *old* around here. Oh, we make our little jokes and do our little things, like Ellen with her art and Davilla with her rotten poetry, but our lives are over."

"You mustn't think that way," Laura said, her instincts going against everything in her therapy training.

"I shouldn't?" Castle demanded with a strange smile. "Don't you know that's how all of us feel?"

"Stoney, you've got lots to live for. You've got years ahead of you."

The faint, derisive smile remained, but his eyes suddenly looked like a winter sky. "What do you think we're doing here? Waiting for a new adventure? What we're doing is waiting to die, Laura. All of us. Whether we admit it or not.''

Laura stared at him in consternation. ''Stoney, I don't know what to say to you right now.''

''Hey, there's nothing to say. And it's no big deal. But look, this is the kind of thing you need to remember if Mrs. Epperman's little edict about using the back path doesn't hold very well. If one of us walks down there like Violet or Dave, and somebody bumps us off, it's certainly no catastrophe. It's not like it had happened to somebody with a lot of time left anyway.''

''Stoney, dammit! Promise me you're not going to disobey the rule.''

He chuckled. ''You're a marvelous young lady, you know that? You really do care about us, don't you?''

''Of course I do.''

''Then try a little harder to understand us, Laura, okay?''

Before she could reply, he turned away from her and went on.

CLEANUP IN THE atrium was finished before the real hour of midnight, the drone of a vacuum cleaner announcing the final step. Lights began to blink out, and Still Bill Mills and his crew left the fake palm fronds and other decorations until morning. Laura and Aaron Lassiter departed, he saying he wanted to follow her home for a cup of coffee, leaving Francie Blake alone near the desk; after they had gone, she stamped a pretty foot and said something no true Southern belle would ever be caught saying in company. Stacy Miller came on duty late, carrying three magazines, a math text, and an oily Domino's Pizza box. The grandfather clock, reset to the correct time, bonged twice; the reset had confused its innards, and its chimes would be all mixed up for another hour or two until the clockmaker's arcane artistry made it possible somehow for the sound gears and cogs to figure out where the hands were now.

On the third-floor balcony, quite alone, Ken Keen moved along, his tennis shoes making not the slightest sound on the thick mauve carpet. He had a key ring in one hand and a flashlight in the other.

Rather than using the elevator as he normally would have, Keen opened the fire exit door on Three and went down to the main floor level via the inside stairs. Once there, he did not go out into the atrium, but entered the back kitchen corridor where he had watched Laura hours before.

The key, which he wasn't supposed to have, inserted into the back door night lock, made it possible to leave without setting off an alarm. He stepped out into the dense, still night humidity and was careful to close the door silently behind him.

Keen took a few deep breaths, standing there in the deepest shadows of the building. He was hyperventilating a bit.

After a minute or two, better under control, he hurried down the steps and across the vacant paved parking and delivery area, heading directly to the rear gate that led to the path in the thicket. The little gate was locked and he did not have a key, but he shinnied over the top with the kind of agility that would have been impressive in a man half his age. He vanished down the path in the dark.

From a darkened second-floor hallway window, August Whitnaur watched Keen enter the wooded thicket. Whitnaur waited, pulse thumping erratically, straining his eyes to see into the darkness down there.

Five minutes passed, then ten. Then old Whitnaur saw it.

Out in the middle of the big black thicket, at least a

hundred yards away, a brief blip of pink-red light shone through the trees. It was gone almost as fast as it came, and Whitnaur rubbed his eyes, doubting them. But in a minute or two he saw it again: a slightly longer flash, definitely red through the branches and leaves, moving a bit horizontally and then again vanishing.

Whitnaur was tremendously excited. Maude Thuringer's suspicions were true, he thought with amazement. Now he had to maintain an even closer vigil—miss nothing—and report to her what he had seen. He knew they did not have enough yet to warrant telling anyone else. But they would. They would.

He sank down onto aching, bony knees and continued to stare out at the thicket where Keen had disappeared.

FIFTEEN

SUNDAY AFTERNOONS were not Sheriff Bucky Davidson's favorite time to hold meetings at the courthouse. But it was drizzling and he couldn't fish or play golf anyway, and he was beginning to get paranoid about all the TV attention being given to the deaths at Timberdale Retirement Center. He had called in Deputy Aaron Lassiter to meet with him and Norman police detective Fred Hunzicker to talk about the case.

"There's the faint possibility that both deaths were accidental," the sheriff observed with the glumness of a man suggesting that he might win the lottery Wednesday night. "They could have fallen. The appearance of possible violence could be our misunderstanding of the evidence. The fact that Violet had lost some petty cash might mean somebody came along afterward and took the money, or she lost it before she fell down."

"You're right, Bucky," Fred Hunzicker growled. He was a middle-aged man with the sallow complexion of a cave dweller and skin that resembled day-old raw pie dough that had been stabbed repeatedly with a fork. Usually he favored very old rumpled brown or gray suits and down-at-the-heel tassel loafers, but today he had responded to the sheriff's invitation in faded Levi's, a Notre Dame T-shirt with a hole over his left nipple, and cowboy boots that clearly explained why such items were sometimes referred to as shit-kickers. "Or they both could have been hit by meteorites, and Mrs. Mayberry's money vanished because leprechauns got it."

The sheriff glared from behind his desk. "Dammit, I'm just raising possibilities."

"Then don't raise *im*possibilities," Hunzicker suggested wearily. "Look, there might have been a minute or two when we could have put out the story those two old folks both fell, and we could have hidden the missing money, and then we could have put out a story that the path was going to be fixed and everything was going to be peachy keen again. But those possibilities damned sure went down the toilet a long time ago."

"Then we've got two old farts killed, and we don't have suspect or clue one," the sheriff snapped.

"Well, Lassiter's got that jerk Spurington working at the JiffyGrub."

"We can hardly arrest his ass because he's working at that convenience store."

Hunzicker stuck his finger into his left nostril and poked around. He found something and examined it, holding it out at arm's length because he had forgotten his reading glasses. "What do you make of that crap the old lady found somebody had buried out there? What was that stuff, Lassiter?"

Lassiter didn't have to consult his notes for this one. "A piece of a Ford muffler, probably a sixty-five model, and what was left of a big metal can, real old, probably older than the muffler."

The sheriff exploded, "What would somebody sneak out into a woods and bury shit like that for?"

Hunzicker wiped his finger on his pants. "Maybe they didn't bury it."

"Of course they buried it! We've all seen the freshly dug dirt and the holes where this junk came from."

"That doesn't mean they buried it. Maybe they dug it up."

"That's horseshit. If they had dug it up, it wouldn't still have been there, would it?"

Hunzicker canted an eyebrow. "True, I suppose."

"What about that peckerwood Aikman going to work for them out there as a security guy?"

Hunzicker lifted one thick thigh over the other. It seemed to require some effort. "I did some checking. He's done other security work. He walked the grounds at night down there at the belt buckle factory in Noble for more than two years. He was a day man at the hospital for quite a while. Lately he hasn't had anything that good, but he's worked some weddings and school plays and shit like that—"

"That pervert around school plays?"

"—and never had any complaints," the Norman detective went on as if he hadn't been interrupted. "We might all have our own ideas about what happened all those years ago, but he's been clean a long time, and going to work out there at Timberdale is not entirely out of line with the kind of stuff he's been doing forever."

"I don't like it," the sheriff grunted.

"I don't either. But there isn't a damn thing we can do about it."

The sheriff wheeled to face Lassiter. "Do you figure Spurington is on the up-and-up?"

"No," Lassiter said instantly.

"Neither do I. Do you figure Aikman is on the up-and-up?"

"No," Lassiter repeated.

"Do you think this whole thing might be somebody inside Timberdale—a resident, even?"

"Yes," Lassiter said.

"Well, what the hell are we going to do about it, then? I am getting real fucking tired of that phone ringing six times a day and it's one of those pricks from Channel Four or Channel Nine asking what progress we've made. We need to make some kind of progress."

Hunzicker uncrossed his thick legs, accidentally bumping a boot toe against the edge of the desk and showering powdery dried manure all over the place. "It's not my case, but if I were you, I'd bring Spurington in."

"On what charge, for God's sake?"

"Check his car. Chances are he doesn't have his liability insurance certificate in the glove box the way state law says. Or maybe his windshield wipers are worn, or his inspection sticker is out of date, or his muffler is too leaky. Shit, bring him in on anything. You can hold him twenty or twenty-four hours, anyway. Grill his butt off. If he knows something he might get shook up and spill it."

The sheriff glowered. "This office does not arrest citizens under false pretenses. We do not violate citizens' constitutional rights."

Hunzicker studied his old friend with eyes that resembled lead. "On the other hand, there's a county election this fall. And I hear a lot of rumors that Buck Johnson is going to file to run against you."

"That phony sonofabitch can't beat me. The incumbent has too much power and name recognition."

"Right. That's what Jed Perkins said about you four years ago." Hunzicker paused and turned the knife. "Of course you'll have a lot of name recognition, all right. The sheriff that couldn't stop some mugger from marauding all over the place and terrorizing the senior citizens at Timberdale."

The sheriff turned to Lassiter. "I want that little prick brought in here by noon tomorrow."

"Charging...?" Lassiter asked.

"You heard what Hunzicker just said. Charge him with violating the Clean Air Act by excessive farting, if you have to. I'll tell the press he's in for 'questioning.' That'll hold them for a day or two, and then after we let him go—unless he really confesses, of course—I'll issue a statement saying we're making good progress on other leads."

"Meanwhile," Hunzicker observed, "maybe you'll get a real break."

"Maybe," the sheriff muttered.

"If I were you," Hunzicker said, "I would make sure I had a man down there around that woods every night."

"I can't afford that kind of manpower!"

"You can't afford *not* to use that kind of manpower, you moron. Your job is on the line."

The sheriff thought about it. He looked sad. "Maybe we'll get lucky. Maybe there will be another attack and we can apprehend the perpetrator."

"If that happens," Hunzicker said, "I hope you won't try to tell the victim it was lucky."

AUGUST WHITNAUR held a hurried secret consultation with Maude Thuringer in one of the back hallways. He felt nervous and silly in about equal proportion.

"So he went out, came back an hour later, and went back to his room," he concluded.

Maude nodded, eyes snapping with excitement. "We're about to crack the case. Watch him again tonight."

Whitnaur stifled a yawn.

Maude added, "Go take a nap. The last thing we need is for you to fall asleep on duty when we're so close to wrapping the whole thing up."

"*Are* we that close?" Whitnaur asked, depressed.

"Sure we are! I can smell it! Now go get some rest, big boy. Tonight is the night of glory!"

MYRA SLATER, THE resident manager of the east-Norman apartment complex where James Aikman lived, was an overweight, bitter-eyed woman of about fifty who had once been blond and was now dishwater. Sitting behind her little pine desk in the apartment rental office, she studied Laura with eyes reddened by smoke and booze, and narrowed by suspicion.

"And you're asking about Mr. Aikman. Why?" she croaked.

Laura maintained her cheerful calm. She had known this was a farfetched fishing expedition that might arouse hostility. "Mr. Aikman has been employed by my employer, Timberdale Retirement Center, in a security position. It's routine in cases like this for us to do a follow-up to the hiring just to make sure we haven't missed anything."

Myra Slater nodded perfunctorily and wheeled her chair around to a lone filing cabinet in the corner. The filing cabinet was olive or avocado, the same color that had been trendy in kitchen appliances thirty years earlier. She opened the third drawer and riffled through some folders, finally pulling one out and turning back to Laura as she opened it.

"Mr. Aikman has been a tenant here for almost a year. It says here he's self-employed. Would that be right?"

"As far as I know, yes," Laura told her.

"He's always paid his rent on time and I've had no complaints about him. He's a very quiet man. Nobody knows him. Did he tell you he prefers to work nights?"

"I don't remember his saying anything exactly like that."

"You say your retirement place hired him recently?"

"Yes," Laura said, suddenly getting the impression that she was no longer the interviewer. "Why?"

"Well, it says in his file here that he's employed by Arco Health Systems, out in the Robinson Crossing shopping center. Did he quit that job, or what?"

"I don't have a clue," Laura told her. "Now, your records don't reflect any difficulty with him here?"

"Not a trace, dear. Of course if they pay their rent and don't tear holes in the walls, they're good people as far as I'm concerned." Slater had relaxed now, and the suspicion had been replaced by chattiness. "Have you ever managed property?" she asked Laura. "You're lucky. Don't. Nothing but headaches. Let me tell you what happened out here a couple of weeks ago, when a bunch of the students decided to have a pool party...."

Twenty minutes later, when she finally escaped, Laura went to her Toyota discouraged that she hadn't learned a thing. She had gone in with little expectation but some hope that she might stumble onto something helpful. You never knew. If she felt a little silly, like a budding Maude Thuringer, she also felt good in knowing that she was doing *something* to try to help in any way she might. It hadn't felt good at Timberdale when she went back this morning to check on the progress of cleanup after the luau. The bad feeling was something hard to put a finger on, but it was there: a deeper quiet, as if some of the residents at least were watching and waiting, nothing like their usual selves. There had been no trace of cheer or optimism this morning, and more residents than usual had stayed in their apartments and not come out at all for Pierre Motard's sumptuous Sunday brunch.

If there was anything she could do to try to raise that cloud of dread and depression, Laura thought, it was worth trying.

Leaving the apartments where Aikman lived, she drove across town in light traffic toward Robinson Crossing and the Arco health club. The city of Norman had exploded toward the west in recent years, and Robinson Crossing was one of the new large shopping centers out beyond Interstate 35 to the northwest. Laura had visited Arco once with the idea of possibly joining, but their rates had been too much for her limited budget. At least now she knew where it was, and that it was open Sunday afternoons.

She reached the shopping center. Most of the stores

clustered around treed islands and small parking areas were closed on Sunday, so there were parking places everywhere except in the immediate area of Arco, where cars were several rows deep. She found a place as near as possible and hurried through the misting rain.

Inside the towering interior of the club, she was confronted by two young amazons behind a curved blue reception desk. Lights blazed in the high ceiling overhead. Laura smelled chlorine, evidence of the indoor pool not far away. Looking past the reception desk, she saw a workout area in the rear of the huge room, Cybex machines, and a dozen or more men working out on them while others nearby hefted traditional weights. On the loft over the weight room, people of both sexes strode along on treadmills, frowning and working hard at it, while others pumped stair-climbers or stationary bikes. Laura felt a slight pang of depression: She needed a place like this: she was a flabby as a cream pie. But you didn't belong to a health club when (a) you didn't have money to pay the monthly fee and (b) your job and school and daughter never left enough time for a spare breath anyhow.

One of the golden girls at the desk gave her a blinding smile. "Hi! Can I help you with something?"

Laura stated her business. "I'm checking out the work references of a gentleman who has applied for employment with my company. Is the manager here today, or someone I might talk with about this?"

"Who's the employee?" the girl blurted with wide-eyed innocence.

"James Aikman. He used to—"

"Oh, wow," the girl groaned. "Shit. Pardon my French." She reached a pink-nailed hand for the telephone beside her. "Let me get Miss Murnan. You're lucky. She usually isn't in on Sunday." She half-turned away as she punched in an internal number and spoke to someone. "She'll be right out, Mrs.—?"

"Michaels."

"Okay. Neat." The girl pointed to a pair of aqua-colored imitation leather couches facing each other in a nearby alcove. Neither was occupied. "If you would like to wait over there...?"

Laura waited over there. She discovered that the health club's magazines were considerably more up-to-date than the ones in her doctor's office. Some of these copies of *Newsweek* and *People* were actually from earlier this same year.

She was glancing through an article about an actress only one husband behind the present when her Miss Murnan showed up from the back area. Wearing lavender sweats and Nikes, Murnan was a lean, athletic five feet, nine inches tall, sunnily healthy. Her red hair was cropped like a man's. She bounded along and plopped down beside Laura on the couch. "Hi! I'm Mavis Murnan. You wanted to ask something about Jim Aikman?"

Laura went through her routine—where she worked, how they had hired Aikman, how it was "standard procedure" to do a posthiring check of credentials and references.

"Well, I'll tell you one thing," Murnan said. "I'm stunned that Jim used us as a reference, after what happened with him around here."

"Trouble?" Laura prodded.

"Well, we had to let him go."

Laura felt a pulse of excitement. "Why?"

"He didn't fit in. We hired him to handle security around here nights, and at first he seemed okay. I mean, he sort of gave me chills, personally, but maybe security people have to be a little weird. He didn't drink or anything, and the people he listed that he had done short jobs for before all said he handled them adequately. But

it didn't take all that long to find out he wasn't for us.
After all, we were looking for building security, not a
gestapo.''

''What did he do?''

''First, early last winter—well, our hours are 6:00 a.m.
to 10:00 p.m. except Sunday, when we're open one to
seven only—early last winter, after Jim had been on the
job about six weeks, one of our regular customers, an
elderly gentleman, came in and walked on the treadmill
not long before closing. When he left, he forgot his duffel
bag. He got home and realized he had left it here, and
drove back. We were closed by that time. He came up
to the front doors and thought maybe somebody was still
inside, and pounded on the door. He didn't get any answer so he went around to the side, because that's where
the offices are, and he thought maybe he could see somebody and get in long enough to get his bag.

''Back there he was looking through a window, I
guess, and Jim Aikman came up and caught him. Mrs.
Michaels, nobody in their right mind would take that dis-
tinguished old gentleman for a burglar. But Jim got him
in a neck hold, knocked him to the ground, and hurt his
back. Then he dragged the poor man into the back room
and called me. By the time I got here, our poor patron
was shaking all over, he had a nosebleed, his back was
killing him, and Jim was strutting around like he'd apprehended Adolf Hitler.''

''So you fired him,'' Laura said, imagining the scene.

Murnan's face sagged in a frown. ''We should have.
But I'm so dumb. I thought he was just overenthusiastic.
We had a talk about it and then we paid our client's
doctor bill. Luckily it wasn't anything serious and he
didn't sue us. So I gave Jim this lecture and he stayed
on.

''A month or two later, though, two of our teenage
clients, two high school girls, got here before we were

open. One had been staying at the other's house and I guess they woke up early. Anyway, they got here about five-thirty or so, and it was still dark outside, and naturally the building here just had the security lights on inside, so they parked right outside in a corner of the lot and were waiting for us to open.

"All at once, I guess they got the scare of their lives. This brilliant flashlight—portable spotlight, I never got clear exactly what—beamed in through a side window, practically blinding them, and the door on one side was jerked open, and the next thing they knew, they were standing beside the car with this light still on them, and Jim Aikman patting them down."

"Patting them down? Even a policeman can't do that to a woman without a terrifically good reason."

Murnan grimaced. "Tell me about it. Of course we couldn't keep him on the payroll after that. And that's the story of Jim Aikman here at the health center."

"I see," Laura said, taking a shallow breath as she realized something else. "It sounds like he's not very stable."

Murnan chuckled without humor. "You hired him? I'd say you got a loser, Mrs. Michaels."

Outside, the rain had subsided. Laura climbed back into her car and checked the time. Trissie was at a movie that would be getting out in less than thirty minutes. Laura turned the Toyota in the direction of the theater, driving slowly.

She did not like what she had learned. Worst of all was the realization—momentary in the health club but now growing into a gnawing certainty—that James Aikman had treated the two teenage girls very much like the old newspaper stories said he had treated lovers' lane couples so long ago.

Maybe nothing at all had changed.

He was still a man capable of brutality, if not violence.

And now he was prowling around Timberdale each night, intent on keeping the residents from using the back path. He could be as serious a threat as the unknown mugger.

How was she going to break this to Mrs. Epperman? If she simply told Timberdale's manager, she could predict the reaction with a high degree of accuracy. Aikman had been Mrs. Epperman's idea. She would get her back up. A person's past was not always proof of what they were today, she would say. He was a good security man, she would say. Laura had been a dreadful girl to snoop behind his back, she would say. He was staying, she would decree, huffing and puffing with righteous indignation.

How could Laura tell her the facts in such a way as to convince her to get rid of Aikman, rather than getting defensive? She felt she had to do it, but right now she couldn't see how.

By the time Trissie larruped out of the theater with her three friends, Laura had the beginning of a headache. By the time she got the kids home, the noise inside the small car had ballooned her small headache into a big one. Thankful to reach her own apartment, but still worried, she went inside and checked telephone messages first. Aaron Lassiter had called twice. No other calls, thank God. She went into the kitchen to start supper.

MONDAY, AT 2:10 A.M., in the deep stillness of the upstairs hallway conversational area, August Whitnaur fell fast asleep.

At 3:12 a.m., Ken Keen went over the third-floor railing and plunged sixty feet to the floor of the atrium below.

He made a terrified little moaning sound as he fell, but night clerk Stacy Miller, alone at her post, did not have time to register it before the loud, sickening crash of impact startled her out of her chair.

Spilling doughnuts and diet Coke all over the place, the girl rushed around the duck-under opening in the desk and ran across the atrium, toward the back and the source of the sound. She got there, looked down at Ken Keen on the floor, and ran back the way she had come, biting her hand to keep from screaming. Seconds later she was on the telephone.

SIXTEEN

DRIVING FAST on the back road to Timberdale, with her sleepy but excited daughter belted into the seat beside her, Laura saw the approaching red and blue emergency lights bearing down on her fast. It was exactly 4:10 a.m. She braked hard and hit the shoulder of the narrow road, giving the big truck maximum room as it raced along, rocking dangerously from side to side, its rack lights getting blindingly bright as it neared. The sound of the siren rose in pitch to a deafening crescendo as the ambulance rocketed past Laura's car, then receded into the distant night.

Laura poked the nose of the old Toyota cautiously back onto the pavement and drove on as hard as she dared. When she turned into the Timberdale driveway, she saw almost every light in the place blazing, and three sheriff's cars and two Norman police cars scattered in front, their red-and-blues still winking.

Skidding to a halt in the side lot, she got Trissie out and held her firmly by the hand as she fled toward the front.

"I want to see everything, Mom!" Trissie piped up excitedly. "You don't have to spare me nothin'!"

"Anything," Laura corrected automatically. "You're going in my office and you're going to sit there, understand?"

"Aw! I—"

"No arguments, dammit. I don't have time right now. You just do as you're told."

Trissie groaned but lapsed into silence as Laura

grabbed the heavy glass front door open and propelled her inside.

The scene in the atrium astonished and dismayed her. More than half the residents, most in nightclothes and slippers, milled around in agitated excitement. Somebody had stretched yellow crime scene tape around the back part of the atrium. Laura saw Aaron Lassiter's familiar tall figure back there. He was not in uniform, so she knew he had been rousted out of bed, too.

"Laura!" Ellen Smith cried excitedly from a group near the door. "Ken Keen took a nosedive off the upstairs balcony!"

Laura nodded and hauled Trissie over to the counter, where she ducked underneath and hurried back to her office. Mrs. Epperman hadn't arrived yet. Laura turned on the office lights and plopped her daughter into the chair behind her desk. "Stay put, young lady, do you hear me?"

Trissie's eyes, astonishingly scared, blinked back at her. Trissie didn't say a word. Laura dug in a drawer, found an old magazine, put it in front of her, and rushed out again, closing the door.

Maude Thuringer hovered in front of the desk. Maude, unlike most of the residents, was fully dressed. Except for a hairnet, she could have been ready for Sunday church, and her dark eyes snapped with excitement. "Laura! I've got some really important stuff to tell you!"

"Not now, Maude," Laura said, hurrying by.

"But—hey! Listen!"

Laura grimly kept going. Several other residents spoke to her as she hurried across from the reception desk toward the back of the atrium, where all the uniforms were. Ordinarily she would have stopped to try to reassure everyone who spoke. At the moment her nerves were screaming bloody murder—just about literally—and she had to find out exactly what had happened, and how.

One of the Norman cops was on guard, keeping people back from the draped tapes. He recognized Laura, however, and soberly held up a tape and motioned her through.

Lassiter, wearing rumpled Levi's and a T-shirt, came over to meet her. He looked grave and solicitous. "I'm sure sorry you had to come in, babe," he told her quietly.

"I met the ambulance on the road. He's still alive?"

"He was when he left here." Lassiter turned and waved to someone. Dr. Fred Which detached himself from a group clustered tightly on the far side of a couch-chair arrangement that blocked Laura's view. He came over.

"Hello, Laura," he murmured. "Hell of a thing. Ghastly."

"Tell me."

Which half-turned and pointed up toward the ivory-colored balconies running around the upper floors. "He fell from up there."

Lassiter added, "The third floor."

"How can you tell it was Three? The railing isn't—"

"We found a flashlight up there that had rolled under a chair. It had Keen's name and apartment number on a stick-on tag on the side."

"And he fell all that way?" Laura shuddered. "How did he survive?"

"He's in a coma," Which replied. "Skull fracture. I'm not at all sure he's going to make it."

Lassiter put in, "He hit on one of those big coffee tables. It shattered. Come over here."

He turned and walked toward the clot of deputies and policemen on the far side of the high-backed couch. Laura followed. As she went around the end of the couch, she saw scattered, splintered wood, the remains of one of the five-foot mahogany coffee tables. An overturned lamp and strewn magazines littered the carpeting all around.

Someone had festooned everything with thick pale plastic sheeting, but she could see easily through it—saw the broad, ugly dark red splotch all over the carpet, too. She felt bile lurch up in her throat and went faint for a few seconds.

Lassiter caught her arm. "Hey!"

She shook her head and fought to regain her equilibrium. "I'm okay. I just got woozy for a second there."

He turned her from the ugly scene and walked her a few steps away. The sheriff, evidently noticing her for the first time, came over. His face looked puffy and glum. "Miz Michaels?"

"Yes?"

"About this man Keen. He was in one of your talk groups?"

"Yes. A regular."

"I need to ask you something. Did he exhibit any suicidal tendencies?"

"Ken?" The question took her breath away. "No. Never. He was—well, everyone here has problems, and he had his down times like everyone else. But he was one of the youngest residents, full of life."

The sheriff nodded grimly. "You don't have to speak of him in the past tense. He was still alive when they left here with him."

"I didn't realize I had," Laura admitted. "God. You think he tried to kill himself? I can't believe that, Sheriff!"

Sheriff Davidson craned his neck, peering up at the high railings. "Nothing broken up there. It's more than waist-high. He didn't fall through and he didn't just walk up there and accidentally fall over. He had to climb the damn thing."

Laura shook her head. Every instinct lay behind her answer. "No."

The sheriff's eyes flared with badly concealed frustration. "Then what happened? Are you thinking somebody flung him over?"

"God, no! I wasn't thinking anything."

The sheriff looked at Lassiter. "Goddammit, Salt, this doesn't make any sense whatsoever."

"They said this happened about three o'clock," Laura said.

"Your girl at the desk says about ten after. She called 911 at three-fourteen exactly. I got the call from them two minutes later."

"What," Laura groaned, "was Ken Keen doing up and wandering around at three o'clock in the morning?"

"Did he have a habit of walking around in the middle of the night?"

"No. Not that I know of." She searched her memory, then repeated more firmly, "No."

"Old people do that."

"Not Ken."

"Sleepwalk?"

"No."

"How did he get along with other people out here?"

"Just fine," Laura said. "Oh, he had fusses with some now and then, but nothing serious. He was...never mind."

"He was *what?*"

She hated to bring it up. "He considered himself a ladies' man. He made passes at some of us. But it never amounted to anything. Everybody knew to be on the alert around him."

The sheriff cocked his head, intensely interested in this. "Made passes?"

"Yes."

"Verbal passes?"

"Sometimes."

"Physical passes? Grabbing, stuff like that?"

Laura liked it even less. "Yes, now and then. But—"

"Then it's in the realm of possibility," the sheriff cut in, "that he ran into some lady in the hall, made a grab, they struggled, she shoved him and over he went, backward."

"No one has told you anything like that happened. Have they?"

His face crumpled. "No. Of course, it could have happened."

Laura's mind raced. "How was he dressed?"

"Sweats. Tennis shoes."

"Was he—did he have any money on him?"

Lassiter muttered admiringly, "All on the same wavelength."

"What?"

The sheriff said, "We thought about that. No sign he had a cent on him. We've already been in his apartment. His wallet and some change are still on the dresser in the bedroom."

"Then it wasn't a mugging for money," Laura said, intensely relieved.

"Not that we can tell."

She took a deep breath and shuddered again despite herself. "What now?"

"It's not going to take long. We've called for witnesses. There weren't any. We'll want to talk some more to your desk girl. The lab boys are going to dust the railing up there for prints." The sheriff's thick face worked with frustration. "Won't bring up anything, but we'll do it anyhow. We're sealing his apartment for the time being. Nobody is to go in. We'll be doing a more extensive search. Otherwise, unless somebody comes forward, I'd say we're put in the position of hoping he manages to survive so he can tell us what happened himself."

Laura became aware again of all the residents standing around beyond the tapes. "What about them?"

"If you can get them outta here, it would be a big help to us."

Laura nodded, disengaged herself from Lassiter's supportive grasp, and walked back around the conversation area and ducked under the yellow crime scene tape. Every face in the atrium stared at her.

She raised her voice, and conversation hushed as her words carried. "Everybody—we've had a terrible accident here. Ken Keen fell off the balcony. He's alive and he's being taken to Norman Regional. There isn't anything anyone can do, so if you would all just go back to your apartments, it would be a really big help, okay?"

For a moment no one moved.

Nervously she added, "We'll be keeping a close check on Ken, and as soon as there's any news, we'll have it at the office. But that might be morning or later, so let's just go back to our homes, all right?" She managed an encouraging smile.

To her relief, a few of the residents shrugged and turned away, sifting toward the elevators and stairs. A murmur of conversation arose, but the crowd definitely began to break up. She spotted Maude Thuringer in earnest conversation with August Whitnaur, and expected one or both of them to hurry her way. To her surprise, they didn't. She saw Maude's head bobbing as she made a furious point.

"YOUR'RE NOT GOING to tell her *anything?*" Whitnaur asked in astonishment.

"No, you ninny, of course not!" Maude stamped her foot. "How's it going to look if we tell her now about watching him? They'll just make *us* suspects, and we haven't done a durned thing!"

"But we weren't watching him when this happened. I fell asleep."

"Exactly! Exactly! How is *that* going to look? Oh, yes,

officer, we had him under surveillance, but please believe us, we were asleep at the switch when he took his nose-dive.''

"You think he killed himself?"

Maude's eyes narrowed. "Maybe he realized he was being watched. Maybe the guilt was too much. Maybe he did, yes.''

"He isn't dead yet."

"He fell more than fifty feet, Gus. You think he's going to survive that, at his age?''

"What do we do now?"

"You heard what Laura said. Go to bed. That's what I'm going to do.''

"And we don't say a word?"

"Absolutely not! Now scoot!''

STANDING BESIDE the plastic-shrouded coffee table and bloodstains on the carpet, Aaron Lassiter watched Laura disperse the crowd. He turned back to Sheriff Davidson. "You're not going to tell her anything else?"

"You mean about the wet dirt and grass on his shoes?''

"Right."

"Hell, no."

"He was outside, Bucky. That's clear, bigger than Dallas. He was out back.''

"We know he was outside," the sheriff said, phlegmatic the way he got sometimes when he was being misleading. "We don't know he was out *back*.''

"Where the hell else would he have been?"

"Keep your voice down, goddammit! Listen. We'll just mosey down there after daylight and see if we can spot definite proof that that's where he was before he came back here and took his dive. We already know there's no sign of him around that back door—of him or anybody else, for that matter. If he was down there, and

we can tell it for sure..." The sheriff paused and his eyes
went far away and then he shifted his dip of snuff from
one jaw to the other. "It won't help us anyway."

"What about Aikman? He's still waiting for us in the
kitchen."

"Let's go talk to the asshole."

A NORMAN POLICEMAN stood watch outside the door to
the kitchen area. He stepped aside to let Lassiter and
Sheriff Davidson enter.

Inside, a single security light over the stainless steel
stoves sent dim geometric shadows in all directions.
Rows of pots and pans, suspended from an area of
dropped ceiling, glinted dully. James Aikman stood near
the sinks, leaning against the Formica countertop. Darkly
dressed in jeans, a lightweight nylon jacket, and heavy
brown hiking boots, he had a glistening black leather belt
around his trim waist. It looked like the kind of belt policemen wore. It had a flashlight hanging on one side and
a heavy leather holster on the other. The butt of a Glock
semiautomatic pistol protruded from the holster.

Aikman pushed himself away from the counter as Lassiter and the sheriff entered. His narrow face seemed to
glow with pallor in the dim light. His eyes resembled
charcoal slashes.

The sheriff walked over. "Thanks for waiting, Aikman."

Aikman shrugged. "Part of the job."

Sometimes the best thing was to pounce, and the sheriff tried that. "What do you know about this deal?"

The surprise tactic didn't work. Aikman never changed
expression. "I don't know anything."

"Were you inside the complex or outside when the
accident occurred?"

The word *accident* registered; Lassiter saw the fractional shift in Aikman's eyes. Aikman answered, "Outside."

"Down in the woods?"

"That's right."

"See anything or anyone unusual down there?"

"No. Very quiet."

The sheriff yawned, so casual and sleepy he looked quite stupid and harmless. "You, uh, get into the building sometimes?"

"Of course." Aikman's eyes narrowed further. "I was issued a key. I make it a point to check all the floors at least three times a night."

"What time were you in there last tonight?"

"A little after midnight. I try to make rounds about that time, then again around three-thirty, and the last time just before daylight."

"Didn't see the old guy roaming around when you were in about three?"

"Midnight," Aikman corrected sharply. "I hadn't made my three-thirty check yet."

"Right, right," the sheriff said, yawning again. "Midnight. Any sign of him then?"

"No."

"And nothing else out of the ordinary?"

"I told you. No."

"Funny thing," the sheriff said sleepily.

"What is?"

"You not seeing him down in the woods."

"He wasn't down in the woods."

"I think he was."

Spots of angry color appeared on Aikman's cheeks. "If he had been down there tonight, I would have seen and apprehended him."

The sheriff nodded. "He had dirt and grass on his shoes. Kind of stuff you pick up walking down into the brush."

"He didn't walk in the woods. If he walked anywhere, it must have been out front somewhere." Aikman watched the sheriff with brightly hostile eyes. "Check the front desk. Residents are required to sign out."

"Yeah. He didn't."

"He broke the rules. These people are terrible about that."

"Yeah. But it's still funny."

"Why? How?"

"It beats us how he could have got out the front doors without that girl at the desk seeing him, or him setting off the alarm."

"Anybody can exit without setting off the alarm. It's coming back in that's difficult."

"That's right," the sheriff crooned. "But he went out, and he came back in with dirt on his shoes. How did he get back in, then?"

"Maybe you people can figure that out," Aikman said, a flat edge in his tone now. "I'm sure I can't. I'm just a contract security guard."

"But you've got law enforcement experience."

Lassiter saw Aikman stiffen again but not comment. Clever, Lassiter thought: The sheriff had let him know they were aware of his background. That would also let him know that he had to be at least a borderline suspect in *some* part of this. A man under the pressure of suspicion sometimes tried too hard...slipped up.

"Well, thanks for your time," the sheriff said now, heaving himself into motion toward the door. "Might have something more to check out with you later. We'll keep in touch."

"Anything I can do, boys," Aikman murmured.

Lassiter followed the sheriff out into the hall.

"I want that peckerwood's history checked out in more detail," the sheriff told him as they walked the dim hallway toward the atrium. "It's been a hell of a long time

since I went through those old files on him. You do that
tomorrow for sure. Make some notes on all the details
about those old murders. Track down where he's been
ever since leaving the department back at that time. Talk
to some people about him.''

"You think he did this?'' Lassiter asked, surprised.

"Don't know. But I know people. The sonofabitch was
lying through his teeth just now. He knows *something*. I
want to figure out what. And why he was lying to us.''

They reentered the back of the atrium. As they did so,
the front doors far at the other end swung open. A sleepy-
eyed boy of college age and a fat man lugging a heavy
TV camera rushed in. The camera had the Channel Four
logo emblazoned on its side. Channel Four chased more
ambulances than anyone else.

"Shit,'' the sheriff grunted. But it was too late to hide.
He headed up to greet them, plastering a big, dumb smile
on his puss.

SEVENTEEN

"I CAN'T DO this!" Trissie wailed at 7:00 a.m. "I'm totally exhausted! I'm just a kid! If I try to go to school today, I'll just disgrace the whole family. This enrichment program is a bunch of bull anyway." She tried to burrow back under the sheet.

Laura firmly pulled the sheet down again. "You didn't have to take the summer program. You said it would be neat. And it is an honor, Tris. So hurry up. We're going to be late."

"Aw, Mom! We were out there at Timberdale until almost five! I'm really fatigued. I'm worn to a nubbin. I can't do it!"

"Up."

Groaning, Trissie swung skinny bare out of the bed and staggered into the bathroom.

"And no closing the door and sleeping on the floor in there!" Laura yelled after her.

The water started running at the washbowl.

The telephone rang. More trouble?

"Hello?"

Lassiter's voice: "Wanted to make sure you're okay."

"Sure, fine, except sleepy, Aaron. Do you know anything about Ken Keen this morning? I tried calling the hospital, and except for next of kin, they won't tell anybody anything about a patient's condition. I don't even know if he's—"

"He's alive and holding his own. They did emergency surgery to remove a blood clot."

"Thank goodness for that!"

"Yes, but they say it's going to be touch and go for

at least another forty-eight hours." She heard him sigh in exasperation. "He's still in a coma. Can't tell anybody anything."

"I'm going to go to work, but then I'm going to try to get away to see him a little later."

"All right. And you're okay?"

"Sure. Maiden of iron and all that, right?"

He sounded puzzled. "What?"

"Never mind. Will I see you later in the day?"

"I hope so. I'm going to be busy as well. I'll catch up with you at some point, even if it's just by phone."

She hung up, feeling down because they might not see each other today. But she realized she faced a big day, too. When Mrs. Epperman had finally blown in last night at four-forty, she had been beside herself to see the TV crew at work in the atrium. She had issued sterner exclusion rules to be enforced by Still Bill and the work crew as well as by James Aikman. Laura had known at the time that it might be the worst thing she could do at the moment, but she had blurted out what she had learned about Aikman anyway. Mrs. Epperman had given her an angry lecture about letting sleeping dogs lie and giving people credit for having the ability to reform and not throwing the first stone unless your own past was flawless. Then she had said they needed more James Aikmans, not fewer. Then she told Laura she was a terrible girl for snooping into someone's life that way. Then she issued some new orders designed to smooth things out at Timberdale as much as possible.

Now as a result Laura was under instructions to get and issue periodic updates on Ken Keen's condition; make herself available to any and all residents who might be seriously shaken by last night's events; hold a special session of the Breakfast Club; see to it that discreet "Danger" signs be printed and mounted on every pillar around the second- and third-floor railings, and "do any-

thing else that needs to be done, child, I can't think of
everything...oh, this migraine is killing me, I may be in
late in the morning.''

Trissie staggered out of the bathroom. She looked better, but not much. She gave Laura the evil eye. "This is
cruel, Mom. Really cruel.''

"Hurry up," Laura told her.

AFTER DROPPING her daughter off at school, she stopped
at a JiffyGrub nearby and bought a diet Coke. She usually
didn't drink soft drinks in the morning, but this was special. The first sip of the Coke stung all the way down
and helped her get wider awake. She thought how close
she was to the hospital here. On impulse she dialed the
Timberdale number.

Stacy Miller answered, sounding more wide-awake
than usual.

"Stacy, this is Laura. How do things look out there
this morning?''

Stacy kept her voice low, a hint that there were already
people in the atrium. "The police and everybody finished
taking pictures and all, and they said Still Bill could clean
up back there, so instead of calling you I just told him it
was all right.''

"Good. You did right. What else?''

"Well, I think some people got up earlier than usual
because there are already eight or ten down here, waiting
for breakfast and kind of gossiping. But nothing special
is going on.''

"Okay, Stacy, listen. I'm going to run by the hospital
on the way in and check again on Ken. I'll be in, in about
thirty or forty minutes, okay?''

The girl sounded dubious. "I'm supposed to be off at
eight, and it's been a horrible night.''

"Do your best, Stacy, and I'll hurry." Laura hung up
before more protests could be voiced.

AT THE HOSPITAL the woman at the information desk said Mr. Keen had been moved from the CCU to the PCCU. Laura knew enough to know that ought to be a good sign: although the Post Critical Care Unit had some horribly sick people in it sometimes, it was not considered quite as serious as the Critical Care Unit. Even more important from her immediate standpoint, perhaps, was the fact that the PCCU was not as strictly isolated, and visitors could wander in at virtually any time if they didn't stay long or create any kind of commotion.

Getting off the elevator on the third floor, Laura headed down a long, carpeted hallway and found the entry doors to the PCCU. The halls were filled with activity—aides bringing breakfast trays, doctors writing orders, nurses bustling about on all the mysterious errands that nurses seemed to do. Laura made it a point to walk into the PCCU area without staring at any of them, or asking for directions. Maybe...

She was in luck. Five doors down, on the left-hand side, and before she reached the sprawling, brilliantly lit nurses' station where inevitably she would be questioned, she came to a room door with Ken Keen's name printed in Magic Marker on the patient ID card. The door stood ajar. The interior looked dim but hardly dark. She went in.

It was a private room, blue carpet, pale blue wallpaper, a single hospital bed at a corner across the far end, light stand above it, an IV stand and tubing running out of connectors on the wall and some kind of bleeping green monitor unit.

Everything seemed to be connected to Ken Keen.

Laura moved close, shocked by how small and shrunken and *old* he looked, lying there under the maroon coverlet. His eyes were closed. They looked discolored—two black eyes from the terrible impact of his fall. His chest moved rhythmically. He had a nasal cannula in his nostrils, white bandages swathed his head. Tubing from the IV stand snaked down and entered a needle taped into a vein on the back of his left hand. He had been catheterized, too. He looked very pale and sick.

Laura reached out a hand and tenderly touched his cheek with her fingertips. His skin felt cool. He did not respond.

She felt a sudden and unexpected urge to cry.

Then, being who she was, she asked herself why this should be so. She had never been close to Keen. He had been an irritant more often than a pleasure. She had lectured herself a thousand times about all the reasons why it was unprofessional to get emotionally connected to residents, why it was bad for them and her both. But he looked so small and sick. She felt her nose get runny.

Behind her there was the slightest stirring sound. She turned and saw a tall blond nurse, quite attractive, coming into the room with a tray of small instruments on it.

"Hi," the nurse said with a smile. "Are you a relative?"

"Sort of," Laura replied.

It seemed to be a satisfactory answer. The nurse moved around to the far side of the bed and put the tray down on the covers. Laura saw that it held some tubing, bandage material and other small metal foil packages, little vials of fluid, and several throwaway syringes. The nurse opened one of the smallest foil packages and proceeded to scrub the inside of Ken Keen's forearm with it. Then she unwrapped a syringe, inserted the needle in the rubber stopper of a vial, and extracted clear fluid.

She bent over Ken's arm and expertly inserted the needle into a vein. "He's a tough old guy," she murmured.

"He hasn't regained consciousness at all?"

"Nope. But you never know in a case like this. He might wake up at any time."

"Then there's a lot of hope?"

"The latest MRI shows no new bleeding or swelling, and the EEG indicates brain activity. I mean, it's not like all the signs are bad."

Laura watched her toss the used materials into a plastic security container. "What happens now? We just wait?"

"Yes." The nurse studied her. "If you or other members of the family have time, there's one thing you might consider doing."

"What?"

"Well, it certainly isn't established medical practice, but there have been suggestions that a patient like this is more receptive to external stimuli than we often suspect. It's good for him to have us in the room and talking, for example. If the family wants to feel like they're doing all they can, they might consider coming in as often as possible and talking to him, or reading him a magazine or something."

"He might hear?"

"He might, and it might help. I know of one case where we had all just about given up, and the sister came in and read to the man every day, hours on end. Then one day he just woke up and was pretty fine. The doctors will say it's a coincidence, but nobody thought that man was going to come out of it."

"I'll pass the word along," Laura said lamely.

With another encouraging smile, the nurse left the room.

Laura looked down at Ken, who had not moved a muscle. *You have to wake up, Ken. You can't leave us like this, dammit. It's not fair—you, one of the few people out there whose physical condition never worried me. And if you wake up you can tell us how this happened. We need to know that.*

She stayed another few minutes. People came and went in the hall outside—voices talking about ordinary events, menus, plans for vacation. She had never understood hospitals or the people who worked in them. How did you endure all the suffering you saw? How were you cheerful and buoying to people all the time when some of them were going to die? How did you understand the crazy illogic behind one person recovering as if by a miracle while another one, seemingly in better condition, suddenly went away?

Ken Keen still slept, deep in his coma. She crept out of the room and reentered the normal lighting and sounds and bustle of the hallway, and headed for the elevators again.

"SOMEBODY," Maude Thuringer told August Whitnaur in her most conspiratorial whisper, "pushed him over the railing."

"Somebody else figured out he was the mugger?" Whitnaur whispered back. The two of them were alone at a breakfast table in a corner of the Timberdale dining room, ignoring dirty looks from several other residents Maude had shooed away, saying they had something private to discuss.

"Maybe he wasn't the mugger after all," Maude said now.

"But he had the physical strength. He made passes at all the women. I saw him go out and down the path, and then I saw the red light."

"Yes," Maude said, her eyes going to suspicious slits. "But what if he wasn't the one making the red light when you saw it?"

"What do you mean? What do you mean?"

"I mean, Gus, what if this is a classic case of misdirection? Another example of the kind of bogus cause and effect that Eric Ambler uses so often? Did you ever read much Erle Stanley Gardner? No, of course not. He used it, too. It's the old post hoc, ergo propter hoc thing. Event

B takes place after event A, so therefore event A caused event B.''

"But that isn't always true," Whitnaur pointed out, puzzled. "It might rain this morning and the wind might blow this afternoon, but the rain didn't cause the wind to blow.''

"Yeah," Maude retorted. "Or the judge might come over here and want to sit with us, and then Ellen might come over a few minutes later, but the judge didn't make Ellen come over.''

"So what you're saying is—"

"You saw Ken go down there. You saw the red light. We both figured he caused the red light. Post hoc, ergo propter hoc.''

"But if he didn't make the red light," Whitnaur groaned, "we're back to square one.''

"Except for this: The maker of the red light must have caught Ken spying on him. Or her. And that's why he— or she—pitched Ken over the railing.''

"Then what do we do?''

"Firstly, we keep our yaps shut. Like I said last night, there's no sense getting ourselves in a pickle here. Secondly, we plan to keep an eagle eye on that thicket down there. If we see the red light again, it tends to support my theory. Thirdly, if we see it again, we dial 911 as fast as we can. Fourthly, we hope Ken regains consciousness and tells us everything.''

Whitnaur frowned as he spooned more sugar into his coffee. Pierre Motard had made it especially bitter this morning. "If it wasn't Ken, who in the world might it be?''

Maude scowled. "I don't know.''

"What if Ken never regains consciousness?''

Her scowl deepened. "I don't know that, either.''

On the far side of the dining room, several residents had risen from their tables to peer out the back windows.

They were talking urgently and watching with great interest. Some others craned their necks from their tables, also trying to see.

Maude got up and hurried across the room. She took a quick look and scampered back. "Cop car out there. Sheriff, I mean. Two of them just went down the path into the woods. Come on."

"Where?" Whitnaur asked, startled.

"Out to follow them, of course! Hurry!"

"We can't do that!"

"Who's going to stop us? The marines? Will you stop messing with that cinnamon roll and come on? We don't have all day!"

In the relative cool of the morning it was dewy and fresh along the dirt path leading down toward the frog pond. Aaron Lassiter and fellow deputy Jim Arwood moved slowly, watching the ground with every step, trying not to overlook or trample anything. Startled birds flew, scolding them as they went farther down. A squirrel went up a tree and peered around the edge at them.

"I don't see anything yet," Arwood muttered.

"Keep looking, keep looking," Lassiter replied.

They moved on down the path, coming to an area where few weeds grew in the perpetually dense shade, leaving the path quite barren: powdered dirt, scuffed by many footprints. Lassiter spotted something and quickly dropped to one knee.

"What?" Arwood demanded, moving in close behind him.

Lassiter pointed. There in the loose reddish powder was a sharply defined footprint, the wavy lines of a rubber-soled athletic shoe, the pattern flowing out of a circular motif in the center of the pad.

"Matches the shoes he was wearing last night," Lassiter said.

"Yeah, but the trees protect this area from rain," Arwood pointed out. "Even if it was his shoes, he could have made that track a week ago. And my God, Salt, I think *I've* got a pair of shoes with that tread pattern. New Balance. I buy 'em because they're U.S.-made, and they're damn nice shoes."

Lassiter felt like cursing. He didn't, but instead climbed back to his feet. "What size shoe would you say made that print?"

Arwood bent over again. "Seven, maybe. Maybe even an eight."

"Keen is small. Those shoes he had on when he took his dive were sevens."

"Maybe he was down here, then. But it still doesn't really—"

"Hey!" a shrill little voice cried out behind them. "Have you guys found a crucial clue?"

Lassiter turned to see Maude Thuringer and a male resident he didn't know standing a dozen paces up the path behind them. Maude hurried closer, all atwitter. "Can we see?"

Lassiter caught her arm. "Stay back. You're not supposed to be down here!"

"It's a free country!"

"Dammit, Mrs. Thuringer—"

"Wow!" Maude cried, pointing to her right and rushing off the path toward a large old elm. "You really found something vital!"

Lassiter bit his lip and hurried over after her. Before he could reach her side, she dropped to her knees at the base of the elm and plunged her hands into the loose dirt of what looked like a giant gopher mound. "Did you excavate it yet? Have you extracted the evidence? Man, this is really a fresh one! What do you suppose you'll find buried in this one? Huh? Huh?"

EIGHTEEN

THE BREAKFAST CLUB convened at ten o'clock: fourteen residents in all, some of them looking somewhat the worse for wear after the night's excitement. Two rows of chairs in a semicircle, most occupied.

"Okay, guys," Laura said with what she hoped was a smile. "Let's get started, okay?"

Side conversations died down. Ellen Smith raised a skinny arm, making multiple bracelets jingle. "Is there any new word on Ken?"

"As far as I know, he's still in a coma." Then, seeing the expressions of discouragement, she added quickly, "I was by there this morning. The nurse said he hasn't shown any more bad symptoms—"

Stoney Castle cut in, "Being in a coma ain't bad enough?"

"I mean," Laura explained patiently, "there hasn't been any more bleeding or swelling, and the tests show good mental activity."

Castle snorted a laugh through his nose. "That's more than he showed out here half the time."

"Stoney!" his wife cried, aggrieved.

"Well, it's true, isn't it?"

"Laura," Sada Hoff said, "you must be totally tuckered. First that horrid test you were dreading on Saturday, and then all this."

"I'm fine," Laura told her. "The test was a booger, but I think I did well on it. I think maybe I'm finally beginning to learn how to outguess the professor sometimes on what he's likely to ask."

"When will you get the results?"

"Next Saturday, I guess."

Julius Pfeister stirred. "Are we still supposed to stay off the back path?"

"Yes."

"Why?"

"Why, for your own safety, Mr. Pfeister."

"It seems to me," the impeccably attired old man said heavily, "shutting us off the back path is tantamount to shutting the barn door after the horse has been stolen."

Stoney Castle beat Laura to the question: "What do you mean by that?"

"It's obvious, isn't it? Someone got Ken Keen right here inside the building. That means we're no safer in here behind locked doors than we are out there in the bushes."

The room suddenly became deathly quiet. Laura saw some of the stricken expressions. "I'm not sure that's true at all, Mr. Pfeister."

Stoney Castle had gone quite pale. "It's either that or Ken tried to kill himself. And I ain't going to believe that."

Laura sensed the fear increasing exponentially. She felt like she was drowning in it. "It could have been an accident."

Sada Hoff said, "I find that impossible to believe."

There was a general murmur of agreement. Maude Thuringer stood, unusually solemn. "This is no time to leap to conclusions. We have to stay calm."

"I couldn't agree more, Maude," Laura said gratefully.

"We also," Maude went on, "need to stay in our apartments after dark and keep the door double-locked and watch all our neighbors for anything that might be suspicious. Also, I think we need to form a vigilance committee."

"Who," Stoney Castle demanded, "are we going to hang?"

"Who said anything about hanging anyone?"

"That's what vigilance committees do, you danged fool."

"No, I meant—"

"This is ridiculous!" Ellen Smith broke in. "We have a killer prowling the grounds and hallways, and we talk about hanging people. Have we all lost our minds?"

"Look," Laura said loudly enough to make them pay attention. "We don't *know* with absolute certainty that anyone has been murdered. Violet could have fallen. Mr. Bell's death could have been a freak happening, too. Ken isn't dead yet. The nurse told me she holds out a lot of hope for him. Shouldn't we all stay calm and not do or say anything rash until we find out about him? He could regain consciousness any minute and talk to us and clear all of this up."

Dot Pfeister spoke seldom, but she spoke now. "It's all well and good to talk about staying calm. But most of us are already really afraid."

Heads nodded.

"Well, of course, we're scared," Laura said weakly. "But we've talked about things like this before, remember? We've all got a right to feel whatever we're feeling. But a person doesn't have to act on her feelings. She can control her actions without denying how she feels."

It was Col. Roger Rodgers's turn to get to his feet. Hands on hips, he glared at his neighbors like a regimental commander might glare at his combat troops. "We have a mystery on our hands. Might be a chain of accidents, as Laura said. No reason for panic. Vigilance. That's the key. Most of us are armed. Vigilance and readiness. No reason why anyone should be in serious danger if proper precautions are taken."

"And that," Laura said, "means to stay out of the

woods out back at night, where an accidental fall could be just as fatal as any attack. And if you're unable to sleep in the middle of the night, stay in your apartment or else find someone to walk with you—the buddy system.''

Pearl Buckingham removed her eyeglasses and dabbed some tears with a tissue. "I hate this. When we moved to Timberdale we thought we would be protected from all the crime and violence out there. The world has had a nervous breakdown. We aren't safe anywhere.''

Laura dutifully tried to work with her. "It seems like there's nowhere to hide, right?''

Buckingham nodded vigorously. "Yes. That's right.''

"You feel helpless.''

"Yes.''

There was a simple trick to take someone out of their emotional state and get them thinking logically again, if only for a minute or two. Laura tried that now. "I know you're worried. On a scale of one to ten, with ten being the most worried, how would you rate your worry right now?''

The round-faced old woman frowned, considering that. "Five,'' she said finally.

"Good,'' Laura told her, and smiled. "That's a heck of a lot better than an eight or nine, isn't it?''

"Yes,'' Buckingham admitted quietly, calmer.

Laura looked around the room. "Pearl is about a five on the worry scale. How many of you would agree that a five is about right for you, too?''

After an instant of hesitation, one or two hands went up. Then most of the others, seeing the first hands, raised theirs, too.

"Okay. How many would rate their worry above a five?''

Sada Hoff raised her hand.

"How many below?''

The colonel stoutly shot up a hand. Stoney Castle followed suit.

"Okay," Laura said coolly. "Good. So all of us are somewhat worried. Gosh, I think we would be crazy if we weren't, don't you? But we've got good security here at Timberdale, and I'm sure of one thing—after last night, it's going to be better yet. I know the sheriff's office is going to be keeping an even closer eye on things. We have Mr. Aikman outside. I'm going to talk to Mrs. Epperman about having Still Bill and at least one of his helpers patrol the halls at night, from midnight to dawn. I think if we all cooperate we're going to be okay. I really do."

For a few long seconds no one spoke, although a few of the faces seemed to relax a little. Then Maude Thuringer piped up. "I betcha they're still checking out clues at the sheriff's office. We could see this case cracked anytime."

"You've all spent your lives being good people," Laura told them. "Good citizens. You know better than anyone what that means. It means watching after yourself, being careful, not spreading false rumors, being responsible. You're all responsible, always have been. We'll get through this thing just fine for exactly that reason: Everyone here knows how to be a responsible citizen."

They seemed to be further reassured by that. Laura felt her heart go out to them. She wasn't at all sure her words had made any objective sense at all. But these oldsters didn't need rationality right now. They didn't need logic or objectivity. What they needed was something they could cling to, some sense of being self-sufficient and in charge of their lives. Her words, as illogical as they might have been, had touched a nerve of pride in each of them, and so had given them some of what they needed.

MRS. EPPERMAN DID a double take. "You told them *what?*"

"I told them we would see about having Still Bill and at least one of his helpers patrol the halls at night."

"That's absurd, Laura! That's—that's counterproductive! In the first place, it's just a tacit admission that it might be dangerous around here at night. In the second place, who's going to work the flowerbeds and mow the lawn if Still Bill and his boys are asleep all day?"

"It's just for a few nights, I'm sure," Laura said.

"You don't know it's just for a few nights, you dreadful girl!"

Laura's frayed patience slipped. "It better be, Mrs. Epperman."

"What? What?"

"It better be for just a few nights at the most. Because if it isn't, we're going to have a full-fledged panic around here, and people will start moving out."

Mrs. Epperman's eyes bulged. She made a gasping sound and rushed out of Laura's office.

It was a total mess, Laura thought. She felt intense discouragement. They didn't have a lead. They didn't have a clue. They had nothing. In her own mind she *knew* two residents had been killed out back, and only a violent attack adequately explained what had happened to poor Ken Keen. There might be a resident here gone over the edge, planning even now to kill again. Once a Timberdale staff member, a woman who worked in the kitchen, had turned out to be terribly dangerous, a true psychopath. The killer could be anyone. Laura couldn't see that they had a prayer of catching that person, whoever he...or she...might be.

Not unless she could bring something out in one of the therapy sessions. Or unless she could pick up some meaningful hint by observing everyone more minutely, by being smarter.

A small sound in her office doorway snapped her out of her funk. She looked up to see James Aikman standing there. He looked angry enough to kill.

"Hi, Mr. Aikman. You're early today!"

His face was so tight that his lips scarcely moved. "I want to talk to you. Now."

"Come in."

He stepped into the office and swung the door closed behind him. As he turned toward her desk, she suddenly felt the smallness of the room and the solid wall, offering no escape, at her back.

Trembling with his rage, Aikman closed the distance to the desk in two strides and leaned over it. His voice rasped low in his throat. "Who gave you the authorization to snoop into my private life?"

Oh hell. Laura instantly knew what had happened: someone she had questioned about him had reported it to him. But she tried pretending innocence. "I don't know what you're talking about."

"You know damned well what I'm talking about! You asked my landlady too many questions. What right did you have doing that? What were you trying to prove? Who's been talking to you about me behind my back?"

"It was a routine posthiring interview," Laura lied. "We do it with all new employees."

"Bullshit! Who's been spreading lies about me? I want a name."

"There isn't any name. I don't know what you're talking about." Laura was beginning to feel the fringes of real panic now. The depth of anger in his eyes scared her. She insisted, "The checkup was routine."

"Who else did you talk to?"

"No one."

"Did you talk to those people at the health club?"

"No. Who are they? I—"

"Am I under suspicion of something here? Have I failed to do a good job for you?"

Laura got to her feet. She felt wobbly. "If you can't stand a routine checkup on your past, Mr. Aikman, are you in the right business?"

His breath whistled in through his nostrils. He started violently, and his hands came up off the desktop. *He very nearly hit me;* Laura realized that instantly, and as clearly as she had ever known anything in her life.

With a tremendous physical tremor he seemed to get himself partly under control. His voice became bubbly and hoarse. "You'll be wise to leave me alone to do my work. If you're as smart as people think you are, you'll stop meddling."

Her astonishment overrode caution. "Is that a threat?"

The eyes that considered her were pinpoints, not focused quite right, terrifying. His mouth twisted at the same time into a bizarre smile. "Of course not, Mrs. Michaels. I would never threaten anyone. I am merely stating a fact."

"I see."

He pointed an index finger at her. "Leave me alone. Let me do my work. Don't pry into things that are none of your business. Have you got me on that?"

"I hear you," she breathed.

He glared at her for another instant, then turned and strode out of the office. The door snicked loudly as he pulled it shut, hard.

Her legs weak, Laura sat down behind her desk again. My God, she thought, what kind of violence had they put on the payroll here? Aikman could be as dangerous as the unknown mugger they were all hoping to catch. He had to go.

But a new thought came, and along with it more fear. If she was instrumental in having him fired now, he would reason at once that she was behind his dismissal.

What might he do to her in retaliation...or to Trissie? The nasty, coppery taste in her mouth was sudden blind fear that went deeper than any rational thought or analysis.

Ken Keen, she thought. *Ken Keen.* He could not be allowed to die. He had to come out of his coma. He was the only one who might tell them anything about any of this.

Which was when she knew one thing, at least, that she had to do.

NINETEEN

IT WAS NOON, and Henry Spurington had been sound asleep in his apartment about five hours when all hell broke loose.

The first thing he knew was incredibly loud pounding on his front door. He swam up out of sleep, dazed for a few seconds. The pounding got even harder and louder. What the hell? He managed to get himself to a sitting position, naked on the side of the water bed. Somebody started yelling on the other side of the door.

Then the door caved in, flying off shattered hinges with an explosive, ripping sound, and sunlight glared in from the outside, half-blinding him, and the shadowy figures rushed all over the place.

"Hey, wait a minute!" Spurington yelled, jumping to his feet.

Two of them hit him, knocking him ass over teakettle to the floor. Panicked, he tried to struggle. One of them held him down, practically jerking his arms out of the sockets, and the other one helped roll him over. He got a faceful of rugburn and blanket lint, and then he felt the cold metal of the handcuffs slam over both wrists.

"You bastards! You sonsabitches!"

They hauled him to his feet as lights went on all over the apartment. His nose was bleeding. He saw uniforms everywhere, Norman police. One of the cops who had handcuffed him shoved him roughly back onto the bed. "Sit there and shut up."

"You got no right!" Spurington protested. He tried to kick the nearest cop with a bare foot.

"Sit still, shithead, or we'll knock you on your ass!" The cop pulled out his billy club.

Spurington knew billy clubs. He froze on the bed.

The police started tearing his apartment all to hell.

THE CLOCK ON Sheriff Bucky Davidson's office desk made a little clunking sound. Then it made another one.

"Two o'clock," the sheriff said needlessly. "Let him cool back there until four. Then you go talk to him."

"The Norman PD didn't find anything but a little grass," Lassiter told him.

"Great! We'll book him on possession as well as suspicion of burglary and that other stuff we had ready for him. We can hold him a lot longer on possession charges. The judge might put the bond high enough on that to keep him in here just as long as we want."

"The PD hasn't found anything else," Lassiter added morosely.

"They're still over there. They might."

Lassiter sighed.

"What's the trouble?" the sheriff asked.

"I'm not feeling real great about this operation."

"Don't give up. We might crack him this way, if he was really involved in the woods out there."

"It's not that."

"What, then?"

"I don't like Spurington," Lassiter admitted. "But that doesn't give us the right to trump something up on him."

"We haven't trumped anything up, man. And he's got a previous record. Don't forget that."

"Okay." Lassiter sighed again.

"The PD might still turn something up. Or he might blow sky-high and confess something about those muggings." The sheriff cocked a cynical eyebrow. "He might, that is, unless your goddamned bleeding heart gets to aching so bad you don't sufficiently scare him."

"I'll do my best, Bucky."

"Thank you very much." Sarcasm dripped from every word.

Lassiter turned to glance at the filthy milk can sitting on the work table against the wall. "Do I question him about this latest thing we dug up out there, too?"

"If it works in right, you can question him about all this crap we've found out there. I would dearly love to know why he—or anybody else—planted any of this stuff."

"It doesn't make sense."

"None of it makes sense, and I'm getting damned tired of it. I don't suppose the old fart that took a dive off the balcony has regained consciousness?"

"I just checked the hospital. He's the same."

"Shit."

"At least he's not worse."

"We need him conscious. We need a break here. If he would come to and implicate Spurington, we could really grill that sucker's butt in that cell after a while."

"I can't think it's going to help much," Lassiter admitted.

"That's the trouble with you, Salt. You're a good deputy. But damn. That negative attitude will be the death of me."

Lassiter balled impotent fists. "The dirt from Keen's shoes matches the dirt down there on the path where we found the footprint. He was outside."

"So what if he was?"

"Where was Aikman?"

"How should I know?"

"He was *outside*."

The sheriff put a boot on the edge of his desk. "So you think Aikman saw Keen, followed him inside, and tossed him over the railing?"

"I think," Lassiter said, feeling like a man about to

go under, "Aikman has become a better suspect than that punk kid down there in fourteen."

"How do you explain the two people killed before Aikman was on the scene?"

"We don't know he wasn't on the scene."

"He wasn't hired yet!"

"That doesn't mean he might not have been on the scene."

"Jesus Christ. Okay. I'll play. Let's say he *was* on the scene at the time of the earlier attacks. Are you saying he was so hard up he mugged those old farts for a grand total of less than twenty dollars?"

Lassiter rubbed his head, which had begun to hurt. "That old lady—the first victim—said she saw a red light. She said she saw somebody with a Weed Eater. None of that makes sense. None of that ties in with anything. Neither does this crap we keep digging up. I could get a confession of robbery out of Spurington, and that wouldn't explain this other stuff either."

"You're forgetting one thing," the sheriff said.

"What's that?"

"This all makes sense to the perpetrator. Nail him and we get our answers."

Lassiter got to his feet. "I've got two hours. I'm going up and read those old files real carefully this time."

"You won't have time to go over everything in two hours."

"I can start."

"Bon appétit."

TRISSIE, STAYING WITH the sitter until Laura's arrival, sounded disgusted when Laura called to say she wouldn't be home before eight.

"Maw-umm! You said we could work on my book report tonight."

"We'll have time, honey. I promise."

"I wish I hadn't ever decided to take summer school! It's no fun at all."

"I'll be home by eight, okay?"

"Where are you going?"

"I have to stop by the hospital for a while."

It had not been a fruitful afternoon. After the confrontation with James Aikman, she hadn't been able to concentrate on much of anything. Even a brief visit with Maude Thuringer seemed to go badly. Maude was curiously reserved and didn't want to talk about Timberdale's latest problems. Laura didn't understand that any better than she understood most of the other things that were happening.

But at least she had two plans of action now, neither very good but *something*. She still intended to do some further checking on Mr. Aikman. And she planned to spend two hours at the hospital every day for a while.

Now, at almost five-thirty, she parked in the Norman hospital's vast parking lot and walked quickly inside, carrying her purse and attaché case. She rode the elevator up to Three as before and went into the PCCU as before and found Ken Keen unconscious, as before.

She pulled the room's only chair over to the bed, moving the IV stand a foot or two to make room. Then she dug the book out of her attaché case and opened it to page one.

She had no idea what kind of reading Ken Keen might like, if any. But she thought everyone ought to like this.

She read, "Last night I dreamt I went to Manderley again. It seemed to me I stood by the iron gate leading to the drive...."

THE SICKLY SMELL of fear made the hot, stuffy interrogation room almost unbearable. Aaron Lassiter wondered how much longer he would be able to stand it in the windowless eight-by-eight enclosure. Across the small table from him, Henry Spurington sat on a straight chair against the wall, his shoulders slumped and his eyes dead. Sweat spread from the armpits of his dark blue jail coveralls. It was the sweat that filled the cubicle with the smell of fear.

"Let's just go over it again," Lassiter said through gritted teeth.

"Fuck you," Spurington said tonelessly, without feeling of any kind.

Lassiter clung to his patience and repeated his litany: "You're two payments behind on your car, and they're threatening to repossess it. You're a month behind on your rent. Your Visa is maxed out. Those pawn tickets the Norman PD found in the back of your closet show two TV sets, a shotgun, and a lot of silverware in the past sixty days. You didn't own that stuff, Henry. They came out of a burglary someplace."

Spurington's red-rimmed eyes flared. "Prove it."

"Oh, we'll prove it, Henry. We're going over all the recent burglary reports right now. They're checking in Oklahoma City and Moore, too. Once we tie you to a burglary and charge you with it after a prior conviction, you're deeper in the can. The marijuana charge will start looking like a greeting card compared with that."

Spurington crumpled deeper into himself. His dead eyes stared at his own bare feet. He hadn't bathed for a while; there was dirt around the joints of his toes. He said nothing.

"Let's just say the money from the burglary ran out," Lassiter said. "Let's just say you've got all this other stuff hanging over you, and the job at the JiffyGrub is minimum wage, not enough to make ends meet or get people off your back. Then you notice these old codgers toddling down that path from Timberdale at all hours. A man could slip over there every little while and watch for one of them. Then—"

"You're crazy! I never did them things!"

"Or maybe," Lassiter added, "he could rig up a simple alarm system. A string across the path connected to a switch that flashed a little battery-operated light, the kind of diode thing you can buy at Radio Shack for three bucks or so. Is that how you knew when to hurry across the road, Henry?"

Spurington scratched in his left armpit and resumed staring at his feet.

"A man might get some kind of plea bargain if he came out with it, Henry. Let's suppose he didn't intend really to hurt anybody. He didn't even have a deadly weapon of any kind. He surprises an oldster and damn if the codger doesn't get startled and fall down and hit her head. A man could get off with involuntary manslaughter in a case like that, maybe, if he copped a plea and admitted the whole deal and how it happened."

Spurington's head jerked up and the tortured eyes burned. "I didn't do it. You can't make me say I did it. You can keep me in here a million years and I won't admit something I didn't do just so you guys can say you cleared a case. Screw you. Go to hell. You can't prove any of it. I ain't confessing a deal I never did."

Lassiter considered starting over again. Although his experience in interrogation was not extensive, he had taken part in enough of them to know that there was a point beyond which continuation only hardened the suspect's resolve, making matters worse rather than better.

Lassiter was not absolutely sure he had reached the point. But he was bone-tired and getting nowhere.

He took a deep breath and got to his feet. It required only one stride to reach the metal door and crack it open. Cooler, sweeter air wafted across his face. The jailer sitting outside the door stood to look at him.

"You can take him back now," Lassiter said.

The jailer came in and signaled to Spurington. Spurington got up and brushed past Lassiter on the way out, giving him a look of utter loathing and superiority.

Left alone, Lassiter gathered up the scattered notebook pages on the table. Most of them had only doodles on them. After some thought, he folded one and put it in his shirt pocket, crumpled all the others, and dropped them into a trash can in the hall outside. He walked to the elevator and rode down toward the sheriff's office.

He was exhausted. Discouragement made it worse. He knew that what he ought to do now was go back to Records and finish poring over the old files on the lovers' lane murders and James Aikman. He was just too damned dispirited, and he felt ashamed and bad about that, too.

Back inside the office, he found a preliminary copy of the report on the search of Spurington's apartment. There wasn't anything new in it. A reporter at Channel Nine had telephoned asking for more information about the arrest. Paper clipped to it was a handwritten note from the sheriff reading "Don't talk to this jerk."

He called the hospital and got through to the nurses' station at the PCCU after identifying himself. Ken Keen's condition was unchanged. He called Laura's apartment and got the recorder. He called Timberdale and was told she had left more than two hours ago. He called the Norman PD and was told they had nothing new. He called the sheriff and reported his failure. He called Pizza Hut and ordered a medium sausage to go.

Outside it had started to get dark. He had been in there with Spurington for five hours with only one short pee break. He wondered if he would ever get that fear-odor out of his clothes. Everything he owned was beginning to smell like fear or cop shop or jail. Maybe he was in the wrong business.

He got into his car and drove south toward the pizza place, using back streets that went by the university. Some of the lots were over half full. Students walked the sidewalks, going to or from late classes. In the old days the campus had been virtually deserted all summer. That had been in the days of the four-year curriculum and the wishbone offense, he thought darkly.

A university police car met him coming the other way. The driver, a young woman in uniform, raised a hand in salute, very macho. Lassiter touched a finger to the stiff, wide brim of his old-fashioned Mountie-type hat, very macho, too. He reached the south edge of the main part of the campus and waited for a light and then turned west, the setting sun turning his dirty, bug-smeared windshield to flaming yellow. Down came the sun visor.

They were missing something, he thought. The procedures with which he had confronted Spurington—ducking across the road to watch between customers, or rigging an alarm string—were absurd. How could he expect to panic the suspect with a cockamamie proposition like that?

Okay. Review. The JiffyGrub had opened and everything was all right for a short time, and then the old lady got robbed and killed. A few bucks out of her change purse, maximum, almost for sure. Then the old boy had gone down there and ended up essentially the same way. Since then, nothing. But of course Timberdale had urged residents not to go that way since that time, and the department had had a car cruising by that woods once or twice a night, and that crumb Aikman was out there all night every night with his flashlight and his shooting iron that probably gave him an erection every time the holster bumped his hip.

The whole thing might be teenagers, members of a gang, even, cruising the back roads and figuring out that they might find an easy mark if they just parked back in the bulrushes, the way Aikman parked his pickup, and waited for an easy mark. Now, with the TV people and everybody else all het up, even teenagers were smart enough to stay away from the area and lay low. Which explained why nothing more had happened in the woods.

But good God, there was the matter of Ken Keen. Teenagers couldn't explain *that*. And what about the red light the old lady had reported, and this crap they kept finding out there at the bottom of freshly dug holes?

The whole thing was stupid—maddening.

But Lassiter had more basis for his frustration than the lawman's normal urge to solve everything. It had all been marginally all right with him, emotionally, as long as two deaths had happened outside, well away from the building, and evidently with a robbery motive. But the Ken Keen thing changed all that. The killer was just as likely to be inside as out.

Laura worked inside.

Laura was talking to her groups and individual clients about the situation.

Some madman, or madwoman, could take her questions and comments as threatening…too close, perhaps, to stumbling onto the truth about whatever was going on. Which could make Laura the next target.

That line of reasoning made Lassiter feel physically ill.

Up ahead, in the neon canyon of Norman's West Lindsay Street, the red Pizza Hut sign made scarcely a dent in the glare. Lassiter wheeled into the parking lot and hurried inside to claim his evening meal.

LAURA LEFT THE hospital. Her throat felt a little scratchy from more than two hours of reading. Ken Keen had not stirred.

She would try again tomorrow.

TWENTY

IN THE MORNING, the usual early crowd for breakfast arrived in the atrium at the customary time, and the usual maneuvering for position got under way nicely on schedule.

Pierre Motard prided himself on his breakfast buffet, which was not large or elaborate, but nourishing and abundant. Still, there had been an occasion seven months earlier when the buffet ran out of stewed prunes quite early on, and people tended to remember things like that. If you reached the buffet late—which is to say the time it was supposed to *open*—you got the toast after it had been out long enough to be cold and crunchy. Only by getting into the line as early as humanly possible could you hope to find the orange juice still nicely chilled. And everyone knew what the grits were like after they sat there awhile, soggy in the milk.

On top of all these factors was the problem of who sits where. Longtime residents had regular places in the dining room: a regular outlook onto the room, a regular chair, a regular proximity to the buffet, regular companions. But Timberdale's resident population underwent constant minor changes as someone died or decided to move back home or got sent to the nursing home, or someone else moved in as a new tenant. That meant you simply couldn't count on holding your usual place if you got there late. There had even been ghastly occasions when some newcomer just waltzed up to a table where the same friends had eaten together for four or five years, and introduced himself or herself, and plunked down in somebody else's chair.

If you hoped to get the right food, in other words, and to protect your turf, you needed to be among the first to enter the dining room when the kitchen staff opened the doors promptly at 8:00 a.m. Not everyone subscribed to the notion that this was vitally important, but enough old-timers did to make things interesting.

The Pfeisters were always down *very* early, she in a mint-condition old Shelton Stroller, he in candy-colored slacks and jacket and ascot. Sometimes they took a brief stroll outside, weather permitting, but they always managed to get close to the back of the atrium, where the closed doors to the dining room were, at a very early hour. They would stand near the doors and talk quietly to each other and await the arrival of their pals, the Buckinghams, who were often second to arrive but never later than forth.

Stoney Castle and his bride also arrived with the early group. If he was worse than sixth in the gathering troop, Stoney Castle tended to be grumpy all day. The Terwiligers liked to come in and sit on one of the couches like they didn't have a care in the world about breakfast, but the couch they chose was always the one strategically located at a prime cutoff point on the carpet in front of the dining area vestibule. From that location, one could simply wait until the proper moment and then cut into the line ahead of a lot of people.

Maude Thuringer, a chronic early riser, liked to fritter around on the edges of the action, but when the lights went on and were visible through the opaque glass doors of the dining room, she was capable of a dash worthy of any running back in the NFL. Sada Hoff was a bit like that, too, although her friendship with Davilla Rose often slowed her down, the pair of them resembling a dreadnought and a canoe as they cruised toward the morning's chow.

It was Col. Roger Rodgers who referred to all food as

chow, incidentally, and he was another early combatant. He liked to come down early and stand off to one side, doing some crisp deep-knee bends, stretches, and jumping jacks while waiting. He and Ellen Smith, another early bird, tended to intimidate some of the more timid competitors, so they never had to use too much muscle to get their proper place in the line.

Everyone knew everyone else's customary strategy. So everyone made subtle moves and experimented with new tactics. It was a given that the Pfeisters and Buckinghams would effectively block the doors, but Maude Thuringer often tried inching along the wall, ready to dart in behind them. The Castles sometimes drifted to their left, ready to attempt to cut off the hard-charging Ellen Smith. There was constant movement and rearrangement of firepower.

This morning, however, the maneuvering was not quite as intense as usual, despite the arrival of all the usual suspects. The Pfeisters and the Buckinghams were having a nice chat near the closed glass doors, and effectively forming a Maginot line, to be sure, and the Terwiligers had taken the high ground of the couch, she sighing and blinking a lot and he pretending unconcern as he perused his morning *Wall Street Journal*. But the intensity wasn't there, somehow.

"It's worry," Maude Thuringer told Ellen Smith.

"About Ken?" Ellen demanded.

"Yes, and about what's going to happen next."

"What is going to happen next?"

Maude set her jaw. "I'm not going to be locked up anymore."

Ellen's bracelets tinkled. "What do you mean by that?"

"I mean I intend to find a partner and walk down there to the JiffyGrub any time I feel like it, that's what I mean."

Ellen looked dubious. "Mrs. Epperman isn't going to like it."

"Well, pooh on Mrs. Epperman, then."

Across the atrium, August Whitnaur emerged from the elevator. He started toward them, moving slowly. He was using his cane this morning.

"And there he is now," Maude said with satisfaction.

"Gus? My land. Can he walk from here to the gate, much less down the path?"

"He can, and he will."

"Do you mean you intend to walk down there at night?"

"Darn tootin'."

"What about Mr. Aikman?"

"He better not mess with me."

"Maude, I'm not at all sure this is a good idea of yours."

Maude stared across the atrium to see Laura Michaels entering, attaché case in hand. "Well, just keep your yap shut, see? I don't want that busybody Laura to hear about this."

The lights went on in the dining room, beyond the frosted glass of the doors. The Buckinghams and Pfeisters formed a solid phalanx across the doorway. Stoney Castle took two quick steps in front of the Terwiligers' couch, neatly cutting them off and knocking Terwiliger's newspaper to the floor. Colonel Rodgers marched across the corner of the room and stuck his chin out at Sada Hoff, who backed off. The doors swung open and the crowd clotted tightly, forcing their way inside, elbows into ribs and heels coming down on insteps, everything perfectly polite and proper, no one so much as grimacing with pain or smiling with the thrill of victory.

Maude Thuringer did not compete as she usually did. She was far too preoccupied with her plans to start walking the path tonight.

"Gus," she told Whitnaur, "stay off of that hurty leg today. We're going to put my new scheme into effect about midnight, and you need to be mobile to help me. I think this is the way to catch our robber. I don't know why I didn't think of it sooner. We'll smoke that sucker out!"

THE TELEPHONE MEMO that Stacy Miller handed to Laura on her way in said her major professor, Dr. Barnett Hodges, had called at 7:10 a.m.

Hodges, a luxury-loving man, never called anyone at 7:10 a.m.

Frowning, Laura turned on her office lights and punched in the return call number at once. Hodges himself answered. He was at home and Laura could hear the *Today* show on in the background.

"What's up?" she asked.

"Good morning, Laura," Hodges's big bass voice boomed. "You sound a bit tense this morning."

Laura modulated her tone. "I didn't realize it, Dr. Hodges. I think, what with the stuff that's been going on out here, it's a perpetual state. What can I do for you?"

"First, I've glanced over the test papers. You didn't perform up to your usual high standards, Laura."

She felt a pang of worry. If she flunked out of the social work program, her entire plan to restart her life was down the tubes. "I was afraid I didn't quite ace it," she admitted.

His chuckle made the telephone vibrate. "Nothing all that bad. You'll have a middle 'B' on the thing. Still every chance to make an 'A' in the course."

"I hope to work a lot harder on the final."

"That's actually what I called you about, Laura."

"The final?"

"Well, no, not exactly. I gave considerable thought to the conversation we had the other day about all the trou-

bles out there at Timberdale. You said you were trying
to use your groups to allay some of the residents' fears,
and at the same time you hoped to elicit information that
might possibly help uncover the culprit."

"That's right."

"And how has that been going?"

"Dr. Hodges, I really think I've done some good work
on the fear aspect. In terms of uncovering any information that might help, or learning something that could
point toward a suspect, I've struck out."

"That's what I thought. Tell me, Laura, do you have
a woman named Maude Thuringer in one of your
groups?"

"Yes. But how did you hear anything about Maude?"

"She called me this morning."

"What? This morning?" Laura groaned. "How did
she—"

"Get my name? I imagine you must have mentioned
me in group."

"Oh, God, I'm sure I did sometime. But I never
thought anybody would remember, and I certainly didn't
think anyone would call you. I'm really sorry. She called
this morning? It must have been early."

"Six o'clock, actually."

"Oh, hell! I'm *really* sorry, Dr. Hodges! What in the
world did she want at that hour?"

He chuckled again, but did not really sound very
amused. "She wanted to ask me about the nature of the
criminal mind."

"My God. What can I say? She's a dear old woman,
but she's read every mystery story ever written, and every
time something the least bit out of line happens, she goes
into her Miss Marple act."

"That's all right, that's all right. I'll admit I was a bit
put off at first, but once I got halfway awake and figured

out who she was, it became rather interesting. The lady has a very Byzantine mind, Laura.''

''Tell me about it. But what—''

''The questioning about the criminal mind is of no consequence. I tried to offer some ideas, but she interrupted continually, quoting everyone from Dashiell Hammet to Mickey Spillane, and generally telling me that she knew more about the subject than I do. The point, however, is that you need to be warned, Laura.''

''Warned? About what?''

''She seems to have some plan up her sleeve to catch the culprit out there.''

''Oh, no!''

''I'm afraid so, yes.''

''What's the plan?''

''I couldn't get that out of her, I'm sorry to say. She started being very cagey with me. About the best I could get out of her was a reference to a book called *Day of Judgment*. She said she was—wait a minute... I scratched this down to make sure I didn't forget it—she said she was going to 'pull a Vaughn'.''

''Pull a Vaughn? Is that 'v-a-u-g-h-n'?''

''I suppose so, although I presume it could also be 'v-o-n'. I judged by her tone of voice and just the way she said it that she meant she had a plan to emulate someone named Vaughn. Or Von. Do you know this book she mentioned, *Day of Judgment?*''

''No, but I'll sure try to find out,'' Laura promised grimly.

''Okay, Laura. That's all I have. Oh. And your man in the hospital?''

''Ken? He's the same.''

''I'm sorry to hear that he isn't better. The longer one stays in a coma like that, as you know, the worse it ordinarily is.''

"I went by last night and read to him a couple of hours."

"You did?" Hodges's tone perked up. "How very interesting. Did he respond in any way?"

"Not that I could see. It was pretty discouraging, but I intend to keep at it."

"That's right, Laura. You never know what stimuli might be going into the unconscious mind in a situation like this." Hodges paused and his voice changed the way it often did when he told one of his egregious old jokes: "Like the veterinarian said when he gave the enema to the dead horse, it certainly can't hurt."

"Thanks, Dr. Hodges. I can really use that encouragement."

He chuckled still again. "Take care, Laura." He paused and then added more heavily, "I mean that." The connection broke.

Laura hung up and started out toward the atrium. Aaron Lassiter walked in through the front doors as she passed the reception desk. He looked wonderful as usual, but tired. Right behind him the front doors fanned again and Francie Blake whirled in on a clatter of high heels and a cloud of shimmery summer dress.

"Oh, Aaron!" she cried after him. "Please wait up."

Lassiter, who hadn't seen Laura yet, stopped in surprise and turned to her. Francie scampered right up to him and made a cooing sound of sympathy and patted his cheek and then went on tiptoe and gave him a fleeting kiss. "You poor man! You look utterly exhausted!"

Laura got around the counter fast and headed in their direction. By the time she got there, Francie was telling Lassiter that he needed to find time for more relaxation, and she had tickets for Pink Floyd, and if he would like to go, why—

"Hi, Aaron," Laura broke in.

He turned and saw her at last. The expression of perplexity on his face changed to a lovely, troubled smile. "Good morning."

She didn't regularly make such gestures in public, but Laura leaned close to him. Startled, he caught her and gave her a quick kiss.

He said, "We have to talk."

"Sure...*darling*." Laura stroked his arm. She wasn't looking at Francie, but knew Francie was having cats. "I didn't return your call last night because it was a little late by the time I got home and helped Trissie with some stuff. I was pooped."

He nodded sympathetically. "We've both been hitting it a little hard."

"Like to have a cup of coffee?"

Francie made a desperation gesture. "Gee, what a nice idea! Let's all three of us go to the staff lounge!"

"No," Laura said with a nice smile, "Aaron and I will go to my office. Come on, honey."

He followed her like a loyal sheepdog. She could have jumped into his arms and kissed him. When they got to her office, she did.

"What's that for?" he asked after kissing her right back.

"Just because I love you," she said.

"This is serious," he growled with pleasure. "I wish I weren't on duty."

"I wish I weren't on duty, too." She pointed to a chair. "Sit. I'll be back in a minute with the coffee."

Amazing, she thought as she hurried to the lounge, how so much could be so wrong in a life and yet be okay if you also had feelings like this.

Taking the two cups of coffee back into her office, she closed the door with her hip, handed him his cup, kissed the top of his head, and went behind the desk. "Okay. What's up?"

"We think somebody tried to murder Ken Keen early this morning."

TWENTY-ONE

LAURA WENT COLD. "You *think* somebody tried to kill Ken? Is he all right?"

"He's fine. Still in a coma. No change."

"What happened?"

"Somebody went in about 5:30 a.m. and took his vital signs, or whatever you call it, and everything was normal. Another nurse looked in about seven to make sure his IV tube and oxygen were all okay, and both of them had been shut off."

"Shut off! How did that happen?"

His forehead wrinkled, Lassiter shrugged. "It couldn't have been an accident. The practical nurse who was in earlier swears he left everything in good shape. But later the oxygen tube thing was shut off at the valve where the supply comes out of the wall behind the bed. The IV tubing—glucose, I guess, to feed him—was cut off at that little monitoring machine hanging on the rack beside the bed."

Laura hugged herself. "It couldn't have been a mistake."

"No. Almost surely somebody slipped in there sometime between five-thirty and seven, and turned them off purposely."

"Thinking that would kill him?"

"That's what we believe, yes."

"But didn't someone on the floor see whoever it was?"

Lassiter sighed. "That time of day is busy. Taking vital signs, weighing patients, getting ready for breakfast. There's a shift change at seven, too, so there are more than the usual number of people milling around, creating a certain amount of confusion. Some of the doctors even get going that early.''

"Then,'' Laura said, visualizing it, ''someone could have ridden up in the elevator, entered through the PCCU area double doors, walked down the hall to Ken's room—''

"Which is, you'll remember, close enough to the doors that a visitor doesn't have to pass the nurses' station.''

"Yes.'' She absorbed the shock. "God. I guess we ought to be thankful that whoever did it wasn't equipped with a syringe full of morphine or something that might have killed him for sure.''

Lassiter nodded. "It was close enough. The old guy's heart isn't as stout as it might be, the doctors told me this morning. Nothing real serious, but decreased function—less oxygen processing than normal. Then you add the flattening effects of the coma on top of that weakness. Until he wakes up and gets his metabolism perking again, Ken Keen *needs* that oxygen to keep him going.''

Laura studied his somber expression. "And there's not a clue.''

"No. We've got a guard stationed outside his room now, of course. It won't happen again. And the hospital is going along with us on keeping the whole thing completely quiet. They're not interested in the furor it would cause if people learned some crazy might be able to walk right into a patient's room and do something crummy. The sheriff sure isn't interested in having all the TV people in our office again. So it won't become public, we hope. But that doesn't make it any less serious.''

"What's the next step?'' Laura asked.

"Good question. I was the first one to arrive at the hospital because I was already down at the courthouse. Couldn't sleep, so I got up and went there to recheck all the old files on your Jim Aikman.''

"He isn't *my* Jim Aikman. If I had my way about it, he'd be out of here."

"And have no outside security?"

"We could hire somebody else."

"Why don't you?"

"Mrs. Epperman. She seems to think he's wonderful because he read about our troubles in the paper and came seeking the job. Also, he's cheaper than the others. Which may be the real reason she loves him dearly."

He sipped his coffee. "I heard you say she pinched pennies, but I thought she was just trying to make this place turn a profit for the owners. Is she really that tight?"

Laura had to sniff. "Is wallpaper?"

"Damn." The scowl came back bigtime. "I don't like the idea of you being close to him."

"The files were that bad on reexamination?"

"Laura, I don't think there can be a doubt in the world that he hassled kids out on the lovers' lanes. He was a sicko, a bully. If they could have found *any* evidence, even circumstantial, to link him to that double murder scene, they would have had him. Some of the old reports—his own incident reports—when you dig deep enough, show what kind of a bastard he was. He loved to write reports on college kids necking in parked cars late at night or allegedly outraging public decency by dancing too close at fraternity parties, shit like that. He cruised the country roads. He hung around the campus, looking for something to butt in to. He just really liked hassling young people."

"But the sheriff didn't fire him for any of that, did he?" Laura asked dubiously.

Lassiter looked disgusted. "No. He always kept a hair inside the law—could claim he was just being a diligent officer. And the sheriff in those days was a drunk and an incompetent, which didn't help matters any."

Laura shook her head, imagining it. "The worst stereotypical small-town deputy."

"It gets worse. I found a number of complaints of that time that told about an unidentified guy accosting kids out on the back roads, sometimes in apartment complex parking lots. It was always the same: a young couple fooling around, up comes this yahoo with a flashlight and a revolver of some kind, demanding ID, hauling them out of the car, trying to get the female to answer explicit questions about her sexual preferences."

"God! Aikman again?"

"I haven't finished checking, and some of the reports won't be explicit enough to help me. But of the few I was able to check, correlating time of the reported incident to the hours Aikman usually worked, these incidents involving an unknown civilian guy all came when he was off duty."

Laura put her coffee cup down. "You mean he hassled kids on his own time, too?"

"I think so, yes."

"Didn't anyone ever identify him?"

"He was clever about that. He kept the big, handheld spotlight in the victims' faces. They were blinded and couldn't see him well. All they usually got was bodily conformation—height, estimated weight."

"Which fit?"

"Which fit."

Laura reached for her coffee again. "I can't believe they just let him rampage around like that."

"It was a different time, babe. A no-good sheriff on his way out, the town a lot smaller, the county a lot less organized. The sheriff in those days had only a couple of deputies. Record keeping was really bad, as I can testify after going through some of this old stuff about five this morning." His face wrinkled sadly. "And nobody wants to say a fellow officer is a bad officer. No one wants to believe that.''

"But you feel sure he was?"

Lassiter heaved a breath. "Oh, yeah."

"Aaron, I'd like to say leopards can change their spots. But I don't guess I can."

His head came up sharply. "What's happened?"

She hesitated, a little embarrassed about her Maude Thuringer imitation at the apartment complex and health club. "I did some checking on Aikman myself."

"When? How? What did you find out, if anything?"

She told him, being especially careful to repeat the conversation at the health club as accurately and fully as she could remember it. As she got to the part about Aikman frightening two young girls, his face sagged in dismay.

"That's our boy," he said disgustedly.

"But what does he want with us here, now?" she demanded. "He's a bully and a thug, and he scares me. I think he's a little crazy. But what does any of that have to do with his wanting to work for us now? He isn't going to find any kids fooling around out in that thicket, is he?"

"No." Lassiter shook his head. "I checked with a couple of other officers. This immediate area has never been known for a lovers' lane, although that old double murder took place only a couple of miles east of here, off Highway Nine."

"I don't know much at all about the murders, for that matter, except what you told me."

He stared bleakly at the wall. "Early one morning, a farmer named Effingham is driving from his spread toward town. He starts past a little dirt turnoff where there's room for parking about five cars—high ground, but partly wooded, a favorite spot for lovers to go park and admire the view back toward town. Our farmer sees one car parked back in there with the front doors both standing open. What looks like a piece of clothing is on the ground on the passenger side. He doesn't see anyone around. Being the curious type, he turns around and goes back and checks it out.

"The clothing item is a girl's lightweight sweater. There's no one inside the car. It looks like a Coke or something has been spilled on the seat——it's still soggy—— and there's popcorn all over the floorboards, although this late-model Ford is otherwise extremely neat and clean inside. The keys aren't in the ignition, but our farmer sees them sticking out of the trunk lock.

"There's something else funny here. The area where the car is parked is partly bare dirt, and this is deep summer and you know how dry and powdery Oklahoma dirt can get at that time. All around the car, and back up toward the road, the bare dirt has tiny groovelike marks all over it. Then the farmer sees several broom bristles in the dirt, and he tumbles: Somebody has swept the area, literally."

Lassiter paused, sent down the dregs of his coffee, and stared at the wall again. "Do you want to hear the rest?"

"Yes," Laura said, her voice sounding thick to her.

"Our farmer calls out several times, but nobody answers. He has begun to get seriously worried by this time. There's the key sticking out of the trunk lock. He goes over and turns the key and the lock unlocks and the trunk lid slowly comes up, opening. Our farmer, I think, at this point wishes he had never slowed down this morning.

"Inside the trunk are two bodies, dumped in together, legs cramped up in the fetal position to get them both in. A boy and a girl. She is naked below the waist and her skirt and panties are stuffed in beside her. The boy has blood on his face from where he has been struck by something. But that doesn't account for nearly all the blood inside that trunk. Both of them have been shot in the head with a .22 caliber weapon."

Laura had been steeling herself as his story progressed, but she shuddered now nevertheless. She watched him and said nothing, realizing for the first time, perhaps, what a brutal world he lived in every day.

He raised his eyebrows in resignation. "Our farmer runs to the nearest house and calls the sheriff, of course. The sheriff is halfway sober this morning and answers the call himself, along with three of his on-duty deputies, including Aikman. One look and they call in the Norman police and the state crime bureau.

"There is no evidence. The couple are identified, university students. The boy has been beat up before being shot and the girl has been raped with some kind of instrument. There are no witnesses and there is no murder weapon. Ballistic tests confirm that the bullets are .22 longs."

Lassiter crossed his legs and patted his tunic pocket, the giveaway gesture of a reformed cigarette smoker. "It isn't clear to me exactly how this came about, but the Norman police suspected Aikman from a very early time in the investigation. Also, he owned a .22 Colt Targetsman pistol. At one point they asked to have the pistol to check it. Aikman said it had been stolen and he hadn't filed an incident report.

"The case got a lot of publicity, and Aikman was mentioned a lot in both the press and the office reports. A week or so after the murders, the sheriff suspended him for allegedly roughing up a motorist. He never came back to the force. I think everybody thought something was going to turn up to provide that final clue linking him to the thing. After all, he had a record for being a bully, he was off duty at the time of the deaths, he owned a gun of the right caliber, one he now conveniently couldn't produce. But nothing ever came to light. The rest you know. He's had several other former officers try to work with him in the business, but he can't get along with much of anybody. He's a loner.''

Lassiter's open palm slammed down on his knee, making a crack that startled Laura badly. ''Dammit! What are we missing? What's going on? How does he fit in? I've got a punk down in the jail that we're trying to implicate, but I don't think we have a prayer on him unless he does one of those Perry Mason spontaneous confessions. This is driving me nuts. To have you right here on ground zero is the worst of all.''

''That's why you got right out here from the hospital,'' Laura guessed. ''Thank you, honey. I—''

''Actually,'' he interrupted glumly, ''I had another reason, too.''

She stared at him, puzzled. ''Oh?''

''I wanted to see if our good friend Aikman was on the job out here. I about half-hoped he would have checked out early. Which would at least make it possible he had gone to the hospital and done the deed.''

''And?''

Lassiter's teeth grated audibly. ''His pickup was parked right where it's supposed to be. He was just getting ready to depart. Said he was tired after a long, boring night. Of course he could have left, gone into town, slipped into the hospital, then driven back out there and resumed his station before I managed to get on the scene.''

''You're thinking more and more that he's somehow involved in all this.''

His quick look was almost hostile with frustration. ''Yes. But try, goddammit, to prove anything.''

It was Laura's turn to sigh. ''Maybe Ken will make it. Maybe he'll wake up, even today, and tell us what happened to him. Then we would know who attacked him and pushed or threw him over that railing.''

"If he saw his attacker," Lassiter said darkly. "And if he remembers."

"He's got to know, and he's got to remember."

They looked at each other. Then he stood slowly. "Got to get moving."

"Will you call later in the day?"

"No question about that, babe. And you're going to be careful?"

She grinned up at him. "Sure."

He leaned over the desk and they kissed quickly. He turned and went out, a troubled man already a thousand miles away somewhere. She stayed at her desk, rather than walk him out as she usually did.

She had not told him about Aikman's discovery of her meddling, and his fury about it. It hadn't seemed like the thing to do. She didn't know why.

LASSITER LEFT the complex via the front entry gate as usual, but instead of turning left toward Norman he turned right and cruised up by the JiffyGrub. A car sat at the gasoline pumps, a swarthy man pumping gas into his mud-covered Dodge pickup. Lassiter got a glance inside the convenience store and saw a young woman behind the counter. An old Harley was parked out at the side, close to a battered Chevrolet, and he wondered who belonged to the motorcycle.

At the next crossroads he saw that somebody had brought in the first heavy equipment for the construction of the nursing home he had heard about. Pulled off the road into the thigh-high weeds were a big yellow Cat, a large bulldozer, and an empty dump truck. Someone had done some surveying, too. He spotted small surveyor's flags stuck at regular intervals along the edge of the road on the Timberdale side. The construction would halt any backdoor traffic down the path to the JiffyGrub if nothing else could, he thought with satisfaction. Once this machinery started tearing out small trees and brush-hogging the entire area and moving massive quantities of dirt around to level the site, strolling down by the frog pond would no longer be a pleasant experience by anyone's standards. It looked like about the eastern half of the old thicket would go under the bulldozer blade right away.

A good thing, he thought, turning around and heading back past the convenience store a second time. Stop the old folks' traffic, stop the danger.

Or maybe not, he thought suddenly, reconsidering. Maybe the only chance in hell they had to solving this case was for another oldster to get mugged, and somebody to see it happening. Aikman was the kind of man who would dearly love to stop such an event, apprehend the attacker, and claim total credit for the breakthrough.

But once the woods were all torn to hell by the construction equipment, Aikman wouldn't have a chance. Neither would anyone else.

MAUDE THURINGER'S eyelids snapped up and down like old-fashioned window shades. "I don't know what you're talking about! I never said any such thing! Somebody is a blabbermouth!"

"You said you had a plan," Laura insisted quietly. She had caught Maude in the mail room just off the atrium, and didn't want to attract attention if it could be avoided. "You said you were going to pull a Vaughn, or something like that."

"You're crazy!" Maude turned and scampered out of the room.

"Dammit," Laura said under her breath.

She had hoped Maude would revert to form and start babbling about how she was about to crack the case. But ever since the accident—or attack—involving Ken Keen, Timberdale's resident literary sleuth had been uncharacteristically silent and even surly. She was not about to volunteer anything.

Which left Laura only one thin hope.

"Yes," the pleasant female voice said. "This is Mrs. Richards, and I'm one of the librarians. How can I help you?"

"Mrs. Richards, my name is Laura Michaels and I'm the assistant manager out here at Timberdale Retirement Center."

"Laura. Of course." The voice warmed. "We've met. You probably don't remember me by name. My great-aunt, Sada Hoff, lives there. We've been out to a few of your Sunday functions."

The voice now clicked. Laura remembered a friendly blond woman, about thirty, with a husband who had an amazing handlebar mustache. "Sure! It's nice to catch you, Mrs. Richards."

"Can I help you with something, Laura?"

"Well, I hope so. I'm trying to track down a book called *Day of Judgment*. I suspect it's a novel or collection of short stories. Could you possibly help me?"

"I'll try. Hang on a sec. Let's see...." Laura heard computer keyboard keys clicking. "*Daily Devotions... Day of the Jackal... Day of—* Yes. Here it is. *Day of Judgment*. It's a novel. Suspense. By Jack Higgins. Holt, Rinehart, Winston. Kind of an old one. 1979."

"Does the fact that you have that information in your computer mean you have a copy?"

"Yes. Let's see. It's on the shelf. Two copies, actually."

A slight sound caused Laura to raise her gaze from her desk. Judith Epperman, eyeglasses perched on the end of her nose, peered in at her and then came on into the office.

The woman at the library asked, "Is this what you're looking for?"

"It sure is," Laura said grimly. "Look, I really need to see a copy of that book. How late are you guys open today? I get off here after five, and could get there by five-thirty."

"We'll still be here, Laura."

"Great. Mark one of those copies to hold for me, okay? I'll be there."

"We'll surely do it. Good-bye."

Laura hung up.

"Were you talking to a bookstore?" Mrs. Epperman demanded.

"The library," Laura told her.

"Don't you have anything better than that to do, you terrible girl? Have you checked with the hospital about Ken Keen this morning? Have you finalized plans to put Still Bill and some other workers around the building for added security, and to watch out for more of those horrible TV people? Francie told me that the deputy sheriff was in earlier, and the two of you were closeted here in your office for a long time. Don't you ever think of appearances? How do you think that looked to some of our nosy residents?"

"Mrs. Epperman—"

"No, now, Laura, listen to me. This is almost the last straw. You *must* start paying closer attention to your business here. Now call immediately and check on Ken Keen."

"I already did. He's the same."

"Oh." The redoubtable woman seemed nonplused. "Yes. Well. How unfortunate. I suppose he's going to die on us. That's all we need, more notoriety. What about Still Bill?"

"We've talked. He's working out a duty roster. He's going to get back to me later this morning. Mrs. Epperman, could we talk some more about James Aikman?"

"Absolutely not! There's nothing to talk about. I just

thank the good Lord we have him. Do you realize that nothing untoward has happened out there in those woods since we employed him? What a godsend he is!'' Mrs. Epperman paused, looked around, fluttered, and started for the door. "As you were, child. Keep up the good work. Cheerio.''

Laura took a deep breath and looked down at the papers on her desk.

Mrs. Epperman stuck her head back in. "Oh. You wouldn't know an eleven-letter word for 'clump,' would you? I think it probably might start with an A.''

"Agglutinate,'' Laura suggested.

Mrs. Epperman winced, and her glasses fell off. "That's horrible. That's ridiculous. Where do they come up with answers like that? If they don't straighten themselves out at *USA Today,* I'm going to stop working their damned puzzles. I am deeply offended.'' She went out again.

TWENTY-TWO

THE BRIDGE GAME got under way late in the afternoon. Ellen Smith, finished painting for the day, joined poet Davilla Rose, Maude Thuringer, and Judge Emil Young at a table in the small activity room. Ellen Smith had the scorepad, pencil, and hardcover copy of Goren, to be used only in the event of controversy. Davilla Rose had the Kem cards. They sat down partners, north-south, giving Maude Thuringer and the judge the east-west chairs.

Ellen Smith began fan-shuffling the blue peacock deck without being asked. Davilla Rose started to do the same with the red deck.

"I suppose," Ellen said, "you've all heard that Still Bill and his crew are to start being bodyguards."

"Bodyguards?" the judge said, blinking sleepy eyes. "I had heard of no such innovation. What pertinent information can you propound in conjunction with this electrifying revelation, if I may be so bold as to inquire?"

As usual, Ellen Smith had not quite gotten all of what he said, but she did not let that stop her. "It isn't general information yet, although Laura did mention it in group. But now it's official. They start tonight. They're going to patrol the halls."

"Hall monitors," the judge intoned. "Shades of junior high school, eh?"

Ellen took it upon herself to deal.

"We don't cut for deal?" Maude chirped.

Ellen kept right on dealing. "I suppose it's a good idea, putting Still Bill and the others out around the building at night. But my goodness. I begin to feel like I'm in a prison around here."

"Oh, you could avoid them if you wanted to roam around," Maude told her.

"Really?" Ellen finished dealing and picked up her cards to arrange them. "If Still Bill and his lads do their work right, you couldn't go very far before one of them saw you."

"There are always the back stairs."

"What good do they do, unless you just want to live in the staircase? One heart."

"There are little glass windows in the stair doors on each floor, Ellen. You could hide there and watch for one of the hall monitors and then sneak out wherever you wanted to go. You said one heart? I'll say one spade."

"Pass," Davilla Rose, sitting north, said.

"Poop," Ellen muttered.

The judge studied his cards. "Two spades."

"Well," Ellen said after some thought, "I'll try three hearts. Maude, you almost make it sound like you're planning to sneak around after hours."

Maude raised her eyebrows in exaggerated surprise. "*Moi?* Heavens, no! I'll double three hearts."

Everyone passed. Maude led the king of clubs, probably indicating a king-queen combination. Ellen had three little ones, but not the ace. She watched tensely as Davilla put down her dummy. She also had three losing clubs and only two jacks in her entire sorry hand. This, Ellen thought, was going to be like the Battle of the Bulge.

Maude kept a straight face. She thought she could see five tricks, and maybe six, depending on how the diamonds broke. She loved setting Ellen. Ellen thought she was such hot stuff at the bridge table.

Talk about Still Bill and internal security was making it more difficult for her to concentrate, however. She and Gus were going to have to be extra careful if they were to get out tonight without being seen. She had to make sure Gus understood how to do it. They would have to synchronize their watches. Gus was going to have to move fast on his cane. It was a hell of a time for his gout to be acting up, she thought.

The judge played a six on her king and it went through. Oh boy oh boy, he had the ace. Maybe this was going to be a real bloodbath now. She led her queen.

"'WITHOUT STYLE, uneducated even, the writing of an indifferent pupil taught in a second-rate school,'" Laura read and slowly closed the book.

Swallowing to combat her dry throat, she looked across the bed at Ken Keen. The nursing staff had turned him onto his side as a hedge against fluid buildup in his lungs, and pneumonia. His unconscious face had never changed expression. Laura felt a pang of hopelessness.

"Ken," she said softly, leaning closer from her chair. "Are you enjoying the story? I know you've probably read it before, and I'm not a very good reader. But I hope it's okay. You need to wake up, Ken. We need you to be better. Wake up and tell us what happened, Ken. Please?"

There was absolutely no response.

She put the book into her attaché case and got to her feet. Her legs felt stiff from sitting in the same position so long. It was past eight o'clock and gray evening stood beyond the drawn open-mesh draperies at the window. Maybe this idea was the stupidest she had ever had, she thought. But dammit, she intended to keep right on with it.

She left the room, went down the now-familiar hall, and to the elevators. She had gotten a parking place within a mile of the building, for a change, and hurried to her car. Once inside, doors locked, she headed for home.

The red-jacketed copy of the Jack Higgins book lay on

the passenger seat beside her. She wondered if looking through a novel for a clue as to Maude Thuringer's scheme was as dumb as reading to an unconscious man. She was grasping at straws.

But she had nothing else, she thought, driving in the dense evening traffic.

She had to get home and skim the Higgins novel all the way through tonight, hoping against hope, because tomorrow night her ethics seminar from six to ten would cut her hospital reading short and leave no time for anything afterward, if she was to have even a few minutes with Trissie.

She felt guilty about her daughter lately. The deal from the start had been that Trissie would stay with the neighbor after school, but Laura would be home by six at the latest and they would have the evenings together except on the one night a week she had class at OU. After the emotional problems Trissie had had in the first months after the messy divorce, giving Trissie a stable, predictable home life had been at the top of Laura's priority list. But since Violet Mayberry's death the schedule had been messed up continually.

It would be nice, Laura thought, to put Timberdale out of her mind and just punch the clock the minimum number of required hours. But she couldn't do that, she wasn't built that way; maybe she would never learn to leave her relationships with people neatly stowed under a paperweight at the office. She might have been less involved if it weren't for the groups and occasional individual therapy sessions. But they made the relationship with many of the residents too personal, too revealing. She could not put Violet Mayberry entirely out of her mind any more than she could forget Mr. Bell, or stop worrying about dumb, lecherous Ken Keen, or ignore the fact that maybe nobody at Timberdale was safe right now, and most of them could never leave the place at all or ever escape from the fear they were trying to pretend did not exist.

Laura's apartment was not far away now. For what seemed like the millionth time, she caught herself reviewing the little they knew about the things that had happened. Petty cash had been taken from the victims attacked in the woods. But that did not explain the bizarre things Violet had remembered: the shadowy figure, the red light, the Weed Eater. For some reason that damned Weed Eater stuck in Laura's mind worst of all. What was somebody doing out there in the middle of the night, chopping weeds? It was crazy! And what did any of that have to do with the newly buried junk they kept finding?

She felt a headache coming on as she parked, gathered up her things, and hurried to the neighbor's apartment to collect Trissie. At home, she started hurrying around the tiny kitchen, preparing Campbell's tomato soup and grilled cheese sandwiches, while Trissie dutifully bent over her school books on the kitchen table.

"So how did it go today?" she asked to make conversation.

Trissie put down her book. "Not bad, I guess, if you like sitting around half the day listening to other kids report on their language arts projects."

"What was so bad about that? Weren't their papers any good?"

"Boy, Mom, are you behind the times! You don't *write stuff* in language arts these days. You go to a show or watch some stuff on TV, and then you get up in front of the class and talk it out."

"Talk it out?"

"Sure. Learn how to think on your feet and be spontaneously verbal."

"Oh." She felt old.

The telephone rang. Thinking instantly of Aaron Lassiter, she hurried to pick it up.

It wasn't Lassiter.

"Laura? I tried you earlier, dear, and got that dratted recorder."

"I just got in, Mrs. Epperman."

"I left a message. Don't you ever check your messages?"

"I hadn't had time yet."

"Not very businesslike, child."

"Sorry. Was there something—?"

"Yes. I had a long and very unpleasant talk earlier with Mr. Aikman."

"Oh?" This was not going to be fun.

"Your actions in snooping into his background were unforgivable, Laura. He wants you to be dismissed. He even spoke of a possible lawsuit, and it was all I could do to calm him down."

"Mrs. Epperman, listen—"

"No, you listen to me, you awful girl. I've tried my very best to go along with some of your peculiarities—those silly gabfests you have with the residents, the way you get so involved in their personal lives, how you let your important administrative duties slide in order to scurry around like a bleeding-heart do-gooder, patching up quarrels, listening to their complaints, et cetera. But this is the last straw. I'm giving you a final warning. If I hear about you meddling into things that are none of your business again, I'm going to have to let you go. That isn't a threat. You understand?"

Laura felt like throwing in the towel. She was so sick of this stuff. But she needed the job, desperately. And no other position would give her the practicum experience of the sessions at Timberdale. "Mrs. Epperman, if you would just talk to Deputy Lassiter about Mr. Aikman, you—"

"No! No! Haven't you heard a word I just said? We should thank our lucky stars for Mr. Aikman! It's been quiet ever since he came onboard. Now tomorrow I want you to apologize to him and promise nothing like that will ever happen again. Is that clear?"

The telephone beeped, an incoming call. Laura gave up. "Yes, Mrs. Epperman."

"You promise?"

"Yes, Mrs. Epperman."

"Good night, Laura. Have a nice evening, dear." Click!

Laura pushed the flash button. "Hello?"

Lassiter's dear, familiar voice. "Laura?"

She felt tears stinging her eyes. "Hi."

"Is something wrong?"

"No. I'm fine." She sniffed.

"I'm out at Timberdale. I'm going to spend a little time snooping around, I think, before I have to go back downtown in an hour or two. I thought you would like to know your custodians are patrolling the halls like Captain Midnight."

It made her laugh. "Good."

"Talk to you later?"

"Great."

The soup was boiling on the stove. She hurried to serve it. On the counter, the Jack Higgins novel waited for her. If she intended to get it all skimmed tonight, it meant the worst all-nighter since spring finals.

IN AN UNOCCUPIED second-floor apartment at Timberdale, Maude Thuringer crouched in the dark by the back window, looking intently out onto the rear parking and service area, and the thicket beyond the fence. Her knees hurt. She had a headache. Despite all her enthusiastic planning, she almost doubted herself.

Behind her, August Whitnaur groaned slightly as he readjusted his position on the floor against the far wall. "I don't like this," he said in a hoarse, muted voice.

"I know you don't, Gus," Maude whispered patiently. "You've made that clear already."

"We shouldn't be in here. What if Still Bill or somebody comes by and catches us?"

"Hush up, hush up. Why should Still Bill or anyone else come poking around in here? The apartment is empty. Nobody is supposed to be here."

"Right! Exactly! Including us!"

"They shouldn't leave the sub-master key on the counter if they don't want somebody to use it. Besides, as long as we keep quiet in here, nobody is ever going to suspect anything." Maude reached for the binoculars on the rug beside her and carefully focused them through the windowpane onto the black void that marked the thicket below.

"I thought we were going to trap the perpetrator," Whitnaur whined, "not sit up here and suffocate in a stuffy empty apartment all night."

"I told you," Maude said, getting short on patience. "If we can spot something first, it will make it a lot easier to get out there and catch him. Especially with Still Bill's border patrol roaming around the halls all night. We'll just watch another hour or two—say until two o'clock— and then if we haven't spotted anything we'll activate the original plan."

Whitnaur groaned. "Sneak out and walk right down there."

"Yes."

"Hope somehow the attacker will be down there and we'll just trap him."

"Sure."

"It's stupid. I don't know how I ever let you talk me into this."

"Why is it stupid?" Maude raked the blackness with the glasses.

"Whoever the murderer is, he isn't going to just walk

right out and show himself because we walk down the path.''

Maude thought she caught a flicker of something—the briefest blip of red—on the edge of the binocular field. She jerked the glasses slightly to the left and saw nothing, but stared hard. "If it's such a stupid plan, Gus, why are you so darned scared?"

"Scared? I'm not scared."

"Good. You've got your gun, haven't you? So there's no reason to be scared."

"I've got the gun," Whitnaur groaned, "but it hasn't been fired in forty years. The ammo is that old, too."

"Don't worry, Gus. Guns and ammo last forever. They're still blowing up stuff over in France that came down during World War One."

Whitnaur said nothing to that. In the field of the binoculars, there was nothing but darkness. Maude felt a stab of disappointment. She had had some hope for a minute, there. But she consoled herself. Hercule Poirot had never had it easy either. Perry Mason always had to get to the courtroom before he cracked the case.

Out in the back lot there was sudden furtive movement. Maude dropped the glasses and looked down with the naked eye. It was dim but not impossible with the back security light on. She made out a uniform—a funny hat and then the gray of the jacket.

Aaron Lassiter walked across the pavement, coming from the direction of the back gate and toward the back security door almost directly below the window. He vanished from view, straight down, and in a moment Maude made out the faint sound of the back door being closed.

Very interesting. Had Lassiter been the source of the red light she had seen, maybe, a few minutes earlier? But by the timing of his appearance in the lot, he would have been far closer to the gate than the spot where she had seen the light, perhaps. What was he doing out here at this hour? Was she wasting her time? Would it work if and when she activated plan A? This was great. She was excited. Even if it didn't work, it would be neat.

THE SMALL CLOCK in the kitchen of Laura's apartment made a clicking noise, and she looked up to see it was 2:00 a.m. She was almost through her speed-read of the Jack Higgins book, and felt thankful he was such a good writer. The suspense made the fast read almost enjoyable, even though she kept getting frustrated because she couldn't see a thing that Maude Thuringer might have meant when she spoke of pulling a Vaughn.

Simon Vaughn was the hero, more or less, of the story. The plot involved digging a tunnel under the Iron Curtain to get a priest and some other people out of the East. But good God, even Maude could not be thinking about trying to build a tunnel. There had to be something else here. Maybe in the last fifty or sixty pages she would find it.

Rubbing her aching eyes, she turned back to the pages in front of her.

AARON LASSITER climbed into his cruiser, started it, and drove away from Timberdale. He poked the button on his Ironman watch and the face lit up: 2:22. He hadn't found a thing.

He drove slowly by the JiffyGrub. Except for the man inside at the counter—the replacement for the jailed Henry Spurington—it looked deserted. Stand around all night, Lassiter thought, waiting for the next armed robbery. What a job.

At the next road crossing he turned around and started back, headlights flicking briefly over the ghostly yellow outlines of the earthmoving equipment parked out in the brush. A minute later he caught a glimpse of Aikman's pickup parked well off the road on the thicket side. No sign of Aikman.

Lassiter had seldom been so thoroughly baffled and disgusted. He was supposed to be off duty long before this. Worry about this situation out here, and the danger it implied for Laura, was driving him nuts. He wasn't even sleeping right, and sleeping had always been one of the things he did best.

He decided to drive back into Norman. The Kettle restaurant on West Lindsay Street stayed open all night. He needed coffee.

LAURA CLOSED the book. The kitchen clock showed a minute or two past 3:00 a.m. She felt extremely tired and puzzled.

There was no question it was a thrilling novel. It seemed funny now to read a story based on the Iron Curtain. But once you accepted the time frame, it was still a nice read, gripping. She liked the character of the priest best of all. There were some really nice touches about that priest. Simon Vaughn had given her chills, a little. He was a classic cold war spy character, she thought, really not a nice person at all.

And yet Maude had said she intended to pull a Vaughn. Do something like Simon Vaughn would do, or did do, in this novel. One thing Vaughn had done was wreak a great deal of havoc and help build an escape tunnel and kill some people. Laura couldn't figure that even Maude could interpret some of her own actions as similar to any of those things.

What else had Vaughn done?

Laura rose and went to the kitchen, where she put a cup of water into the microwave to make tea. She reached into the cupboard and got out the Lipton's, debated sweetener or sugar, and got down the sugar bowl. She was starting to feel a bit dumb and sorry for herself.

Maude's remark, after all, might have been one of those random Maude Thuringer generalizations that meant darned little at all. Maybe she had simply meant she intended to be tough and mean and succeed. That was a discouraging idea.

Laura reviewed the plot again in her mind. The priest needed help getting out. They dug the tunnel under the fence and had to go under a churchyard, where they dug under old graves, and one of them collapsed into the tunnel, then Vaughn got them out okay.

The microwave dinged. She removed the cup of water and dunked her tea bag into it. Then, because the woman he loved was still back on the other side of the wall, after he was out and completely safe, the darned dumb, heroic fool had turned around and gone back to the other side, walking into certain danger. His adversary had known he would be back.

Wait a minute. Laura's teaspoon clattered on the sink-board.

Vaughn *had gone back*, putting his life on the line.

Oh, no, Laura thought. This was too farfetched even for Maude Thuringer.

But Maude had been down in the thicket on several occasions.

What if, by saying she would pull a Vaughn, she had meant she would *go back down there* in order to smoke out the attacker?

Was even Maude that reckless?

Laura knew the answer the moment the question formed itself in her mind. It never occurred to Maude that a dangerous situation might be dangerous to her personally. Sure, characters sometimes died in the mystery novels and thrillers she thrived on, but one could always go back and read the story from the front again, and everybody was back alive again. Death was abstract in the mysteries. No matter how harrowing the story, it had never shed any of Maude's own blood. That was the beauty of reading a story; you could vicariously experience mayhem and yet never really be touched.

Was it possible that Maude might plan some really crazy gambit like going back down into the woods, thinking she would catch the killer, without ever fully realizing that this was real life, and she might end up dead?

Sure, it was possible.

There was a way to find out.

The Timberdale residents' telephone directory was in the kitchen drawer under the telephone. Maude's number was on it. Laura dialed the number. It rang four times and then a hollow-sounding recording came on: ''Hi, this is Maude. Leave a message after the beep.''

Beep.

Hurrying now, Laura dialed again the main number for Timberdale. She got a busy signal.

She slammed the telephone on the hook. Damn Stacy, talking to her boyfriend half the night on the only line they left activated in the wee hours. Now what?

It was possible she was jumping to an outrageous conclusion. But the telephone and answering machine in Maude's room were on the table right beside her bed, and Maude was a light sleeper. She wasn't in there. She was *out* someplace.

Pulling a Vaughn.

Aaron Lassiter's answering machine was on, too. She left a message and dialed the courthouse dispatcher's number. Georgie, the night deputy on duty, said Lassiter was off. Would she try him on the radio anyway? Sure, hang on. No response. Dammit.

''What?'' Trissie groaned as Laura awakened her.

''Honey, I've got to go out to Timberdale for a minute. I've called Barb and she's coming right over to stay with you until I get back. I just wanted you to know everything is all right.''

"Oomph." Trissie rolled over and went back to sleep.

The doorchimes sounded, a very sleepy baby-sitter arriving from across the courtyard.

Laura rushed.

TWENTY-THREE

HE WAS OUT there.

Maude knew it. Three times in the past hour she had definitely seen a wink of red down in the woods below the retirement center. It was time to do something about it.

Behind her, August Whitnaur snored softly. Sitting against the bare wall, he looked crumpled and helpless in the dark, his chin deep down on his chest. Maude almost hated to wake him.

"Gus! Gus! Wake up!"

He started violently. "Wha—?"

"It's time to move, Gus. Get yourself together."

She expected protests and complaints, but Whitnaur immediately shook himself and climbed unsteadily to his feet. She felt a flush of admiration and something like jealousy. Her plan of action sounded a little screwy even to her, and the good Lord only knew how screwy it must sound to him. But he wasn't griping a bit. He must have loved poor old Violet very, very much to be willing to undertake an operation like this one. Maude wished somebody could love her like that.

Well, no time for that kind of thinking now. She slung her binocular strap around her neck and slipped across the room to the door. Being infinitely cautious, she turned the knob and peeked out through the narrowest crack. The hall stood empty, dim and empty.

She pressed the door closed again, but did not allow the lock to catch. She turned to Whitnaur, who had edged closer with anxiety.

"Gus, we'll wait until Still Bill or one of his guys goes

past the next time. As soon as he's out of sight, we make our move. Understand?''

Whitnaur licked his lips and nodded mutely.

They waited.

About five minutes later, a slight sound beyond the door alerted them. Maude opened the door even more narrowly than she had earlier. Through the pencil-thin opening she saw Still Bill Mills himself move into view. Wearing his usual overalls and work boots, Still Bill looked sleepy in the extreme. He moved along slowly, zombielike, scarcely seeing. Maude pressed the door the last eighth of an inch closed as he got close. Her ear pressed against the paneling, she heard him shuffle on by. Then the soft click of the stair door only a few feet farther on told her he was gone.

She opened the door and risked sticking her head out. No one in view. She turned back to Whitnaur. "Okay, Gus. This is it.''

Her heart pounded along at about 140 as she led the way out of the safe confines of the empty apartment and into what felt like the spotlight brilliance in the hall. Still Bill Mills had gone down to her left, using the regular carpeted staircase. She turned right, hurrying along toward the red EXIT sign halfway down. Whitnaur lurched along behind her, relying heavily on his cane. His face betrayed his discomfort. She could sympathize. Her knees hurt, a lot.

Reaching the fire escape door, she swung it open and entered a barren paint-and-tile staircase. Hanging on to the metal railing, she started down. Whitnaur stayed close. Their feet seemed to make an ungodly racket despite every effort to move silently. But there was no yell of alarm anywhere as they reached the first floor.

She opened the door into the back hallway near the kitchen. The hall stood empty. Motioning to her partner, she hurried out, across the hall, down the side corridor, and to the back door.

Nobody challenged. She almost wished they had.

Well, no help for it now. They had come this far and her pride wouldn't let them turn back this far into the game. She grasped the big metal doorknob and looked back at Whitnaur, gray-faced behind her. "Ready?" He nodded.

Her hand was so sweaty it slipped on the metal knob. She had to stop and wipe her hand on her sleeve before she could get the thing to turn. Then it turned easily, however, and the door swung outward into the night.

The humid warmth of the air at this hour surprised her. The sky overhead appeared almost completely clear, only a touch of high haze, and starlight made the back paved area seem as bright as day. She couldn't see a soul around. She stepped outside onto the small concrete back porch and went down the three steps to the pavement. Whitnaur stayed right with her.

Nobody around, still, and no excuse to do anything but keep moving. Maude hurried out onto the asphalt and half-ran across toward the deeper shadow of the back fence and gate area. Whitnaur fell a bit behind her but caught up, breathing bubbly hard, as she caught her own breath in the shadows.

The gate lock stood open, the gate ajar. She wondered where Aikman was. She wondered if they might run into him. Maybe, she thought, he had had the same idea she did: Stay in the woods until the killer showed that red light again, then home in on him.

Or maybe Aikman was beyond planning. For all she knew, he might be lying dead down here someplace. Now *there* was a comforting prospect.

Whitnaur bumped into her from behind. "What's wrong? What's wrong? Why are we just standing here?"

"Take it easy," Maude whispered. "Have that gun

ready.'' She pushed the gate open and took the first step
down the path. Maybe none of this had been such a good
idea after all, she thought. Chills ran up and down her
back.

AARON LASSITER LEFT the Kettle at about three-fifteen.
Even Lindsay Street lay deserted at this hour. The early
breakfast felt like lead in his gut, and sleep seemed no
closer than it had before.

Getting into his car, he hit the ignition and stayed
parked a moment while he called the dispatcher. "This
is Unit Three off duty. I've been out of contact for a
while, just wanted to let you know I'll be home shortly
in case anything develops I ought to know about."

The dispatcher's female voice came back: "Three, you
had a call from Mrs. Michaels at 03:11."

What the hell? "Did she leave a message?"

"Negative."

"Ten-four. Three out."

He turned the engine back off and returned to the restaurant. There was a pay telephone on the wall inside the
entryway. He plugged in his quarter and punched the
number.

"Hello?" a sleepy, unfamiliar girl's voice answered.

"Laura?" He knew it wasn't, but worry made him
think at less than 100 percent efficiency.

"This is Barb. I'm the sitter. Who is this?"

"Barb? Hi. This is Aaron Lassiter. Can I speak with
Laura, please?"

"Gee, Deputy Lassiter. She isn't here. That's why I'm
sitting."

"Where is she?"

"She went to Timberdale. I don't know why—"

Barb might have said more, but Lassiter had already
hung up. He didn't know what was going on, but he
didn't like it. He sprinted for his car.

LAURA JUMPED OUT of her Toyota under Timberdale's front canopy and hurried for the door, fumbling in her purse for her master key as she ran. Her billfold and reading glasses and two lipsticks spilled out on the pavement and she had to stop and gather them up, murmuring to herself with worry and frustration. But she had the keys in hand now and got the front doors unlocked quickly.

Even though she had used a key, the alarm system was set so that an alarm light began blinking on the console in front of Stacy Miller at the reception desk. Laura was pleased to see Stacy notice it at once and jump up, startled and alert, to peer her way. Laura rushed over. Stacy turned off the alarm.

"Gosh, Mrs. Michaels, I—"

"I tried to call you, Stacy, but you were on the damned line as usual. Where's Still Bill? Have you seen Maude Thuringer?"

Stacy's eyes went large with alarm. "Bill's on Two right now. I saw him go along the atrium balcony just a minute ago. But I haven't seen Maude."

Laura pointed at the telephone, just out of her reach on the far side of the counter. "Call her room."

"Now? Jimminy—"

"Two-eight-six. Call, Stacy. Now."

Stacy plucked up the phone and punched in the numbers. She listened. "It's busy."

"Busy? Damn." She thought a second. "Go find Still Bill. Have him meet me at her room right away."

Without waiting for a reply, she turned and fled across the vast silence of the atrium to the stairs. Waiting for a Timberdale elevator was like watching the sap rise, and she didn't have time for it.

On the second floor she exited the staircase corridor and looked right and left, hoping to spot Still Bill Mills or one of his aides. The hallways stood dim and vacant in both directions. She ran down the hall to the north, heading for Maude's room.

The door stood closed, everything normal. She tried the doorknob and it didn't budge. She pushed repeatedly on the doorbell button and heard the chimes inside. She waited. No one came.

It was just like Maude to "pull a Vaughn," she thought. Just as Simon Vaughn had walked back into danger in order to achieve his goal, Maude would walk back into the woods at the most dangerous hour, hoping to lure the killer and somehow identify him without getting herself killed in the process. Maude would never think about losing her own life. She would see only the great victory after she "cracked the case."

If she got Maude out of this one alive, Laura thought, she was going to get her some kind of a damned psychiatric evaluation, or at least a personality profile test.

Thinking about the future didn't help right now, however. She pushed the doorbell again, and again nothing happened. Disgusted and scared, she fitted her master key into the stout lock and turned it. The bolt clattered loudly, shooting back open.

She entered Maude's apartment. "Maude?"

No answer.

An old-fashioned brass floor lamp glowed in the living room—overstuffed furniture, Oriental throw rugs on top of the Timberdale carpet, books all over the coffee table, the wreckage of a pizza. Laura hurried first into the bedroom, flicking on the lights. The bed had not been slept in. Why had the phone been busy? Returning to the living room, she saw it on the end table. The receiver had been left off the instrument, making it impossible to call in.

A futile glance into the kitchen and even the bathroom revealed no trace of Maude, of course. Laura already knew, with a mounting sense of horror, where Maude was going to be found. She turned toward the apartment door and took a step and collided with Still Bill Mills, breathless and worried, rushing in from the hall.

"Stacy said you wanted to see me," he panted.

"Bill, Maude isn't in her room. Have you seen her?"

His good eye rolled. "Land, no. I've been by here ten times, her door was always secure, looked like. How did she get out without one of us seeing her?" He shook his head. "It's a conflagration."

"Bill, go get your other guys. Quick. Meet me at the back door behind the kitchen just as fast as all of you can get there."

"Well, I've only got Harvey. Jack got to feeling poorly. Diarrhea. I had to send him home before he instigated a cervical aneurysm, practically."

"Get Harvey, then. But hurry!"

Still Bill lumbered out of the apartment and down the hall, heading for the elevator lobby. Laura took to the stairs again, rushing down them two at a time. On the main floor she took time to hurry back to the desk, where Stacy Miller stood worried and helpless.

"Stacy, get the front doors locked again, if you haven't. Stay off the phone. We may need to use it fast. If by any miracle you do see Maude wandering around, put her in her apartment and come back out and give us a holler from the gate, okay?"

Stacy shivered. "Out back? You're going out back?"

"I'm afraid so."

"Why?"

"I think that's where Maude went."

By the time she reached the back hallway behind the kitchen, Still Bill and his hulking Harvey had arrived. Still Bill had a big flashlight in hand, and sleepy-eyed Harvey at least looked reassuringly bulky.

"I think Maude went out there," Laura told them. "We're going to go look for her."

"She shoulda never gone out there," Still Bill groaned. "That woman is peripatetic!"

Laura shoved hard on the horizontal metal bar inside the security door, unlocking the door and shoving it open in one motion. Warm, humid night air gushed in. She led the way out, onto the tiny concrete porch, down the steps to the pavement. In the dim gray illumination of the security lights, the area lay vacant and silent.

She started across the pavement toward the back gate, Still Bill and Harvey close behind her. About the time she had crossed half the space, figures appeared out of the dark on the other side of the gate, coming into the feeble light. Laura stopped and stared, totally shocked and relieved and puzzled at the same time.

The first one through the gate, August Whitnaur, limped badly on his cane. He was shaking terribly and had dirt and grass all over his old-fashioned suit pants and shirt. Right behind him, Maude Thuringer darted through, hair standing on end, her face twisted by fear.

Close behind the two of them came a lean, darkly dressed figure—James Aikman. His face, twisted in anger, seemed to glow in the dimness. He had a very large pistol in his hand, trained directly on Maude's back.

AARON LASSITER locked up all four wheels of his cruiser, loudly skidding to a halt under the front canopy behind Laura's little sedan. Piling out, he ran for the front doors, unsnapping the leather flap of his holster and pulling out his revolver as he ran.

The front doors were locked. He rattled them violently, making a huge noise, and then started hammering on the frame, making even more of a racket.

Across the atrium somewhere, visible through the scrolled glass, he saw Stacy rushing in his direction. She hurried nervously into the foyer and fumbled with the security lock for an instant and then opened the door for him. "It's a good thing you're here. We've—"

"Where is she?" Lassiter rasped.

"In her office. She's—"

He ignored whatever else she was trying to tell him. Running across the atrium, he ducked under the end of the reception desk and plunged into the corridor that led to Laura's office. The hall light wasn't on, but her office light was, spilling out into the dark. He reached the door and looked in.

Laura stood behind her desk. Still Bill Mills and one of his slobby helpers stood against the right-hand wall. Maude Thuringer and an old gent Lassiter didn't recognize stared at him with vacant, shell-shocked eyes from where they stood in front of Laura's desk. The old man had dirt and grass all over him. To Lassiter's left, just inside the door, James Aikman stood with his hands on his hips, the butt of his Glock semiautomatic sticking out of his open holster. Everybody looked like hell, and Aikman had the pallor of a dead man, his eyes like black holes.

"What's going on?" Lassiter demanded. His gaze went back to Laura. "Are you all right?" Intense relief went through him like hot fluid.

"I'm fine," Laura said hoarsely. She looked like she had been scared half to death, and her voice trembled. "We've had some excitement."

Lassiter glanced at Aikman. The security man licked paper-thin lips and inclined his head toward Maude and her partner. "These two violated the security orders. I found them out back in the woods, apprehended them, brought them back here for disposition."

"He practically killed us!" Maude Thuringer cried. "Look at poor Gus, here! This man knocked him down and *kicked* him."

"Didn't know what we had at that point," Aikman clipped. "Can't take chances."

Lassiter focused on Maude. "What the hell were you doing out back at this hour?"

"Looking for the criminal," she chirped defensively. "What else do you think anyone in their right mind would be doing?"

"Stupid," Aikman said, his lip curling. "If it hadn't been for me, you could have both been killed out there."

Lassiter studied him. "Did you see anything else suspicious tonight?"

"Nothing. Just these two old fools."

"If you didn't see anything else," Maude told him angrily, "you must have been asleep at the switch. I saw that red light of Violet's two or three times."

Aikman studied her with an expression of sheer loathing. "You're senile," he told her. "You imagined it."

The filthy, shaky Whitnaur braced himself up. "Now see here. You can't talk to a lady like that."

"Shut up, old man," Aikman said with quiet venom. "You've caused enough shit for one night."

"Okay, okay," Lassiter said, stepping in quickly. He turned back to Maude. "Are you hurt?"

"Me? No."

"Then isn't it about time you went to your apartment? And stayed the hell in there?"

Maude crouched like she expected to duck a bullet. "You're not going to bust us?"

"Maude, I'll tell you the truth. If I could think of some charge, I might. I really might."

She pointed at Aikman. "How about him? Assault. Attempted murder, I'd call it."

"You old—" Aikman began.

"Just go to your apartment, Maude," Lassiter cut in. He glared at the old man. "And you, too, sir. Unless you require medical attention."

"I believe I am all in one piece, sir," Whitnaur said with grave dignity. "I require no ministration."

Lassiter glanced at Laura. "All right?"

She hugged herself. "Fine."

Lassiter jerked his thumb over his shoulder. "Out."

Maude scurried past him and out of the office. The old man limped after her, wobbly on his cane.

"Okay, Bill," Laura said after a moment's silence. "You and Harvey can get back to your patrolling."

Still Bill Mills and his helper silently left the room.

"Goddamned old fools," Aikman said softly. "They could have gotten themselves killed out there."

"Did you have to rough him up like that?" Laura watched Aikman with eyes made bright with anger. "Was it really too dark to see it was just a couple of old people shuffling along the path?"

Aikman looked at her with sheer hate. "My job is security. Keep people off the path, out of those woods. It isn't coddling their ass. They're lucky I didn't shoot first and ask questions afterward."

"You must have been pretty edgy," Lassiter observed, testing.

"Wouldn't you be?" Aikman shot back. "Out there in the dark where two people have been murdered?"

"What do you intend to do now?"

"Get back on duty."

"Back there?"

"Of course, back there. Where else?"

"Nothing else unusual? No red lights, anything like that?"

"The fucking old woman is hallucinating."

"Okay," Lassiter said, breathing deeper. He looked at Laura. "I don't think there's anything else to be done right now."

Aikman somberly considered both of them, then turned and left the office without a word.

"Jesus," Lassiter said. "What a character."

"He didn't have to beat Mr. Whitnaur up," Laura said, hugging herself again.

"He had to apprehend them, Laura. Just like he said. How was he to be sure it was a couple of your old kooks?"

"Old kooks?" Her eyes flared. "My old kooks? Is that what they are now? *My* old kooks? Are you on his side now?"

"No, goddammit. I'm saying he was justified. I don't have to like it to say he was justified. They shouldn't have been out there."

Her eyes went bright with moisture. "I was so scared—"

"Hey, I know you were." He went to her and took her in his arms.

"Now what do we do?" she sniffled. "The guy you've got in jail isn't admitting anything, and Aikman is doing his job, and nobody else is showing up as a suspect, and Ken Keen is still in that coma. Are we just going to have to sit around forever until somebody else gets hurt?"

Lassiter held her closer. He didn't say anything. He had seldom felt so helpless. He didn't see much hope for anything.

TWENTY-FOUR

THE DISTANT ROAR of earthmoving machinery came heavily through the trees, like the rumble of a beginning earthquake, when Laura drove back into the Timberdale parking lot at nine-thirty the next morning. She had been home long enough to shower, change, apply makeup, and get Trissie off to school. She ached all over.

"Laura!" Mrs. Epperman pounced on her before she was halfway to the desk. Hurrying across the atrium from the building postal center on the far side, Timberdale's manager looked especially formidable in a new red dress that matched the plastic frames of a new pair of reading glasses. "I want to hear details of last night's escapade, dear. Come into my office at once."

She seemed to be in an extraordinary good mood, especially considering that she obviously had read the brief report Laura had left for her on the desk. When Laura went into the office she was even humming something that might have been the Georgia Tech fight song.

"I read your note, Laura, and I must say I believe you did a fine job of helping to avert another catastrophe around here. Of course it was really Mr. Aikman who did everything, but you couldn't know the situation was already well in hand. I spoke to Still Bill before he toddled off home for a few hours' sleep, and he confirmed my impression that you were Johnny-on-the-spot. Bully for you. I'm proud of you. This gives me hope you're finally really getting up to speed around here. Now tell me, how do you propose to deal with Maude and Gus's nonsense in your little talk group today?"

It was nice to hear praise for a change, but the question

at the end took the bloom off things. "Ordinarily we wouldn't meet today," Laura pointed out. "And when we do meet—"

"Oh, I think you must meet today, child. Rumors are rampant about last night. I believe Still Bill's helper talked to several residents and staff members early this morning, and they are all gaga about it. You need to downplay the danger of last night's little episode and emphasize the additional danger that will now be faced by anyone who tries to take the back path to the JiffyGrub."

"Additional danger?" Laura echoed.

"Yes. Surely you heard the noise when you came in. They're starting to clear brush and move dirt back there. Of course they're starting at the far-east end, but they'll be up this way in no time. Once they get a little farther up this way, it will be impossible for anyone to walk out there; it will be full of Caterpillars and brush hogs, and all kinds of big, dangerous diggers. Won't that be nice? But in the meantime, if you can just emphasize to the old darlings that construction is already under way, then Mr. Aikman might not have to prevent any other midnight madness around the grounds."

"I'll stress staying away," Laura replied. Then she couldn't resist adding, "After all, they might not get run over by a bulldozer, but they might run into Mr. Aikman, and that could be more dangerous if he's feeling like beating someone up."

Mrs. Epperman glared at her the way the Babe had once glared at opposing pitchers or bartenders who tried to tell him he had had enough. "That will be sufficient criticism of Mr. Aikman, Laura. I had the unhappy task this morning of meeting with him about all this, and telling him that now, with the construction project getting in high gear, we probably won't need him for more than another week or two. The poor man seemed quite sad about leaving us.''

"He knocked old Mr. Whitnaur down and kicked him," Laura pointed out.

Mrs. Epperman seemed not to hear, a trick she often used when she didn't want to hear something. She was quite good at it. "Won't it be grand when that nursing home is finished and into operation, dear? We'll have the retirement center here, and when they get too old or feeble to stay with us, they can just move next door and not even leave the corporation. I think it will help our sign-up rate, don't you?''

"I guess I hadn't thought about it, Mrs. Epperman."

"With any luck, we'll have a few residents sick enough to transfer right over as part of their grand opening. Wouldn't that be fun!"

"I THOUGHT," Laura told the Breakfast Club when their special meeting began at ten-thirty, "we might just get together a few minutes to talk about last night.''

All the regulars were in attendance, including Maude Thuringer. She looked crestfallen and worn out, but piped right up when Laura glanced at her. "I don't think anybody has anything to be ashamed of.''

"I'm sure you're right," Laura told her. She addressed the group. "Maude was outside last night and Mr. Aikman, our security guard, found her there. He brought her back inside, which is his job. I don't think there's really a lot more to it than that.''

Stoney Castle stirred. "I heard he beat the dickens out of Gus Whitnaur.''

"Gus fell down," Laura lied quickly.

"Yeah," Maude chimed in. "He fell down."

Col. Roger Rodgers cleared his throat. "Not much chance of that happening again. Heavy equipment on the prowl. Ground being cleared for the nursing home down there. Big expansion for this outfit. Walk down there now and you get taken out by a twenty-ton earthmover.''

"I think you're right about that, Colonel." Laura scanned faces. "Nobody will try walking down that way again, right? That heavy equipment is going to be all over the place, and there might be ditches to fall into."

"The roar of those engines is exhilarating," Davilla Rose said. "I have been inspired to write a poem about it."

Ellen Smith jangled her jewelry. "This is the kind of change that results in a burst of creative energy on everyone's part. I plan to set up my easel on the third-floor balcony. I'll be able to see everything. I've never done a landscape scene with earthmoving equipment in it. It will be exciting."

"Would you like to hear my poem about it?" Davilla asked.

"No," two or three voices chorused instantly.

Davilla looked hurt. "I'll never understand why there is such hostility to the arts in this institution."

"Madam," the colonel rapped, "no one is hostile to the arts. We are hostile to your poetry."

"Well! I never!"

"Precisely, madam."

Laura said, "Maybe we can change the subject?"

"Be pretty neat when they get that place built next door," Stoney Castle observed.

"Yes, Stoney, it will."

"Put a person here at Timberdale, then later move them down the road to the nursing home. Then, if the company would just put in a funeral home on the far side of the nursing home, they would have the whole shooting match."

"That's sick," Julius Pfeister said, drawing back offended.

"That's realism, bub."

"But now," Sada Hoff said out of left field, "we'll never know exactly what happened to Violet."

"Or to Dave Bell," Dot Pfeister said sadly.

"If it was one of us who did the deeds, the danger won't be over just because the back path is closed."

"I've thought about that," Mrs. Pfeister replied. "I can't believe it was any of us. But it was probably kids, marauding around. Any time we go out to get in a car after dark, the same thing could happen to us."

"Oh, I really think they were isolated incidents," Laura protested.

"Well, of course you're paid to believe that, Laura. Part of your job is to keep all of us pacified."

"But you don't have to go out to that parking lot after dark," Stoney Castle put in.

Maude said, "They'll still catch the guy, they'll still catch him."

There was a gloomy silence that said nobody shared her confidence. Laura was about to speak when the door into the atrium opened, something that was never done. She looked up.

Kay Svendsen, LPN, peered in. "Laura? Sorry to interrupt." She paused, clearly waiting for Laura to come over to the door.

Laura got up and went over.

"Now what?" Laura whispered, already imagining all sorts of new disasters.

"The hospital just called," Svendsen said. "They'd like you over there. Ken Keen is showing signs of regaining consciousness."

TWENTY-FIVE

BOTH AARON LASSITER and Dr. Fred Which were standing in the hospital hallway outside Ken Keen's room when Laura arrived out of breath.

"Somebody called and said he was regaining consciousness."

"Calm down, calm down," Which urged. "He's showing signs of regaining consciousness. He hasn't done it yet."

"How soon?"

"There's no way to know that. It might be hours or even days yet. Frankly, Laura, calling you at once, when the first stirrings came, was the deputy's idea."

Laura turned to Lassiter. "How come?"

Lassiter's forehead furrowed. "Two or three reasons, I guess. First, you've been coming over here, reading to him. It seems like you have the right to be here. Second, we need all the information we can get out of him as soon as possible. He might trust you more than some of the rest of us."

"I'll do whatever I can. Can I go in and peek at him?"

Which nodded. "Just don't expect too much, Laura. The signs of consciousness have been on the monitor. You'll probably see him as the same."

Laura turned and went into the room. The overhead lights blazed, and a nurse was in the process of attaching a new IV bottle of glucose solution. Keen lay just as deathly still as he had on Laura's earlier visits. Despite having been warned, she felt sharp disappointment.

The nurse smiled at her. "He's not exactly up and dancing yet."

"All his vital signs are good—everything like that?"

"He's an amazing guy. He's healing like a twenty-year-old. He had signs of a serious infection somewhere, but the doctors finally tracked that down. He had an impacted wisdom tooth that was really badly infected. We had a dental surgeon in this morning, got it out of there." The nurse made a little face. "He must have been grumpy as the dickens for days before his fall. The surgeon said it must have been hurting like everything for quite a long time. But I guess if you've got to have an impacted wisdom tooth removed, maybe the only decent time to do it is when you're in a coma."

"I would just as soon not have it done at all," Laura said.

"Hey, me too. Excuse me." The nurse bustled out.

Laura leaned closer to Keen, examining his face carefully. The swelling of his jaw on the left side was quite noticeable. She wondered if it might have been visible before she had looked for it.

Some people at Timberdale, like Sada Hoff, had wanted to make him a suspect in the attacks, she remembered, because he had been short-tempered and hateful to them, not at all like his usual self. Now there was a reason for that. This tooth must have been driving him batty.

He continued to lie perfectly still, a wax figure.

"Ken?" Laura said softly. "Ken? Want to wake up?"

He did not respond.

Out in the hall, Lassiter paced and frowned. "I've got to get back on duty. Are you going to stay here, Laura, or go back to work?"

She checked her watch. "I think at this hour I'll just stay put. By the time I got back to Timberdale it would be almost too late to accomplish much, and then I'd have to come right back to read to him later...if he hasn't woken up by then."

Lassiter looked at Which. "Are you staying, too?"

"Wish I could, Salt, but I've got patients waiting."

Lassiter turned back to Laura. "I'll leave word at the nurses' station to holler for me the minute he wakes up, if he does. Okay?"

"Okay." She went on tiptoe to kiss him.

"And you don't stay too late if he stays unconscious, right?"

"Okay," she repeated, and pecked his chin again.

"And—"

"Hey, go already." She grinned at him. "You act like you don't want to go back to the courthouse, and you must have a bunch to do."

DRIVING THE SHORT distance from the hospital to downtown, Lassiter reflected that Laura didn't know the half of it. He had one more chance at Henry Spurington. Then the DA was going to file the charges that could be justified and make Spurington bondable. One of his pals had already been in twice, along with a bondsman, to get him out.

Lassiter did not think he had a chance with Spurington now. Maybe at first, when the shock of the raid and arrest was still fresh, but they had nothing to link him to the attacks across the road from the JiffyGrub, and Spurington knew it. He had laughed at Lassiter earlier today. He was ready to cop a plea on the marijuana charge, and the sheriff thought the DA would drop any possible burglary charges in exchange. Spurington would get one to three, or maybe—if the judge felt cranky—five to seven after a former conviction. Spurington would breeze through it, proving the criminal's adage "If you can't do the time, don't do the crime," and with Oklahoma's prison population density problem he would be back on the streets in less than a year anyway.

No wonder he wouldn't cooperate with Lassiter.

For which Lassiter could be irritated and discouraged, but hardly heartbroken. Spurington had been a long shot, a product more of hope than evidence, from the beginning.

But hell, what did his release leave them?

Come on, old man, he thought, visualizing Ken Keen in the hospital bed. *You're all we've got now.*

LEFT ALONE AT the hospital, Laura went to the cafeteria and had a ham sandwich and coffee. Going back to Ken Keen's room in the PCCU, she imagined what it might be like to find him awake, to have him tell everything he knew, and solve this thing once and for all. But it was a hope, not an expectation, and she was not that surprised when she went back into his room to find everything exactly as before.

She sat down and got the copy of *Rebecca* out of her attaché case, opened it at the bookmark, and resumed reading. Keen slept.

After an hour or so she took a break. While she was walking in the hallway and sipping ice water, a doctor came by and went into Keen's room. She followed him back inside.

He was young, with a toothy smile. "Hello! I'm Doctor Abernathy. Are you a relative?"

"As close as one gets, I think," Laura replied.

Abernathy leaned over the bed, raised one of Ken's eyelids, and shone a small flashlight beam into the unmoving eye. Then he did some mysterious feeling around on Ken's throat, his elbows, and his wrists. He raised one corner of the coverlet and probed Ken's ankles. Standing up again, he studied the monitor for a long minute before nodding satisfaction.

Laura was unable to contain her curiosity. "Is he better?"

"No question," Abernathy said.

"When will he regain consciousness?"

He looked surprised at that. "Oh, my. No telling about that, or even if he will."

"But I thought—"

"That he's better? Yes indeed. Every sign indicates better brain function. From every test we have, it looks like he's merely in a deep sleep now. I'm very optimistic. But I'll be honest with you, miss. This could go on for weeks yet...or forever. There's no way I can promise he's going to come out of it."

Laura stared at him in dismay.

He reached over and took one of her hands, clumsy bedside manner. "Please don't look so sad. And don't give up. As I said, every sign looks encouraging. I'm personally optimistic. I expect him to come around within the next forty-eight hours."

"I've been reading to him," Laura confessed.

Abernathy frowned mightily and then nodded. "I've read about cases where that evidently helped. Keep up the good work." He sailed out of the room.

Feeling vaguely patronized, Laura sat down and dug out her book again. She resumed reading.

OUT AT THE construction site across the country road from the JiffyGrub, dirt foreman Jake LaRue throttled back the big Caterpillar and climbed down to speak to the skinny little guy who had been watching him with great patience.

"Howdy," LaRue said. "You want something?"

"I was just wondering how you plan to proceed," the man told him. He had a pale, cold face and the bleakest gray eyes LaRue had ever seen. The man pointed uphill in the direction of the retirement center. "You plan to work right up alongside the road and clear north to south?"

LaRue pointed toward the two big, snorting bulldozers

clearing brush fifty yards up the slope. "They'll clear to the pond. Then they'll swing back to the road. We'll get this much done, including rough smoothing-out. Then we'll take the other half."

The man nodded and watched the distant work with slitted eyes. He seemed as tight as a valve cover.

LaRue couldn't resist probing. "You an owner?"

"No," the man told him. "I work for the retirement center up there. I provide security. I was just wondering when the entire area will be worked over, when you'll get a construction fence in place up at the far end, so I don't have to worry about the old people wandering down here and getting themselves hurt."

"Oh, I get it," LaRue said. "Well, we ought to have scalped all the way to the top by Saturday. Then we'll start the heavy digging. That end is a hell of a lot higher. We got a surveyor coming again Friday, but I can tell right now we'll be digging down at least eighteen inches up there beyond the pond, moving all the dirt down to this end to make a level building site."

"I see," the man said, eyes even more chill as he looked over the site. "You'll be digging up there in a day or two, then."

"We'll be started then, right. At that point we'll put up the plywood fencing and your old folks won't be able to get through no matter how stubborn they are."

"I see," the man repeated. "Well, much obliged."

"Don't mention it, friend." LaRue climbed back up to the cabin of his big machine. The skinny little guy walked away, headed for a pickup parked on the side of the road a half block on West.

Weird guy, LaRue thought. Bad vibes.

He did not analyze it. He pushed the throttle and the big diesel engine roared to life again.

"'I BEGAN TO walk upstairs,'" Laura read. "'My heart was beating in a queer excited way.'"

She had reached the end of the chapter. Her throat felt like emery paper. Closing the book, she placed it carefully in her attaché case.

It was past five. The sunlight beyond the hospital room windows slanted at an angle that turned the redbricks of the near wall a golden brown. She hated to give up, but Ken Keen had not moved a muscle. She was tired and discouraged, and too little sleep last night had left her feeling numb. She had to go back out to Timberdale long enough to make sure Maude and Gus were all right, and Still Bill's evening security patrol was ready to function. Then she could get home and pick up Trissie at a decent hour for a change.

Maybe tomorrow he would wake up, she thought, getting to her feet and turning away from the bed. She picked up her purse, applied lipstick.

The raspy voice startled her: "Hey, baby."

She spun around. Ken Keen stared up at her with beady-bright eyes. "Ken! You're awake."

He looked puzzled. "Have I been asleep?"

"How do you feel?" She looked around for the call button.

"I feel good," Keen told her, licking his lips. "Thirsty. My jaw hurts. I guess I'm gonna have to see a dentist with this damned tooth. Hey, baby, you look really hot. You wanna get in here in this bed with me?"

"You're awake, all right," Laura said. "Ken. Listen. What *happened* to you?"

He blinked. "Did something happen to me?"

"You've had an accident. A bad fall. Do you remember?"

He frowned and his eyes looked far off for a moment, and then his face tightened. "Hey. Last night. I went outside because I seen the red light, just like Violet said."

"You went out and down the path?"

"Yeah. Right. Wow, it was dark and spooky out there."

"Then what happened, Ken?"

"I was walking down the path, going real slow and careful...." He scowled and frowned, remembering. "Saw the red light again. Got in the bushes, wanting to see better. Then, pow! I remember now. Geez, somebody had got around behind me someway. I hear him, and I decide I'm going to get outta there, see, so I get up and haul my fanny back up to the gate and across the back lot and back inside, where I'd left a card stuck in the lock so I could get back in whenever I want."

Keen drew a deep breath and shuddered. "But I hear somebody else on the pavement outside just as I go in, see, so I hotfoot it to the elevator and punch 'three' and ride up, out of breath and kind of shaky. So I get out of the elevator and I start down toward my room, but I hear a movement behind me, and shit, he had come up the stairs faster than that stupid elevator could run, see, and I start to turn. I wish I had never started this by now, believe me, but it's too late, see, and wham! He hits me with something. My bell gets rung, I mean seriously. Then..." Keen's doughboy face tightened, then went slack in confusion. "After that I don't know. Hey, maybe I remember my face hitting the carpet. But that isn't exactly clear."

"Do you remember who hit you?" Laura asked, desperately hoping.

"No, I sure don't, honey."

"You're sure you didn't see him?"

Keen's face screwed up. "Well, I don't know if I seen him or not. All I know is, if I did, I don't remember it."

Laura looked down at him while her hopes collapsed.

He leered and moved over in the bed. "You wanna snuggle?"

"No, Ken, thanks." She found the call button and pushed it.

LAURA HAD BEEN standing in the hall for a long time when Dr. Abernathy came out of Ken Keen's room. Abernathy looked exhilarated. He walked over. "He's doing wonderful."

"He seemed fully alert."

"Yes. No question about it. He seems to have some short-term memory loss, but perhaps he had that earlier?"

Laura smiled. "He did."

"Hum. Alzheimer's, perhaps?"

"Perhaps."

"He seems young for that, but it happens. Any erratic behavior, compulsiveness, other symptoms?"

"Some, but part of his recent grumpiness might have been that bad tooth someone extracted this morning."

"Well." Abernathy patted her arm paternalistically and started to turn away.

"He doesn't remember anything about his accident," Laura said.

The doctor turned back. "Might be another aspect of the short-term memory loss you say he was already experiencing. But temporary amnesia after a severe concussion is hardly unusual. We'll keep a close eye on him for a few days. The memory might come back by the time he can get out of here with those cracked ribs and the sprained back."

Laura studied his expression. "So he might remember...or he might not?"

"Looks like it." Abernathy gave her a blinding smile and hurried away.

She swallowed her disappointment and went back into Ken's room. The lights were all on now and early-evening light stood at the windows. Keen had turned the TV on and was watching *Hard Copy*.

"Hey, sweetie, you're just in time," he said brightly. "This is a nifty report, here."

"Ken, I just wanted to say so long. I'll be back to see you, all right?"

"Sure. I'll be here, heh-heh."

She turned back toward the door.

"Hey, Laura?" he called after her.

She looked back. "Yes?"

He frowned. "What kind of a place is this?"

"You're in Norman Regional Hospital, Ken."

"How come I'm in here?"

"You had a bad fall. Do you remember that?"

"Huh. Skiing, or what?"

"In the atrium."

"Huh." He looked around, puzzled. "This isn't my apartment, is it?"

"No."

"Where was it you said I am?"

THERE WOULD BE no help from Ken Keen, she thought later, driving crisply through the gathering gloom of the country road that led to Timberdale. Now about the most they could hope for was that there wouldn't be any new incidents, that whoever had done these things was gone now, scared away. But of course if it had been a resident or staff member they would *not* have gone away. And there would be a recurrence.

She felt really tired. She had to get a good night's sleep for a change. The upcoming test in policies and procedures at school would be tough. She was far behind in the readings. It felt like everything was closing in on her.

Reaching the side road that led directly through the rolling, blackjack woods to Timberdale, she caught herself going back through the endless cycle of theorizing about why Violet Mayberry and Davidson Bell had died, and what lay behind the attack—if that was what it had been—on Ken Keen. Violet had been the only one who had offered any kind of clue, in those hours before she died, and what she had said might represent the confusion of her injuries. Why would there have been a red light? My God, how did a figure with a Weed Eater make any sense at all? Then those little mounds of fresh dirt and objects like an old car muffler hidden in the ground. Didn't it all have to be the work of some deranged resident suddenly gone over the cliff into senile dementia?

She neared and then reached the Timberdale entrance gate. She turned in, negotiated the long curving driveway, and parked under the front canopy. The front doors were locked in good order and she used her master key.

Inside, a half-dozen residents sat around the atrium, visiting or working jigsaw puzzles. A couple of them waved as she entered. She went directly to the desk.

Stacy Miller said everything was quiet. Still Bill Mills crossed on the second-floor balcony, looked down and saw her, and came down. He had a full crew on security tonight, and James Aikman was on the job outside. They had conferred and Aikman had told him to keep his people inside so that Aikman could be reasonably sure any activity outside might be the mugger, not a friendly security patrol.

"You won't have to handle this much longer, Bill. Surely things will calm down."

Still Bill's good eye looked south. "That'll be good. The photinia out front need a trim, and so do the Chinese holly. And that number-two cooling unit in the kitchen isn't going to last much longer. It could quit or go interruptional anytime."

"I'll talk to Mrs. Epperman about your schedule tomorrow."

"Thankee."

A quick trip to her office showed no new crises. She gathered some paperwork that she might find time for at home. A telephone call told Trissie she was on the way home in another minute. Outside in the atrium again, it was just as before, the same residents, the same deep quiet. There was a kind of wave motion in the average age of Timberdale residents. Laura could remember a year earlier when there had been a number of younger people, in their sixties, as residents. Then there had been someone at the piano in the large activity room almost every evening, and some others singing along, and a bridge game or two, or even poker. Mrs. Epperman's edicts about keeping it down for the sake of the older folks, along with a raise in rents, had run some of those people away. It was not quite as lively or as much fun now.

Some of the younger residents had left Timberdale with some bitterness and anger. It crossed Laura's mind that one of them might be their attacker here. But she dismissed the theory as quickly as it hopped into her mind. Maybe, she thought, it was a measure of her fatigue and depression that such an idea occurred at all.

Sleepy and numb with fatigue, she had another word with Stacy Miller and left the building. In her car, the driveway in the glow of her headlights looked blurry. She yawned, fighting sleep.

This, she decided, would not do. Driving to the entry gates, she turned right, heading down toward the JiffyGrub. A cold Coke would startle her awake a little, the cold and the caffeine both helping.

It was pitch black on the narrow back road past the woods where so much had happened. Up ahead glared the lights of the convenience store. There were two cars parked in front. On the right, in the reflections from all the brilliant lights, the huge yellow earthmovers crouched like prehistoric monsters, waiting to pounce.

On the right, closer to her present position, there was another light that registered for a split second in her peripheral vision. It was not even possible to be absolutely sure she had seen it, but her foot hit the brake instantly, slowing the Toyota to a crawl.

There, in the same place, she glimpsed it again.

A wink of red or pink light, the briefest glimmer.

Tingling all over, she pulled her car off the road onto the shoulder and switched off the headlights and engine. Her heart beat sluggishly in her throat as she waited, staring with painful intensity into the dark woods, hoping to see it again.

TWENTY-SIX

THE RED LIGHT did not blink again. But Laura knew she had seen it.

Well out in the woods, perhaps almost as far downhill as the frog pond. Either being turned on and off very quickly, or moving behind trees that blocked any continuous view.

But she had *seen* it.

Now it had vanished again.

She felt cold sweat on her forehead, and her entire body chilled. She knew she had two choices. One, the sensible one, was that she could start the car, hurry back to Timberdale, and call the sheriff's department. That was the safe, sane, reasonable option. But while she was gone, whatever had caused the red light down there could vanish again.

The second option was to try to see what had caused the light.

No, no, no. That's crazy.

Maybe not. Maybe not. This might be her only chance. Something had to be done. Was she going to let a little fear get in her way?

There was more than fear involved, dear. There was sanity. No one in her right mind would climb out of the car and go down there.

But, she told herself, she had a number of advantages over anyone else who had been involved. First of all, she felt sure she had the element of surprise. Second, she would not be bumbling along the path, practically inviting an attack; she would be creeping along with caution, fully alert. And perhaps most important, she was forty years younger than others who had come down here and gotten attacked; if worse came to worst, she could run for it. Fast.

She stayed right where she was, her seat belt not even loosened. If there were so many fine reasons she could risk poking into the woods, why was she scared half to death?

Her view out through the windshield took in the dark right-hand side of the road and up ahead the unholy white glare of the lights of the JiffyGrub. The same two cars remained in front, both nosed in by shoppers, she guessed, picking up convenience items. The pumps out front stood vacant. A stray beam of light glinted off the panel of the pay telephone in its cubicle on the corner.

The pay telephone.

Laura fumbled in her purse and found some change. Then, digging around under the seat, she came up with the slightly rusty, L-shaped tire tool she had carried there as a last-ditch weapon of self-defense ever since buying the car. The tire tool and fistful of change in her left hand, she removed the ignition keys with her right, clicked her seat belt open, and reached for the door handle.

The dome light threw shocking brightness all over everything as the door cracked. She had forgotten that. She got out fast and closed the door hurriedly but gently to avoid noise. The interior light went out, leaving the Toyota in blackness.

Turning, she looked on all sides for possible trouble. The weeds stood quiet, unmoving, and farther away the first willows looked pale in the starlight. A slight night wind rustled their branches, making a spooky movement.

Gulping in air, she hurried up the right-hand side of the road, staying close to the weedy margin. Nearing the convenience store, she crossed over and walked fast across the concrete ramp to the telephone kiosk. Under all the lights she felt naked, like she was being observed by a million people.

Her hand shook as she punched the coins into the telephone and selected the number.

"Sheriff's department, Hazelton speaking."

"Hello, is Deputy Lassiter on duty right now?"

"No, ma'am. He just went off a few minutes ago."

"Look, could you try to get him on the radio? Is this Max Hazelton? This is Laura Michaels, Aaron's friend. We met recently when we had some trouble at Timberdale, where I work."

"Oh, sure, Mrs. Michaels, I remember you. The frequency is tied up right now, working an accident. I could give him a shout as soon as I can get in."

"Okay, great. Look. Could you give him an urgent message?"

"Sure."

"Okay. Tell him I'm out here at Timberdale, and I see something in the woods. I'm going to try to check it out."

Hazelton sounded dubious and concerned: "We strongly advise against any citizen taking action in a crime-potential situation, Mrs. Michaels. We—"

"I know, I know. But whoever is over there might get away again. Just give him the message, okay?"

"You will really be better advised to remain—"

She didn't have time for this. She hung up.

IN THE BASEMENT communications room of the courthouse, deputy Max Hazelton gave a hand signal to his dispatcher and reached for the microphone. "Unit Four, are you still listening?"

Aaron Lassiter's voice came back quickly. "Ten-four."

"Unit Four, public service this office ASAP, ten-four?"

"Roger."

Hazelton pushed the gray Motorola microphone back across the desk to the regular dispatcher and looked at the telephone. Lassiter was not one to mess around. It would ring within two minutes, he thought.

It started blinking as it rang.

LASSITER SLAMMED the telephone back onto its cradle in the booth and sprinted for his cruiser, parked a few steps away with the lights on and the motor running. Try to check it out? Was that how Hazelton had said Laura phrased it? Damn. Double-damn. This was horrible.

The car door slammed. Still messing with his seat belt, he jerked the shift lever down into drive and floorboarded the accelerator. The big Ford engine howled and the back wheels screamed, burning rubber as the cruiser fishtailed out of the lot and onto the asphalt street.

THE TIRE TOOL clutched in her sweaty hand, Laura walked back up the far side of the road toward her car. Her footsteps on the gravel shoulder sounded to her ears like a passing infantry brigade. She realized all her senses had been heightened by her tension. She tasted pennies; she could see her car up ahead already, although the night was dark; she felt the night wind cool on her sweaty face; every pea-sized piece of gravel underfoot slid and poked at her through the thin soles of her flats; the road beside her, still hot from the day, smelled strongly of tar; crickets yammered all over the woods, and she heard the bass-drum *groink* of a big bullfrog down by the pond.

She couldn't see any more strange lights, or anything else, for that matter, back in the thicket. Maybe she had been mistaken, she tried to tell herself. It didn't work. She kept moving, slightly out of breath from her fear, hurrying along.

She reached her Toyota. It smelled hot, vaguely of oil

and metal. Standing beside it in its scant shadow, she thought about getting back inside and just waiting for Lassiter. But hell, she had no guarantee they would even contact Lassiter right away. Off duty, he was under no obligation to monitor his radio. He might be in his favorite hangout, the Kettle on Lindsay, having a number sixty-six with the eggs over easy, his favorite. He might not come out for an hour if the owner happened to be there and they got to talking sports.

She couldn't wait. Any advantage she might have would be dissipated.

Swallowing hard, she left the comforting closeness of her little car and struggled down into the weeds choking the shallow borrow ditch beside the road. She climbed out on the other side and walked slowly toward the deeper vegetation ahead, the hairs on the back of her neck bristling. The weeds made her legs itch. Some kind of small animal darted away from her in the brush, startling her badly. Heart racing faster, she moved on.

Except for the crickets and daddy bullfrog, her movement through the summer-dried brush was the only source of sound. She cringed at the amount of noise she felt she must be making. It sounded deafening to her. Her eyes stung from the effort of staring ahead into the blackness beyond the willows, trying to see the red light again.

Reaching the willows, she stopped a minute to try to get her breath. The wind moving the limbs made a whispering sound. Many of the willows had dense branches starting all the way down at the ground, so they resembled giant shrubs more than trees. She started working her way through them and found it hard going. *Be careful. Be careful.*

The line of willows was not very wide. On the far side she found a flat area, grass only, perhaps the route of the original dirt road through here. Beyond the narrow grassy band, the weedy vegetation and bigger trees of the real woods began. She couldn't see a thing in there. She knew the end of the Timberdale path could not be far off to her right and slightly upslope.

Starting forward, intent on getting across the open strip as quickly as possible, she almost missed the pickup truck parked in the brush to her right. The moment she saw it, she knew it belonged to Aikman. She stopped and then hurried over to it, hiding in its shadow.

It was deserted, no sign of Aikman. A faded color, it looked beat-up and sad in the starlight. A film of dirt showed on the narrow windows in the low-slung camper shell on the back. The back door of the shell had been swung up to the full-open position.

She went around to the back. Inside the shell were some hand tools and gardening implements, a couple of flattened fertilizer bags, other miscellaneous trash, two fishing poles, and a metal box that might contain fishing tackle. Nothing helpful.

Where was Aikman? Well, she couldn't worry about him. She had enough to worry about otherwise, thank you.

She wondered if the dispatcher had found Lassiter. Maybe, she thought, this was a good place to wait for him, right here by the truck. But wouldn't that be splendid, standing here an hour or two while the dispatcher tried to track him down. And she was just as vulnerable here as anywhere else. Might as well move on. Or go back. No, move on.

She left the side of the pickup and crossed to the brush-choked heavier woods. Suddenly the trees on all sides became more visible, pale silver in a faint light. She looked up and saw that scattered clouds had been covering a silver moon. The added moonlight seemed like a spotlight to her night-adjusted eyes.

She crept into the deeper brush. Downslope ahead, and not all that far, the bullfrog racketed at the pond. Maybe this was a wild goose chase, she thought, taking another step.

Her foot stepped on something round that rolled a little under her, almost tripping her up. She staggered and stopped and looked down to see what it was. A long-handled shovel, its blade crusted with dried dirt, lay in the grass.

That was when she heard the slight movement in the brush behind her. Every nerve wanting to scream, she whirled. She couldn't see anything back under the trees. It was just too dark.

Then a male voice, so near it made her jump, said out of the deep shadows, "You had to do it, didn't you. You couldn't leave me alone."

TWENTY-SEVEN

JAMES AIKMAN stepped out of the shadows. He had his gun in hand. Laura could not quite make out his expression, but the tone of his voice had been enough to send chills through her body.

She knew, before anything else was said or done, that he was the one. But she tried weakly to pretend: "It's you! I'm so relieved."

Aikman came a step closer, shaking his head. "It won't work."

A red light—a flashlight with red plastic over the lens—beamed into her eyes, temporarily blinding her. Then it went out again, but all she saw were dancing white stars in her vision.

"Drop the tire iron," Aikman's voice ordered tonelessly.

"It was you," she blurted. "All along it was you."

"I said drop it!"

She had forgotten the heavy steel tire tool was in her right hand. Panic shot through her and without thought she hurled it at the sound of his voice. It hit something. He grunted and the weeds rustled violently. Still mostly blind, she turned and ran into the thick brush at her side. Creepers and thistles tangled around her legs, almost throwing her to the ground. She staggered ahead, fear making her stronger, and came to a little depression in the earth that she plunged headlong into with shocking force.

Behind her, but slightly off to one side, she heard Aikman thrashing after her. She scrambled to her feet and staggered ahead. Her vision had started to come back but she couldn't see exactly where she was going. She thought it was downhill, toward the pond. The enormous sound of her movement through the dry brush drowned out any other.

She didn't know where he was. She felt she couldn't stop but she couldn't keep going. Up ahead, moonlight glinted on the black surface of the pond. She veered to her left, running between larger trees, going faster because no high weeds could grow in here and she ran on thin grass and lichen.

A sudden sharp declivity yawned in front of her. She tried to veer but it was too late. Her right foot went off into nothingness and she plunged forward, out of balance again, tumbling down the embankment of the pond and rolling to a stunned stop in waist-high reeds.

The stink of perpetual mud rose up around her. She had fallen into it and then rolled, and she was covered. Something squirmy moved sharply away from her. She shuddered and started to push herself to her feet and then heard the movement of a heavy body just above the place she had fallen. She froze, fighting to keep her spasmodic breaths quiet.

Just over her position, perhaps six feet higher, the weeds rustled and crackled. Her cheek in the dank mud, she did not dare move more than her eyes. She saw Aikman's booted feet on the lip of the embankment, moving parallel with it. He rushed past her spot and kept going, moving hurriedly into the bushes farther on.

She stayed put. She did not trust her legs to carry her much farther, and any movement would make noise. Guardedly turning her head, she saw that she had fallen over the lip of the earthen bowl that contained the pond. Water glinted not ten feet from where she lay in the reeds and brush. She could not go that way and she could not climb back without making an unholy noise. She was stuck. But she couldn't be stuck. She had to do something.

Raising her head a few inches, she looked around in the half-light. Aikman was well off in the woods now; she could still hear the sounds of his rushing around. She needed something—anything—she might use in desperation as a weapon of defense.

A muddy rock about the size of her two fists stuck out of the muck a foot or two nearer the water's edge. She reached over and grasped it and pulled. It came out of the wet mud with a loud sucking sound. It wasn't quite as big as she had hoped. She grasped it, grateful for anything.

The sounds being made by Aikman in the brush were closer again now. He was coming back this way. Everything in her said to jump up and run. But if she gave in to that panic, it was all over. He had missed her once down here. Covered with mud from her fall, she must be virtually invisible. Her only chance was in lying still, hoping he would overlook her again.

His sounds grew closer, deafening. She lay still, quaking inside, fighting tears of sheer terror. Maybe if she closed her eyes it would be all right. Maybe if he looked down and her eyes were open he would see them. But did eyes gleam in the dark, or did they only look that way when you were out driving at night because your headlights were reflected? Eyes couldn't really shine. They didn't have an internal illumination, like fireflies. *Oh God, I'm going crazy.*

The noise of Aikman's movements reached a crescendo. Bits of dirt and brush showered down off the lip above and tickled her face. They made her have a convulsive need to sneeze. She bit her lip and held her breath. The sneeze was held back. The movement over her hiding place stopped.

She did not so much as breathe. Seconds ticked away.

All he had to do was shine his damned red-lensed flashlight down, she thought, and he would see her. Then it would be the end of her.

But the light did not come. Was he afraid to use it because he didn't know where she was, and feared the flashlight would tip off his position? She didn't know, couldn't think. She realized there was a rasping, uneven noise nearby somewhere: his breathing, just above where she lay in the mud.

Holy Mary, mother of God, pray for us sinners....

More dirt and brush showered down. His booted feet had moved. The sound of his stentorian breathing became less oppressive. She heard him working his way along, farther from her again. She remembered to breathe.

Minutes passed. She began to feel like she had been lying in this sticky mud forever. Once she heard him well off in the thicket, making what seemed like an awful lot of noise. Then he came closer again, and she froze all over again.

It couldn't go on, she thought despairingly. His sounds now indicated that he was walking back and forth in straight lines—west, then east, then west again—covering the woods like a hunter searching out wild game. When he got to the edge of the pond he would climb down the embankment this time, and walk the edge. She knew that. And that was where he would find her.

The noise of his movements became louder again, then moved farther away, then louder again, then farther away. Oh, he was being so patient now, so systematic. He must realize she could not have escaped, had run the wrong direction to escape to the road, and the JiffyGrub. He would keep walking back and forth, combing, until he came upon her.

She wondered how deep the pond was. She thought about trying to wade it silently. But even if she could do such a thing, she would be totally in the open while she did so. He could not possibly miss her then. No. She had to stay where she was. She thought she knew now what a little rabbit must feel like, crouched under the broad leaf of a big weed, hearing the hunter's footsteps.

His sounds approached again. He was making some kind of new noise that her fear-sensitized ears picked up, a faint wailing sound, as if from an electronic gadget of some kind. Did he have some kind of weird, space-age gadget to help him hunt for her? It was getting louder, rising and falling in pitch.

Heat flooded through her veins as she finally identified the sound: a siren, no, more than one siren, coming closer from a great distance. Thank God.

Aikman must have heard them, too. She heard his voice mumble an obscenity, and then the sound of more violent movement. It moved away from where she lay. He was running away from her hiding place, running through the thicket.

The sound of the sirens grew rapidly, shrilling through the woods. Then she heard the roar of engines approaching, and the squeal of tires as they made the curve in front of Timberdale. The racket practically deafened her. The cars—there had to be at least two—made rubber squeal up on the road near where she had parked. The sirens wound down toward silence. Car doors slammed and she heard men shouting to one another. Then more shouts, and quiet again.

Pulling herself out of the mud, she stood and managed to drag her body up through the loose dirt of the nearby vertical embankment. She saw that weeds choked the lip, sticking out more than a foot over the edge. The weeds had partially blocked Aikman's view—they had saved her. She would never pull another weed as long as she lived, she thought fervently.

Another flurry of shouting echoed through the woods, and then a single sharp yell and the distant sound of the violent movement of bodies through the brush far up toward the road. She pulled herself up over the lip of the embankment and lay on the drier dirt, catching her breath. She couldn't think of anything except her intense relief.

That was when she heard the sound of men's voices, talking loudly and urgently. Someone yelled hoarsely. A car door slammed. After a moment of silence she heard the noise of someone coming down the slope from the road through the weeds.

A voice called sharply, "Laura?"

Lassiter's voice.

She staggered to her feet. "Here! I'm over here!"

A brilliant white light bounced through the trees, approaching fast. Then he ran into view, a big flashlight in one hand and an even larger gun in the other. The beam of the flashlight danced over tree limbs and leaves and bushes and then darted along the ground and found her. He rushed up and caught her in his arms.

"Jesus! Are you all right?"

"Yes," she said, hugging him as tightly as he was hugging her. "I'm fine. I'm fine now."

"You crazy idiot! I ought to—!"

"I know. I know." She was crying.

His arm strong around her waist, he walked her back up the gentle hill toward the road. They reached the area where she had passed Aikman's pickup truck. It was still there, but now the headlights of two sheriff's cruisers bathed it in brilliance. Two deputies stood there beside Aikman, who was already handcuffed.

Laura's attention was drawn to two objects leaning against the front fender of the illuminated pickup. One was a long-handled shovel, possibly the one she had stumbled over earlier. The other object, with a D-shaped plastic grip at one end and a flat cylindrical protuberance at the other, looked a lot like a Weed Eater.

But it was not a Weed Eater, she saw now. It was a walkaround metal detector.

BY THE TIME things had even remotely begun to straighten out, half of Timberdale's residents were milling around the atrium in their nightclothes, old ladies in frilly nightgowns and floral robes, men in everything from smoking jackets and trousers (Julius Pfeister) to silk pajamas colored like jungle fatigues (the colonel). James Aikman was gone, taken off to the courthouse by two of the deputies, and only one car in addition to Lassiter's remained in the front driveway. That one belonged to Sheriff Davidson.

Laura, flanked by Lassiter and the sheriff, stood behind the reception desk with the public address system microphone in hand. She had washed her hands and face, but was still covered with smelly pond mud.

She keyed the mike and her voice echoed back to her from speakers around the atrium. "Okay, everyone. The excitement is all over. What's happened is, the sheriff's department has caught the person responsible for the troubles we've been having around here lately. It's all perfectly safe now. You can calm down and get a good night's sleep. We'll have some more information for you by morning. In the meantime, how about going back to your apartments and trying to get some rest? Thanks."

They all stared at her, some of them whispering to one another. Then something less than half the crowd began to disperse. Maude Thuringer, who had been fluttering around nearby, rushed over.

"It was Aikman, right?" Her eyelids racketed. "I knew it. I knew it all the time. He needed money, right? He took this job so he could rob all of us with impunity, right, Sheriff? I *knew* it!"

"He didn't do it for the money," Lassiter said.

Maude's eyes snapped. "Of course he did! Don't be a sap! He robbed them. Nothing else makes sense."

Bucky Davidson considered her for a moment, his weathered face grave. "You've got it just right, ma'am," he said solemnly.

"I knew it!" Maude repeated, and dashed off.

The front doors whisked open and Mrs. Epperman, a brown corduroy robe thrown over crimson pajamas, sailed in. Her fuzzy slippers were the type designed to look like elephant feet.

"You caught the murderer?" she demanded, charging up to them. "You said on the telephone it was Mr. Aikman? Are we safe? Is he in custody?" She turned on Laura. "You're the one who hired that man, you dreadful girl! I thought you were supposed to be the one who could judge character. What are we paying taxes for, if the university can't even teach you how to judge character?"

The sheriff spoke quietly. "Mrs. Michaels caught the man, ma'am."

Mrs. Epperman's eyes bulged. "What? What?"

"I said—"

"I heard you, but I don't believe it!"

"Oh, you can believe it, all right." The sheriff turned a phlegmatic gaze to Laura. "Of course she tried to take the law into her own hands, which was stupid, and almost got herself killed for it."

"I didn't like him," Laura admitted, "but I still can hardly believe it."

Lassiter put a protective arm around her. "When you look back on things, it all makes good sense."

"How?"

"A red light doesn't show as well as white. He needed some light, a flash now and then, to show him what he was doing. He was combing the whole woods with that metal detector, desperately looking."

"Looking for what? Why was he desperate. I don't—"

"Remember the murders years ago? It's the only theory that makes sense. He must have committed those, just like a lot of people always suspected. Was out cruising around, spotted those kids parked a few miles from here, stopped to hassle them. Probably got in a scuffle with the boy, which would explain why he was roughed up. Then shot one of them more or less by accident, and had to kill the other one, too."

"I still—"

"It's the metal detector that makes it all fit. What probably happened was, he did the killings with his own small target pistol. He wasn't stupid; he got a broom out of his car and literally swept the entire death scene to leave no footprints or tire tracks. Wiped the car down, too. Then he headed back to town. This is one of two or three country roads he might have used on the way back to town."

The sheriff nodded agreement. "But he gets this far, see, and he realizes he's still got the gun. He stops and buries it where nobody will ever find it."

"And you mean when we found those freshly dug spots with metal objects in the bottom—"

"He had detected something, dug it up, reburied it, disappointed."

Laura thought about it. "Why now? Why, after all these years—" She stopped. She saw the likely answer.

"Right," Lassiter said, reading her expression.

Mrs. Epperman stamped an elephant foot. "Why *what?*"

"The construction," Lassiter told her. "Right, Bucky?"

The sheriff nodded. "Makes sense."

"He heard or read about the plans to scrape and level the woods down here and build a nursing home," Lassiter told Mrs. Epperman. "That meant they might damned well turn up the old murder weapon—*his* weapon. He had to find it before they did, and get rid of it somewhere else, once and for all.''

''After all these years,'' Laura said, ''how bad would it be for him if the old murder weapon showed up?''

''With the other stuff they had on him? Enough to convict him, probably.''

''But he didn't find it.''

''He hadn't yet. He might have. He was damned sure trying his hardest. Your residents that died down there must have come upon him without warning. He had no choice but to do them in.''

Laura thought about it, seeing the pieces fall into line. ''So he was out desperately searching with his metal detector, taking an awful risk, and Violet stumbled upon him.''

Lassiter nodded. ''And then the old gent.''

''And he killed them. Taking Violet's money was just to confuse the issue.''

Lassiter's smile looked tired. ''How about joining the department?''

Laura ignored that. ''Then,'' she went on, ''he got himself hired as the security guard so he could keep on looking.''

''Right. Keep everybody else out, and keep on looking. What could be better for him?''

''But Ken must have gotten too close.''

''I would think so. Aikman spotted him.''

''And Ken must have run back inside and Aikman followed him and threw him over the railing, hoping it would look like an accident.'' She had another thought. ''But why was Mr. Bell's body found all the way up in the service area behind the building, when he must have been attacked on the path where we saw the blood?''

The sheriff shrugged. ''Maybe Aikman will tell us that.

But I figure it was to conceal a connection between the lower part of the path and the attacks.''

Laura took a deep breath. "So it all makes sense, sort of. If all the guesswork is right.''

"Yep.''

"But if he doesn't confess, how are you ever going to prove it?''

Davidson's yawn was enormous. "Once the construction crew or our boys dig up the gun, we'll have the proof of just about all of it.''

"What if they never turn it up?'' Laura asked.

"Oh, they'll turn it up,'' the sheriff said with quiet confidence.

Two days later, they did.

JAMESON COLE

"Jameson Cole has created a
masterwork...a must read."
—Clive Cussler

It is the summer of 1957 and Bob White, Oklahoma, is a
dry rural town. Illegal moonshine is a hot commodity, and
fifteen-year-old Mark Stoddard decides he's going to find a
local bootlegger and win the respect of his older brother
Jake, the local deputy sheriff.

But the peaceful appearance of the lazy little town is only a
facade, and Mark soon becomes snared in a deadly game of
vengeance being played by a killer who has nothing to
lose. To find his way out alive, Mark must confront truths
about the end of innocence, about young love...and
murderous hate.

A KILLING IN QUAIL COUNTY

1997
COLORADO
BOOK AWARD
WINNER

Available in October 1997 at your favorite retail outlet.

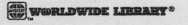

WJC251

Worldwide Mystery™
is on the case...

We've taken the guesswork out of finding the very best in mystery entertainment—and every month there are three* new titles sure to please!

From spine-tingling suspense to unabashed hilarity, every Worldwide Mystery™ novel is a guaranteed page-turner! Criminals always have something to hide—but the enjoyment you'll get from reading your next Worldwide Mystery™ is no secret.

Worldwide Mystery™—
stories worth investigating.

* Not all titles are for sale in Canada.

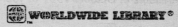

Jo Bannister

First Time in Paperback

FATAL ATTRACTION...

The first victim is a young prostitute—an easy, accessible target for a killer's lust. The second victim is another young girl. The killer is skilled, seasoned and enjoying himself.

The detective team of Liz Graham and Cal Donovan is on the case as suspicion falls on a charismatic traveling evangelist. Who would benefit more from a town's tragedies than he?

Among them, though, wearing a mask of decency, a killer is once again deciding who lives and who dies....

Charisma

A CASTLEMERE MYSTERY

"Superb character work."   *—New York Times Book Review*

Available in October 1997 at your favorite retail outlet.

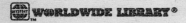 **WORLDWIDE LIBRARY®**   WCHARISMA

Just the Fax, Ma'am

First Time in Paperback

A MOLLY MASTERS MYSTERY

To Molly Masters, the whole situation was absurd. As a cartoonist and mother of two, she was surprised—and a little angry—to find that the only risqué drawing she'd ever done has appeared in the pages of a porn magazine. Not quite surprising was the fact that Preston Saunders, the husband of her arch rival, had stolen the drawing and submitted it to the magazine.

Molly begins receiving hate mail from antiporn groups, then Preston is found dead. In search of a killer, Molly goes undercover—posing as a high school student—and is forced to dodge a hail of bullets. But it's only a matter of time before she finds the killer...or the killer finds her....

Leslie O'Kane

"Excellent." —*Poisoned Pen*

Available in November 1997 at your favorite retail outlet.

 WORLDWIDE LIBRARY ®

WLOK254

Clare CURZON

First Time in Paperback

Monday was going to be a killer...

It's the worst day of the week for many people, but this particular Monday is brutal for Annette Briers. First, she finds out that her boss, Miranda Gregory, was the victim of a hit-and-run accident and is now hanging on for dear life. To make matters worse, she finds a dead stranger slumped over in her office chair.

As the police team tries to link the two crimes, they discover that the elegant Miranda Gregory is a mystery woman without a past, or so it seems. And it also becomes apparent that she holds the key to a secret that could lead to a murderer....

PAST MISCHIEF

A THAMES VALLEY MYSTERY

"...ingenious narrative...a true teaser."
—*New York Times Book Review*

Available in November 1997
at your favorite retail outlet.

 **WORLDWIDE LIBRARY**® WCC256

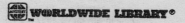